HELLBORN ANGEL

KISSED BY BRIMSTONE BOOK ONE

LEIGH KELSEY

For one of my favourite authors
Sarah Rees Brennan
who encouraged me to keep writing
when I was young and very bad at it.
You probably don't remember, but I've never forgotten that
kindness.

And I'm still in deep, obsessive love with
the Ryves brothers.

I'm pretty sure my demon addiction
is your fault.

BLURB

Hell hath no fury like a demon psycho scorned.

The first thing you should know about me is I'm completely cuckoo. Two hundred years ago, a monster of abusive proportions killed my fated mates. And me.

Don't ask how I've been reborn. All I know is I still have my memories, my rage, and the power to make blood boil in someone's veins. Both literally and because I'm a sarcastic little shit.

Emlyn, Malakai, and Harveil held me together, and without them, I've hit breaking point. Probably when I stole that porcupine demon's quills and made them into a tiara. (Looks cute; tragically impractical.)

But in positive news, my insanity helped me become Lucifer's best assassin. Now, I spend my days taking out hell's enemies and my nights scouring every forsaken city for my mates.

Because if I've been reincarnated, they have too. And someone thought it was a good idea to keep me from the men I love.

Hellborn Angel is a paranormal romance with psycho men, a ruthless revenge-driven FMC, twisted romance, and lots and lots of bloodlust. Deadly archdemons, cutting sarcasm, epic reincarnation romance, and gruesome murders fill these pages, so get ready to laugh, cringe, and swoon.

This book is medium burn, with moderate heat, and multiple love interests, and set in the same world as Lili Kazana - but this series stands completely separate.

HELLBORN ANGEL

LEIGH
KELSEY

NOTE

This book contains mentions of past abuse and sexual assault that could be incredibly triggering for some readers, plus it deals with infertility, so please proceed with caution. Don't hesitate to skip this book if it's safer for your mental health.

As always, don't recreate any sexy times in this series without doing your research, communicating with your partner, and discussing aftercare.

This series also contains some spoilers for the Lili Kazana trilogy, which takes place a year before this series, but nothing too major that doesn't appear in the books' blurbs.

Oh, and this series will break your heart. Fair warning.

Leigh x

P.s. don't forget to read the footnotes for added hilarity!

PART I - MERCENARY

1

"Of course it's fucking raining," I grumbled, taking my frustration out on a puddle.

This town was a shitheap of crumbling houses, worn-down shops, and as many pubs as you could squash onto two dirt roads. Sometimes I hated my job. But I was a single woman in her twenties with no family, few friends, and an empty purse. If I wanted to eat this month, I had no choice but to be here.

It was slightly worrying that no one else had taken the job, though. Usually mercenaries clamoured for anything with this hefty a reward. Not to mention it didn't require a murder—it was a simple retrieval mission.

"It's probably nothing," I dismissed, checking my weapons before I approached the squat cube of an inn. Warped windows threw squares of light on the ground, catching yet more puddles. "Just think of the ten thousand gold crowns."

Inside, the pub was as delightful as I expected. A heavy scent of stale beer filled my lungs, accompanied by the familiar sensation of my boots sticking to the floorboards as I let the door fall shut behind me.

Rough voices and coarse language came from people sitting at chipped tables a week away from falling apart, and every liquid behind the bar was cloudy, brown, and unpalatable. But at least there was a fire roaring across the room, so a wall of pleasant heat sank through layers of travel-dirty clothes and into my body.

It sucked that I couldn't let it bleed the tension from my bones; I needed to be alert while I searched for my mark.

I'd been given a shitty amount of information about Wane Van Khama, the man I was here to take back to my client. All I knew was a vague description—he looked to be in his late twenties, though my client had notably left out his true age; he was a demon with bat-like black wings, spiralling black horns; and deep bronze skin. And I knew he was an experienced fighter, so I needed to be on my guard.

I didn't know what he'd done, or what my client would do with him. But *fuck,* ten thousand gold crowns. That would set me up for a whole year. Maybe two if I was clever about it.

Maybe I could get a house, buy myself a sweet husband and a family. The devil knew I wasn't getting one without paying for them—I was a foulmouthed, bad-tempered bitch who preferred stabbing to singing and combat to cooking. Men wanted a sweet, romantic girl, not one who came home dripping blood and got into fights on a Friday night because she was bored.

But hey, if I *paid* a guy to like me, problem solved.[1]

I hopped onto a bar stool and flagged down the portly, moustachioed man currently cleaning a cloudy glass with a rag.

I didn't make the mistake of asking after Wane in a place like this; everyone would close ranks, maybe even throw me out on my ass. My ass was already too cold to land in a muddy puddle, so I asked for a beer and canvassed the place while I waited for my drink.

The single room was filled with the usual assortment of scowling and sneering demons in grungy clothes. Some stared into their pints while others scanned the pub like I did, although for entirely different reasons. In the back, a woman in a frothy purple dress sat energetically in a man's lap, leaving little question about what was happening under her skirts. There were a number of winged, horned men, some with brown skin and others pale, ruddy, or crimson, but I knew which one was Wane van Khama when my eyes skimmed over him, and a clang went through my chest.

"What the fuck?" I hissed under my breath, jumping when the bartender set my beer in front of me. I *never* got jumpy on a job. But what the hell *was* that clang? I still felt it echoing through me, like someone slammed a fist into my chest. Only instead of hitting skin, muscle, and bone, they hit my vulnerable insides.[2]

There's still time to turn around and leave, I told myself.

But I accepted the job, and fuck knows what would happen if I returned emptyhanded. I might have been a vicious bitch with very few hard lines, but my client was powerful—and a total psycho. I couldn't predict what he'd do. One thing was for sure: if I walked away from this, I'd have to find a new career.

But let's be real, there's no chance in Hell I'm walking away from this.

Ten thousand fucking credits.

So I sipped my beer and discreetly watched the slim, black-winged man. His lithe body was wrapped in shadows like a huge fur coat, and my gut cramped as I watched him. My chest fluttered. It was alarming as fuck. It wasn't a flutter of fear, but *excitement*, and my heart needed to get its head in the game.

Sure, his bronze face was carved by the gods, and there

was a visible corona of power around him, but come on! *You're working, Halwen, get your shit together.*

Retrieval. Probably fisticuffs. Definitely trouble with capital T.

Wane van Khama wasn't alone; he sat with three other men that gave me the same deep, resonating clang in my chest. These three looked every bit as intimidating and deadly as Wane, with an assortment of horns, claws, wings, and tattoos. I almost slipped off my stool.

Whatever that warning clang was, it was not. Fucking. Good.

I needed to get Wane alone, because his buddies were *massive*. Muscle wrapped around muscle, and bulged from shoulders, arms, chests, and *thighs*. One was so thick his arms were like tree trunks. I briefly entertained the thought of climbing him like he really *was* a tree, and hissed at the immediate pounding between my legs.

So what, they were hot? They were still trouble. Still in my way.

When I next glanced their way, the oldest (and biggest) man watched me.

Oh, shit!

I panicked, and batted my lashes, covering up my reconnaissance with pathetic flirting.

This bastard was every bit as hot as Wane, his features more rugged and his jaw covered in a salt and pepper beard to match the hair that curled slightly at his shoulders. The grey, long-sleeved shirt he wore hugged muscles my hands were desperate to trace, and the fabric clung to the unmistakable shape of weapons. *That* dunked cold water over me; I spun back to the bar and my pint.

Okay, I reasoned. *Just go over there, flirt with them, get Wane alone, and cuff him. Easy.*

I had enhanced metal cuffs that would bind even a furious, magical rhinoceros, but something told me Wane wouldn't *let* me snap them around his wrists. There'd be a fight.

Why did my blood spark?

Why did my stomach change from churning nerves to excitement?

Oh, because I was crazy. Yeah, that explained a lot.

Like why I took another sip of beer[3] and sauntered over to the table of four clear predators, swishing my hips and channelling the woman getting lucky over in the corner. *Good for her.*

"Hello, boys," I purred, my voice already raspy enough to be sultry. No one had to know it turned that way by screaming while my 'trainer' hurt me to make me a good little soldier.[4]

Interest lit in the eyes of the older man, and he leaned back in his seat, grey feathered wings spreading as he eyed me up and down. I doubt he saw much; I'd been on the road for days, and my leather trousers were caked in as much dirt and dust as my heavy jacket. Fuck, I hadn't thought this through. I needed to be alluring.

But the interest in his vibrant blue eyes only flared, as if I was attractive to him even covered in the grime of travel. Yet his arms remained crossed over his chest, and he wasn't the one to reply.

"And who might you be?" a shaggy-haired, bronze-skinned Adonis asked, his chin tilted at a cocky angle and molten silver eyes meeting mine in a sultry look. I'd never seen eyes like that before, otherworldly and shining like mirrors. I fought a shudder.

"Jynn," I answered, curving my mouth in an inviting smile. I could play sweet and flirty if I wanted to; mercs had to play so many roles that I'd lost count. It was all part of the job.

"Pretty name," the bronze god replied. "But I think I'll call you sugarplum."

I couldn't control my reaction; my mouth fell open. "You fucking *won't.*"

"Try and stop me," he taunted. "Now, are you joining us or going back to your lonely seat by the bar?"

I was tempted to go back to my lonely seat by the bar just to spite him. But my eyes drifted to the other two men—to Wane, who was a near identical copy of the smirking bastard —and a man who sat a head taller than the others, with ultra-pale skin, deep red eyes and matching crimson hair, and a body *covered* head to toe in scrawling ink—writing. He watched me like he'd enjoy cutting my body apart to see how it ticked, so I avoided his gaze and met the challenge in the smug bastard's.

"Fine." I shrugged, "I suppose you're not the worst company in this place."

The big guy grunted, his beard twitching with a smile.

"*So*, sugarplum," the cocky bastard said, taking great pleasure in the glare I shot his way, "what brings you to our little town?"

I came to kidnap your brother. But I couldn't exactly tell him that.

"I'm here for work," I replied expertly. "What about you? Do you live here? And you haven't even told me your names."

"We live here—ish," he replied. "As for names, I'm Harvey; this is my brother, Wane; the stern, silent bastard is Emlyn; and this is Malakai, our resident psychopath. Don't make any sudden moves," he whispered. "Kai tends to get a little twitchy and choke people until their heads fall off."

"It's really good to meet you all," I bullshitted. "Thanks for letting me sit with you."

Malakai grinned, a slow spreading, chilling thing. "Little liar."

He gave the others a meaningful look and angled his horned head at me. "She's from the guild; it stands out a mile."

Uh-oh. The guild as in the guild *of mercenaries.*

"What guild?" I asked, my eyes big and innocent.

The look Malakai gave me could have scalded iron. My heart skipped when he shoved his chair back, throwing it to the sticky floor.

I jumped automatically to my feet—my instinct wouldn't let him tower over me. But I gave myself away with my fast response.

"For fuck's sake," Harvey spat, silver eyes flashing. "We've barely been here a week. What did he offer you?" He dropped his hand, giving me a loathing look. "Fame? Fortune? A city?"

I snorted. "You're way off the mark, buddy."

"She's struggling to survive," Emlyn, the big, bearded guy spoke, and I gasped at the low thunder of his voice. I was having inappropriate thoughts again, and it couldn't have been worse timing. "They offered money or food."

"Ding, ding, ding," I replied, and *shrieked* when Malakai launched at me

He moved so fast, I had to pump my wings to leap out of his path.

The rest of the pub's patrons jumped to their feet, but not to help me. Not even to help Wane and co.

Wane hadn't spoken a single word, and only stared at me, half wrapped in shadows.

People moved out of the way, clearing space for Malakai to throw himself at me. Generous of them.

I dodged, scanning for an exit that *wasn't* blocked by a crimson-haired psychopath. This job was impossible with Wane's entourage around him. I'd have to leave, and later follow them to get him when he was alone.

I pumped my wings and reached inside my jacket for my

knives. They were old and mottled, but I sharpened them regularly and they could cut as well as any new, pretty blade. I slashed one at Malakai when the pale, inked bastard hurtled at me again, moving faster and far more graceful than he looked. That was the benefit of being a demon; we were faster, stronger, and with magic in the mix, *anything* was possible.

"Fine," I growled, throwing my hands up and giving the red-haired man a scowl. "You win; I'll leave you alone. Happy?"

Judging by the way he slammed into me, wrapped both hands around my neck, and squeezed until my eyes almost popped out of my head ... no, he was not happy.

"Kai!" a raspy voice called, gravely and raw like my own voice.

My gaze snapped to Wane as the bronze-skinned, sleek-haired man came toward us. His face was the only visible feature, his shadows wrapped around him like a shield. Or like a child's comfort blanket.

"Stop," he ordered tiredly.

I took advantage of the pause to angle a knife up into Malakai's gut, but when I tried to slam it home, my hand refused to budge.

"What the fuck?" I spat, trying my other knife to the same effect. "Who enchanted my knives? Undo it *now!* These are my best pair, you salty cumrags."

Malakai scoffed and glared at me, his eyes dark crimson and *seething* with murder. "*You're* the one who's enchanting."

"Aww, thanks, that's so sweet of you," I preened, batting my lashes. Sometimes I thought I had a death wish.

"Whatever you've done to my hands," he hissed, deep and throaty as he snapped sharp teeth at my face,[5] "I'm going to kill you for it."

His scent of amber and crackling firewood invaded my senses, annoyingly pleasant.

"Stop," Wane said in that same quiet but forceful voice, footsteps approaching us and the other two guys right behind him. "It's not an enchantment, it's *nature*. Instinct. You can't kill each other, because you're mates."

I laughed.

Malakai's upper lip curled back.

"Didn't you feel it?" Wane went on, looking at *me* now. My stomach squirmed at the eye contact, and I was a little embarrassed when my heart skipped. "When you first saw me? I know *I* felt it, like a bell rang through my entire soul."

That clang...

A chill went down my spine.

"You're—you're our mate, Jynn. You're mine, and Malakai's."

"And mine," the burly, older man grunted.

Harvey flashed me a blinding grin. "Guess that explains why I want to fuck you into submission so badly."

"You wish," I hissed, trying to stab Malakai and failing miserably. "I wouldn't touch you if my life depended on it."

Wane sighed, his shadow-wreathed shoulders drooping an inch. "It might, actually. You can't kill any of us, but the man who sent you to hurt me? When he finds out you haven't done the job, he'll do unspeakable things to you. It's worse than death."

I frowned, unable to get a read on what kind of person Wane was. Something about him registered as genuine. And it made me think he'd personally experienced those unspeakable things.

"Son of a goat-fucking whore," I muttered, and removed my knife from Malakai's stomach.

I had four soulmates.

2

"*My* name is actually Halwen," I told the guys on a sigh. We'd righted the pieces of furniture that got pushed over when me and Malakai tried to kill each other, and the ambience of the pub went back to normal. Now, we sat at the same table with refreshed drinks in front of us—I sipped my beer, but it still tasted like a pig's bathwater—and my knife was openly in my hand instead of hidden inside my mud-splattered jacket.

Malakai still glared at me, his unnaturally pale face twisted with hatred. Fair enough—I was pissed that some law of nature had stopped me killing him, too.

"What does this mate shit mean, exactly?" I asked, some bitterness leaking into my voice even as I tried to mask my emotions. I was in a full scale panic, my heart hammering my ribs, my breathing jagged, and my black wings refused to stop twitching with nerves.

I looked to Wane, who'd broken the news of me being their mate in the first place, but he'd retreated into the dark corner and was now so wrapped in shadows that I couldn't make out his hands or even his face.[1]

Harvey, the bronze Adonis, wasn't smirking anymore, but this was worse. *Oh*, so much worse. Mercury-silver eyes tracked my every movement in awe, like I was a goddess. But this was Hell and there were no gods here, only Lucifer ruling us in his fancy-ass city.

"You're telling me you've never heard of a soulmate?" Harvey drawled, but the bite in his voice was drowned out by the way he propped his chin on his hand and *gazed* at me.

I made a throaty sound and sipped my beer—and wished I hadn't. Gods, it was gross. "Of course I've heard of a soulmate. But how does this *work*? What power does it give you over me?"

Emlyn snorted, his beard twitching as he smiled. The giant was a man of very few words, but he noticed *everything*, and the way he kept scanning the room for threats told me he was used to fighting. Maybe was used to protecting his friends from people like me.

"You can't use it to control us, Halwen," Emlyn said with gruff amusement, instantly figuring out the true root of my question.

Dammit.

"Bonds don't work that way; they're a link forged between souls. We can sense each other anywhere, find our way back together, and it's ... a comfort. A feeling of safety like no other."

I tapped my knee with the flat of my knife. "I make you feel safe?"

Malakai's vicious grin grew, red eyes flashing with the promise of another tussle. To my horror, my blood heated in eagerness.

"You were sent here to kill us; you're hardly safe," the psycho breathed, his voice sending a chill down my spine.

"Not kill, just pick up and deliver," I replied flippantly, my heart drumming faster. Antagonising Malakai came as easily as breathing, and gave me the same rush as a bar brawl.[2] "But it's a shame I can't kill you; I had so many pretty plans for you."

"She's just winding you up," Harvey told Malakai, reaching out to ruffle the psycho's wine-red hair.

Malakai turned slowly enough to make even *my* stomach squirm, but Harvey only smirked and patted his head before letting go. It was impossible to believe this upbeat, golden nuisance was Wane's brother, but the resemblance was undeniable. Well, when my mark wasn't wrapped in shadows and trying to disappear into the wall, that was.

"You still think you can finish the job," Emlyn rumbled.

I stiffened unconsciously in my seat, swallowing at the deep thunder of his voice. "Well, obviously I can't with all this mate business."

Malakai's upper lip pulled back from his teeth—sharp, deadly rows of teeth— and he hissed so viciously that a few patrons slipped out the pub door behind us.

"You even *think* about touching him, and you die."

I leaned back in my wooden chair, giving him a lazy stare. Like I gave a shit about his threat. I'd been threatened too many times, almost *died* too many times, that it had lost its edge. If I died, so what? My life wasn't exactly sweetness and light; I wouldn't miss it. And no one would miss me.

"If Wane's right, you can't kill me," I taunted, giving Malakai a wink that had him shooting out of his seat. Harvey and Emlyn dragged him back down.

"*Enough*," Emlyn growled, and again I responded with a base, primal instinct. A deep shudder worked through me, my breathing abruptly short. The man might have been quiet, but he was dominant as hell, and *powerful*. Demons didn't have a hierarchy of power per se, but we had damn good instincts, and all my warning sirens were flashing and screaming, telling me to back the fuck down.

"Halwen, you can feel the pull to us as much as we can feel it to you; stop trying to convince yourself you can't."

I grumbled and glared at the table, but there was no ignoring the clang I felt through every part of me.

But just because I felt the bond didn't mean I had to be all in with this *soulmate* shit. They still hadn't properly answered my question. *No power over me, my ass.*

"You're a part of us now," Emlyn went on, scowling at the table even though we all knew his scowl was meant for me. "We're part of you. Live with it."

Well. That was a bit harsh. Then again, I'd come here to kidnap his friend. It was a wonder I was still alive, honestly.

"You're not taking Wane," Harvey warned me, the awe wearing off his mercury gaze. He crossed his arms over his chest, and I noticed for the first time the homespun but sturdy clothes they all wore. Nothing fancy or expensive. Weird; criminals usually paraded their riches in front of people's noses.

"Look," I sighed, "it's not my fault he pissed someone off and they hired me to hunt him down. Whatever he did—"

"Nothing," Malakai snarled so fiercely that his red eyes flashed and power trembled around him, making my bones quake. The inn windows rattled in their frames; a few pint glasses vibrated off their tables and shattered. Malakai didn't flinch. "He did *nothing.* You don't know a damn thing about him."

In the corner, Wane vanished entirely. I knew he was still there, but I didn't want to examine why and *how* I knew that too closely.[3]

"It's fine, Kai," a barely-there voice whispered.

But Malakai was too angry to back down. His nostrils flared, the ink scrawled across his skin shifting, *moving.* I jerked back in surprise—and cursed when I found my arms bound to the chair arms by invisible chains, my torso similarly wrapped.

Well, that answered *that* question. We might not be able to kill each other, but the space between life and death was a big playground. And I couldn't wait to play with this mean bastard.[4]

"Whatever you're thinking," Harvey said, his eyes once again fixed on me but with an intensity that made me squirm, "you're wrong. Look at Wane. *Look* at him."

I frowned, wrenching against the invisible bindings tying me to the chair, sweat dripping down my forehead. "Fuck off, Harvey."

"Actually, I've changed my mind about that," he fired back, his cheerful persona stripped away to reveal something that made me nervous. "Only my friends call me Harvey. You can call me Harveil."

My eyes widened; my breath hitched. Oh no. *Ohhhhh no.*

"Yeah," he laughed, entirely devoid of humour. "*That* Harveil."

The Harveil who slaughtered his way through a whole town, decimating their council and leaving buildings in rubble? No one knew what kind of demon he was, or the limits of what he could do, but he left destruction in his wake. And then he vanished.

"Maybe my client meant for me to kill *you*," I mused.

"No," a soft, raspy voice disagreed, and I startled, my eyes shooting to the corner where a swath of shadows unwrapped from Wane van Khama. "It's me he wants."

"He's not getting you," Emlyn swore, something like protectiveness threaded through the violence of his voice. It rattled me to my core. "She won't hand you back to him."

Oh, wouldn't I? Emlyn had *clearly* never been promised ten thousand crowns before.

"You think I'm a criminal, don't you?" Wane asked, catching my attention again with his soft, husky voice.

I shrugged. "Most people are criminals, buddy. I'm not gonna judge you for it."

"Your client, it's—it's Cassander Locke isn't it?"

"I don't know his name," I admitted, my voice gentling on instinct, my bravado and attitude softening around the edges. There was something broken about Wane. Hiding in his shadows, speaking in murmurs, his voice as raw and husky as my own.

Had I completely screwed up, coming here? My stomach twisted up until I was nauseated.

"I know it's him," he replied, his eyes lowered, the same molten silver as Harvey's. "It always is. And whatever he told you about me—"

"Not much, to be honest," I murmured.

"Let him *speak*," Harvey snapped, every bit as protective of his brother as the other two were.

I made a show of sitting back in my seat. Not that I could go anywhere with Malakai's magic trapping me. Should I have been more worried about that? It bound me but didn't hurt. The psycho could have squeezed the air out of my throat, or cut off the blood circulation to my feet, rendering me unable to walk. He did neither.[5]

"Whatever he told you about me," Wane began again, shadows wrapping around him until I could see only his shining silver eyes, "it's a lie. He wants to drag me to his council and force me to tell everyone I lied. But I *didn't.*"

I blinked. "What didn't you lie about?"

Wane shook his head, visible only as a scatter of inky shadows and chestnut hair a few shades darker than his brother's.

"He hurt you," I guessed.

He mentioned a fate worse than death; maybe he told

everyone what my client had been up to. Was it an experiment? Everyone knew there were fucked up labs and cages in Hell's seedy underbelly, where people experimented to make faster, stronger, weaponised demons. They called them a new breed of alphas—the unnatural variety.

"Yes," Wane hissed. "And I told everyone what a fraud he was. What he's *really* like. Now he wants me to lie to save his reputation."

I blew out a hard breath, tightening my fingers around my knife.

Fuck.

"I'm not a good person," I told him unapologetically. "I don't usually give a shit what my marks have done to deserve being grabbed or killed or whatever. This is Hell; we do whatever screwed up shit we need to survive. And that's what my client is offering me; survival. It's not personal, and I'd rather *not* haul you in, but I need the money."

Malakai and Emlyn exchanged a glance.

"How much is he paying you?" Malakai demanded, leaning across the table. Dark ink scrolled in words I couldn't read across his skin, and I stiffened, waiting for the magic trapping me to cinch tighter. It didn't.

"Ten thousand," I replied.

Malakai spat a curse I hadn't heard in a long while. I smiled, reminiscing; when I was a teenager, I knew a red panda who used to use it constantly. Of course, no one spoke her language so they didn't realise how colourful her words were. Man, I missed her. Dad and I had been forced to move out of that neighbourhood and into a shittier place when it cost too much.

"But," I sighed, wondering what the fuck was wrong with me, "if you're thinking of paying me off, I'll take half."

That would set me up for six months. And all I had to do

was walk away from this pub and never see these people again.[6]

"Five *thousand?*" Harvey demanded, his face slack with disbelief. "Do you think we're loaded, sugarplum?"

"Of course not, buttercup," I replied, heavy on the sickly sweetness. I even batted my long lashes at him, and wished I had a hand free to twirl a strand of pale pink hair around my finger. "But you could *get* the money, if you were really determined."

"But I'm your mate," Wane breathed, the words striking the vulnerable squishy flesh of my heart like he'd gored me with a spear.

I swallowed hard.

"Three hundred," Emlyn muttered, disapproval clear in his eyes.

Three *hundred?* Was that a joke?

"Two thousand," I countered, flexing my fingers around my knife and ignoring the sickly twist in my chest at Wane's hurt.

"He'll kill you if you don't bring me to him," Wane said abruptly, leaning closer. "You won't ever be safe; he'll find you like he found me."

"A thousand," I sighed before they could even shoot down my demand of two.

I was hot and clammy and miserable, and I was pretty sure it was because I planned to walk away from these bastards. Well, these bastards and Wane. Wane wasn't a bastard; he hammered at my protective instincts like no one ever had.

"Five hundred," Malakai spat, nostrils flaring and power thrumming around him. He was thinking about killing me again; it was obvious.

"Fine," I groaned. "Five hundred and I'll leave you alone."

"*No,*" Wane blurted, his shadows scattering until I saw him

—*all* of him. He was remarkably like Harvey, his features the same and his clothes similar, but the rest of him was covered in pale, overlapping scars, and my stomach turned over at the sight of them.

"He did that to you?" I whispered, my heart slamming against my ribs.

Wane nodded, dark chestnut hair tumbling into his strikingly elegant face.

I'll kill him.

I couldn't explain where the thought came from, or why the need to exact blood and vengeance beat at my chest like a war drum.

Because he's your mate, dumbass, an inner voice drawled.

My shoulders slumped in defeat. I flicked a glance at Malakai and watched his pale face tighten with a threatening snarl.

"Set me free; I'm not gonna hurt any of you," I murmured.

Malakai's head tilted in an unnatural swoop, crimson eyes scanning me. I had the unnerving sense that he saw through my skin to the red, sinewy bits inside.

A line of text spun around his pale, muscle-corded forearm and he nodded. The restraints fell away, and I could *finally* drag in a full breath, finally move my damn body. When I looked at Wane next, he was wrapped in his shadows again. It was like he wasn't even there.

Emlyn dug his purse out of his jacket and threw a pouch of coins on the table. But my heart was tight with compacted pain, and I kept glancing at the shadows in the corner.

Gods fucking dammit, I growled at myself as I stood and backed away from the table.

"Keep it," I grunted, and could have cursed myself. Since when was I a selfless bleeding heart? "Use it to get as far away from here as possible."

"What?" Malakai spat.

Yeah, I shocked myself, too. I was broke, and hungry, and I *needed* that money. But like a complete idiot, I turned and walked away.

"You're serious?" Harvey demanded as I weaved across the room, tucking my knife back where it lived.

"Yup," I replied without turning, and tried to ignore the pain that carved itself into my chest as I took one step after another.

I tried to tell myself it was because I was walking away from the money, but I knew that wasn't true.

Maybe they really were my mates, and I was a complete bloody idiot for leaving them behind.

But like I said, I wasn't wife material—and I certainly wasn't soulmate material. It was better this way.

3

Sixteen days later

I'd like to say I slept deeply and dreamt of happily ever afters, but like the paranoid, jumpy woman I was, I slept with my hand wrapped around a knife under my pillow, and woke at the slightest creak of the house beneath me.

I was back home in Sarishon in East Hell, barricaded in my second-floor room in a building tucked between a *delightfully* perfumed butcher's shop and a rowdy pub. The other rooms in this building were rented by a single mother, a drunk, and three guys who were either brothers or lovers. Not the place anyone would expect to find a merc. It was almost always safe.

Even so, I never slept easy, and tonight I was glad for it. I knew beyond a doubt I'd locked the window, so the low, sultry creak it made when it opened had me shooting out of bed.

My covers ended up tangled around my legs as I assessed the bastard climbing into my room. Tall, slim, and moving quietly and competently enough to tell me we were in the same field of work.

Great. Someone had been sent to kill me.

The second his feet touched my floorboards, I kicked out my leg and threw the covers at him, momentarily blinding the merc. He was distracted long enough for me to kick him into the middle of my living room/kitchen area.

He sprawled onto my table, snarling as he ripped the covers off his face, but I was already jamming my knife into his ribs and angling up into his heart.

"Bye bye," I taunted, a little breathless.

He dropped heavily to the floor, and I had a moment of relief before I spotted the blood spreading across my rug. It was a rare impulse purchase I made in a market town a few months ago while hunting a mark, and it was my favourite damn possession. I wanted to kill this bastard all over again for daring to stain it.

I was so consumed with the blood crawling across my rug that I missed the second assassin climbing through the window, and the *four* that snuck through the door I'd also locked when I got home.

Five against one. Wonderful.

I wasn't overly attached to my knife, so I threw it into the skull of the man who dropped from my window.

I needed to get better locks. If I'd been paid ten thousand crowns, I could have had better locks.

I exhaled a hard breath and dove into the kitchen. Well, kitchen was a stretch; it was two cabinets and a stove in the corner of my room. Two cabinets, a stove, and a *knife block*. I grabbed two knives out of it, measured the weight of them in my palms, and threw them with force. One hit a black-clad woman in the shoulder and the other downed a man with a blade to the dick—my favourite move.[1]

While they were distracted, I lunged across the sofa to the

box of weapons I stored under it—one of three in this room. I crossed my fingers that no one found the stashes under my bed or in the bathroom. Dragging the wooden box out, I threw up the lid and closed my fingers around my beloved dagger. It had seen much, much better days but it was special to me.

Rough fingers ensnared my hair before I could use the dagger, and pain tore across my scalp. I spat a clever insult about the man's father as the bastard wrenched my head back.

Cold steel kissed my jaw as he angled it for my throat.

The good thing about being clinically insane was no one could ever predict what you were going to do next.

"Harder," I purred. "Lower."

His grip faltered in surprise, and I laughed as I shoved the knife easily away.

"Boring," I critiqued with a pout, spinning and burying my knife in his gut.

It was a nasty, slow death I dealt him, but in my defence there were two women and four men running at me and—

Wait, there shouldn't have been that many.

"Where the hell did *you* come from?" I demanded as a tall, brawny woman barrelled into my right side, slamming me into my small kitchen counter, wrapping her hands around my throat.

"Now *this*," I croaked, "is more like it."

The good news was my breath play kink was satisfied. The not so good news? I was going to be murdered. Life was cruel sometimes.

I rammed my knee up into her ladybits, slashing with my knife at her arm for good measure. Holy shit, she didn't budge. The tanned woman only grinned, her mean face lighting up like I got on one knee and asked her to marry me.[2]

But she didn't know I had a secret talent, a party trick I liked to pull out on special occasions. Like, when someone was trying to murder me. I could make the blood boil in someone's veins until it roasted them alive.

I matched my attacker's crazy grin, and reached for the well of cruel power that burned inside me, slamming it into her body and—

"What the hell?" I croaked, my mouth parting. My power couldn't touch even a drop of her blood. That had never happened before.

"Nothing can hurt me," she took great pleasure in informing me.

Well, wasn't that just *typical?*

Black spots crowded into my vision, blotting out my attacker's satisfied smile. My arms were getting weak, and I was too woozy to correctly aim my knee into her vagina. My knife barely glanced off her stomach instead of burying deep in her gut.

Great, was I actually going to *die?* That was annoying.

But then, what did I have to live for, really? A rug I was emotionally attached to and a job that paid in as much violence as it did coin?

The black spots wrapped around my vision like a blanket of menacing death.[3]

"I curse you," I croaked as the other intruders began breaking my shit. If I was going to die, I was at least going to scare the shit out of everyone here. It sounded like they'd ripped my door off; they deserved a curse. "I curse *all of you.* You'll never know sleep, never know peace—"

In my head it sounded profound. Aloud, it was a slur of syllables barely pronounced, but the intention was the same. The woman choking me snorted—and then gurgled.

Uh. What?

Her hand tore away from my throat. I learned, quite suddenly, it was the only thing holding me up.

My knees slammed into the hard wooden floor—not the rug, because I had shitty luck—and I groaned as I collapsed onto my side.

Yay, not dead.

Nay, I didn't know what the fuck was happening.

"Halwen," a soft, breathy voice rasped.

I groaned unintelligently in reply, falling into a warm body when they lifted me off the floor. I felt liquid, like my body forgot how to be solid; I poured over whoever had grabbed me, and jumped when a soothing cold wrapped around me. It was like going outside at night when you were too hot. I wilted into the sensation, even if the more intelligent side of me was screaming, *you're being attacked, you woolly yarmouth.*

"Are you okay?" that whispery voice demanded, soft and sharp at once. "Are you hurt? Where did they cut you?"

I made a throaty sound of protest as the cold seemed to surge, sweeping over my legs, my stomach, my back, and my chest, before pausing on the trickle of blood at my throat—and what was already no doubt a nasty ring of bruising.

"Harvey!" he hissed.

I groaned for a whole new reason, trying to drag myself out of the comforting cocoon. "Not you lot."

The floor shook as someone slammed to their knees beside me. Oh, were we still on the floor? That was nice.

A new set of hands grasped my face, ignoring the teeth I snapped. I needed to open my eyes, but they'd glued together when the world started going dark.

"This might hurt," Harvey said, sounding more concerned than smug. It was the only thing that kept me from killing him as fire blasted through my face and down to my throat. I clenched my teeth on a scream as the burn travelled lower, finding all the places I'd slammed into furniture.

"Bastard," I gasped, forcing my eyes open.

Harvey leaned over me, gloriously handsome with his bronze skin and wild brown hair, his eyes flashing as he scanned my face.

"I was completely fine without your help," I muttered, which was a total lie, but my pride wouldn't allow me to thank him.

I scanned my body for wounds and jumped when I noticed both the thick shadows wrapped around me and the scarred, dark gold arms around my waist. Fuck, I really wanted to relax into that hold and take a nap. Oh no, my eyelids were fluttering.

"It's okay," Wane said in his comforting rasp. "You're safe with us."

I fought the closing of my eyes, managing to glimpse Malakai storming through my small living room, throwing his hands at my assailants and doing something evil and invisible until they dropped dead. I didn't see Emlyn anywhere, but something crashed in my room behind us, and I swore I heard wings beating.[4]

"You break shit, you pay for it," I slurred and passed out.

4

"*H*alwen." An unfamiliar voice stirred me from the dream I'd been having about a donkey heist. Not riding into a heist *on* a donkey—stealing six of them. They were my beloved family now. "Haley."

I groaned, batting my hand at the scalding hot body splayed against my front. "Not now, I've got donkeys to save."

A snort stirred my hair, and I realised all at once that I should have been alone in bed.

"Mother*fucker*," I gasped, snapping my eyes open and lurching up and out of bed.

At least I was in my own bed, and I was still dressed in my pyjamas. I could have done *without* the arrogant bastard splayed on my mattress like he owned it, a cruel smirk on his mouth and inked fingers tapping on his knees.

Malakai was hot as sin, and I despised him for it. His crimson hair looked incredible against my pillow, but the sharp tips of his horns left a scratch on my headboard, and my eyes narrowed at the pale slice.

"You're buying me a new headboard," I growled.

Malakai shrugged, lines of ink winding around his

arms. I waited for him to strike me with magic, but nothing happened. Maybe the tattoos were alive? Fuck if I knew.

"Get off my bed, you cockroach."

He made a contemplative sound, and then said, "I like the name."

I made a throaty noise. Of course he did. Bastard.

A glare was glued to my face as I reached out and grabbed his arm, surprised by the thick layer of muscle I could feel under his skin *and* by his scorching temperature. I had a sleepy memory of being surrounded by delicious heat, and tried my hardest to stamp that memory out. But fuck, it had felt good.

"Out," I ordered, hauling on his arm. It was a tiny bed, and he looked damn near comical splayed across it. He also didn't budge until he threw a crooked grin my way and deigned to climb off the bed himself.

I realised far too late that he'd boxed me into the corner of my bedroom—well, the sad space I *called* my bedroom. He loomed a head above me, his curved black horns adding another seven inches, and menacing dominance coming off him in waves. Crimson eyes narrowed, his mouth pressed thin, and his shoulders blocked out the light from the window.

I shuddered.

"Here's the deal, Halwen," he said in a voice that oozed danger. "Fourteen assassins broke into your room with a single intention."

"To kill me," I agreed, stealing his thunder.

By the twitch in his jaw, he'd been about to say the exact same words. I tried not to preen in satisfaction.

I froze when he reached out to tuck a wayward strand of pink hair behind my ear.

My heart sped.

Dammit, now we were even. He didn't even *try* to hide his smirk.

"Exactly," he agreed. "And they're going to *keep* trying to kill you, because you pissed off a man with limitless power, dangerous connections, and zero morals. The guys and I are what you might call morally grey, but we *do* have morals unlike the bastard who hired you. You're a loose end."

Yeah, I realised that in the middle of fighting the intruders. But I shrugged. "I'll go on the run, set up somewhere new."

"Good plan," Malakai agreed, watching me too intensely for comfort. Like a viper fixed on its prey.

My stomach squirmed; I glanced over his shoulder at the rest of my home, planning my escape. Emlyn and Harvey were laid on my sofa, cuddled close like kittens. Aww, cute. I didn't spot Wane or his shadows anywhere, though, and a pang of worry went through my heart.

"I'm sensing a *but* coming," I sighed to Malakai.

"*But* you're alone, and easily overpowered."

"Hey!" I snarled, teeth bared and my feathers ruffled. Literally—my wings twitched angrily. "I was not *easily* overpowered. I'll have you know I killed *five* of those bastards before they got to me."

"At which point, you were easily overpowered," he drawled, red eyes glittering in his harsh face.

"Fine," I muttered, my ear tingling with warmth where he'd brushed my hair back. I viciously ignored the heat. "But only because she was indestructible. What's your point?"

"Our souls are the same," he replied, which was not what I expected to come out of his cruel mouth. "The idea of you getting hurt makes me want to set the entire realm on fire and toast marshmallows over the embers."

"I've never had marshmallows," I told him, my mood brightening.

Malakai snorted, but his lips lifted in a genuine smile. "You're fucking crazy."

"Takes one to know one, psycho."

He snagged another strand of my hair, giving it a hard enough tug to make me hiss; I snapped my wing at him in warning. "I'm trying to have an actual conversation here."

"You're pretty bad at it, aren't you?" I taunted, my whole body lighting up when he released the strand of hair only to grab a fistful, gripping tight enough that sparks leapt down my body.[1]

"Would you shut the fuck up?" he groaned, exasperation flattening his gaze.

"Dubious," I quipped, and let out an embarrassing whine when Malakai slammed his mouth onto mine.

He kissed me so fiercely I could barely catch a breath. When I *did* draw air, his fingers tightened in my hair until it hurt. My hands shot up, grabbing fistfuls of the black tunic he wore.

The wicked man distracted me from the sharp hurt by sucking on my tongue.

Holy fucking fuck.

I could count on one hand the number of good kisses I'd had in my life. Good sex was easier; all you had to do was pay attention to your partner and you were gold. But good *kisses?* Holy *Hell*, they were rare. And this was better than good; this was explosive and violent and for a second I forgot how to breathe.

"Better," he grunted, releasing my hair to glide his hand down my spine, pressing his hot palm to the small of my back. "Now be a good girl and stay quiet while I explain our proposition."

All I heard was he thought I was a good girl.

"More assassins will be sent after you, because you dared to disobey Cassander Locke. By happy coincidence, those same assassins are being sent after *us*, and we've learned a few tricks over the last year. You took us off guard, but that's the first time an assassin has gotten that close."

"Technically, it was a retrieval mission," I murmured, wondering if I could con Malakai into more kisses.

"No," he argued, but his anger was directed elsewhere, "trust me when I say you'd kill Wane by dragging him back there."

I had so many questions, but my head was too mushy to sort through them.

"Have you got to the proposition bit, yet?" I asked sassily.

Malakai groaned, dragging me flush against him. Heat and pleasure pounded through my clit when a hardness pressed against me. "Here, grind on this and keep quiet."

"Maybe I'll keep *you* quiet," I threatened.

"Maybe I'd like it," he whispered, his face close to mine.

I should probably be stabbing him and running away, shouldn't I? He was an obvious threat, and clearly crazy. Anyone else, and I'd have been out the door before they could touch my hand, let alone kiss me senseless.

"Come with us," he urged. "Instead of fighting off the assassins on your own, come with us. There's safety in numbers."

I made a face. "I'm not a people person."

Malakai chuckled, the sound vibrating into my chest. "And we are?"

Eh, he had a point.

"How do I know you won't stab me in my sleep?" I asked, squinting suspiciously.

"Because we're your mates, stupid woman," he groaned.

"Call me stupid woman, and I'll make you infertile for the rest of your life," I threatened. I controlled blood; it wasn't an idle threat.

I went still when he jerked forward, dragging his tongue up my cheek and groaning at my taste.

"I almost want to," he breathed against my wet skin. "But that would deprive us both of a delicious future."

Oh man, he was *really* crazy. I thought he was a little insane, but this was asylum-worthy.

"We can't hurt you," he echoed his point, drawing back to look at me and flicking his tongue against his lips, as if there was still a taste of me there. My pussy clenched hard. I wished, not for the first time, I had a normal, safe taste in men. Sadly, this level of sheer madness did wicked things to my body.

"Because of the mate bond?" I guessed. I'd heard of mates, but never met anyone who had one.

It was like marriage, friendship, kinship, and unconditional love rolled into one magical fusion of souls. It was the stuff of legends and fairy tales, and I highly doubted a fairy tale would choose four coarse, psycho bastards and a mercenary to play out its fabled story.

"Can you feel it?" Malakai asked, his focus honed on me and sharp enough to make my belly squirm. "The bond?"

In a rare moment of sense and logic, I disentangled myself from the six-foot-tall package of unhinged violence and stepped back. Not that I had far to go; my place wasn't exactly roomy.[2]

"I can't feel anything. Sorry, cockroach."

The flash of challenge in his eyes made my stomach twist into an even tighter knot. I slipped across the room away from him, pulling clearer air into my lungs. His heady scent of amber and crackling firewood muddied my common sense.

I sighed when I looked at Emlyn and Harvey on my sofa, feeling a strange combination of emotions. Like a kitten had destroyed my room, clawed up my curtains, pissed on my favourite rug ... but then fell asleep in the cutest possible way.

I was alarmed by the soft feelings in my chest, and even more unsettled by the cannonball that hurtled against my ribs from the inside.

"What the fuck?" I demanded, my hand flying to my chest.

Malakai laughed. "Good. You felt it."

I shot him a seething glare which intensified in heat when I saw he'd helped himself to my bed. *Again*. He sprawled across it like a lazy prince. At least he'd taken his boots off; if shoes had met my covers for even a second, he'd be dead, mate or not.

"And since you felt it," he went on with a crooked grin, "you can stop denying the bond's existence."

My expression went flat. I let him see all my exasperation. "I want you out of my home."

"That's nice," he murmured, getting comfier in my bed. His horn left another scratch on my headboard.

I took a threatening step towards him, but paused when he spoke.

"You'd be dead if we hadn't been watching you. You're lucky we got here in time; you were thirty seconds from death. It would be a shame if we weren't there to save you again." He met my glare from across the room, his red eyes urging me to agree with his madness. "Come with us. We're setting up a permanent safe house so we don't have to run forever. As our mate, you have a place there."

I ground my teeth. "I'm not settling down with you fuckers. I'm no sweet housewife."

"More like a panther," he teased.

I raised my eyebrows in agreement, trying to hide how he'd poked at my insecurities. "So you agree. You're better off by yourselves, and I'm perfectly fine alone."

"Who said being a panther was a negative, sweetheart?"

"Well, that's a step up from *stupid woman,*" I muttered, but his meaning finally processed and I blinked. "So you're into women who want to scratch your eyes out?"

Malakai gave me a cocky grin. "I bet I can have you clawing my back instead."

"Don't antagonise her, Kai," a quiet voice murmured, and I jumped in surprise.

Wane had materialised out of his shadows; I watched him climb to his feet in the corner of the room and understood *exactly* why he slept over there. It had a good view of the door, and with both walls behind him no one could sneak up on his vulnerable back. My heart thumped with sympathy.

"Not antagonising," Malakai replied, crossing his ankles on my bed. "Just convincing her to come with us."

Wane's silver eyes flared with panic, and he snapped his attention to me as shadows bound tighter around him. "That's up for debate. We *have* to stay together. Locke will get you, and he'll—he'll—"

Malakai shot off my bed and stormed across the room, reaching through the blanket of shadows for Wane.

Shit. What the hell had Wane been through, to be so traumatised? My instincts battered at me, urging me to approach the shadows and haul him into a tight hug. I took a step forward, but logic held me back. My client, this Locke, had obviously hurt Wane; he'd hardly want a mercenary like me touching him.

I sighed and dragged a hand over my face, rubbing the crust of sleep off my eyelashes. Malakai was right; Locke would keep sending people after me, and it would get tedious real fast. I'd almost been strangled to death, and I might have had the inflated bravado of a housecat, but it had rattled me.

These four could be biding their time, playing me, but if they *were*, I had my weapons and my magic. I could take them down before they hurt me.

And yet ... two of them were asleep on my sofa, one of

them was in the midst of a panic, and the other was trying to calm him. They were pretty unlikely murderers. And there was no ignoring the soulmate thing.

"Fine," I sighed quietly. "I'll come with you. But the second any of you lays a finger on me, I'm cutting body parts off."

The shadows around Wane's face thinned enough for me to see the relief there. "Thank you. You'll be safer with us."

Malakai tilted his red head, considering me in a way that made me nervous. "What about a finger *inside* you?"

I rolled my eyes and went to wake the cuddling demons. They could help me pack up my shit.

5

Two months later

*E*verything was rosy and rainbows for two months, if you didn't count clashing with Kai and getting scolded by Emlyn for stealing shit, starting fights, and taking on dangerous jobs.[1] It turned out the gentle, bearded giant wasn't quiet because he was mild mannered, but because he measured his words carefully. And when he went on a rant, he went on *a rant.*

I sensed him building up to one now as he shot Harvey an *I told you so* look. To be fair, he had warned us this job was too good to be true. The posted info only said we needed to pick up a package and drop it off on a street corner uncomfortably close to Akstrang. Five thousand silver for an afternoon's work? Of course we signed up.

But Akstrang? I'd only spent two years in the children's home when I was sixteen, but it was long enough to leave its scars. I'd left enough scars on other kids—and adults—too, but I still preferred to stay away from his place.

Harvey edged closer, brushing my arm. He'd been finding

little excuses to touch me for weeks, and I was growing more used to it each time. I was starting to crave the touches, which was dangerous as fuck. They kept looking at me like I was their perfect woman, and I kept waiting for them to wake up and see what I really was: not a beautiful doll but a wolf with bared teeth.

The only issue was they'd seen me fight, and even seen me kill an assassin that hunted us last month, and their eyes *still* followed me when I walked into the room.[2] I was so used to not forming connections because men usually preferred their women meek and submissive, or at the very least *polite*. This was ... strange.

"Are you okay?" Harvey asked, his voice dipped low and stripped of its usual laughter. He was always more serious, less himself, when we went on jobs. At least until the fighting started, and he seemed to thrive in the chaos of violence. Especially with Kai goading him; those two bickered like an old, married couple.

"Fine," I replied, and jumped when his fingertips skimmed mine where they were curled into a fist at my side. "I'm just uncomfortably acquainted with this part of Hell," I added, and patted myself on the back for sharing something personal.

"You're safe with us," Wane's raspy voice came from my left, making my heart jump out of my chest. Fuck, he was so quiet and so completely covered in his shadows that he was a talented sneak. "Always, Haley."

"I know that," I replied, dismissive. It wasn't that I didn't feel *safe*. They were being dramatic.

But Harvey's fingers skimmed my knuckles, and a knot I didn't realise had formed in my chest unwound a fraction. "Anyone who even *thinks* about hurting you will die instantly," he assured me.[3]

"Thanks," I replied gruffly, and hoped he didn't notice the

heat that flooded my face when Wane's shadows brushed my other hand, filling my head with all kinds of indecent ideas. Sandwiched between them, sunlight and shadow on either side of me, two cocks filling me—

Nope. Bad Halwen. Bad, bad Halwen.

"You know we care about you, don't you?" Wane asked, shadows thinning over his face so I could see his big, silver puppy eyes. I fought a groan, my heart softening. "You're our mate, Halwen."

"You can call me Haley," I said, disturbed by the emotions fluttering in my chest. "If you want," I added quickly, and internally cursed myself. *A little handholding and you're acting like a bashful teenager?*

"What about me?" Malakai demanded, stopping where he walked with Emlyn on the dirt road ahead of us and spinning to face me. His jaw clenched; he crossed his arms over his chest. I waited for his red tail to start swishing like an angry cat, but it was sadly still, hanging behind him. "Do I get to call you Haley?"

Unlike the others, Kai refused to give me space and time to get used to the whole *mate* thing. He seemed to think that little M word gave him permission to touch me whenever he wanted, climb into my bed in the morning, and kiss me even if I was busy reading, or training, or even defending myself from the mercs Cassander Locke sent at us.

"No," I replied just to piss Kai off.

Crimson eyes flashed and glowed. He stalked closer. My heart skipped, instincts blaring that a predator had me in his sights.

Harvey snorted and let go of my hand. "You're in for it now, Sugarplum."

I shot him a sharp look when he went to stand beside Emlyn. "Traitor. Wane, you'd never leave me, would you?" I asked his brother, matching his wide, pleading look with my own.

Wane wrapped a tendril of shadow around my wrist and —and brought my hand to his mouth. When he kissed my knuckles, my heart legitimately skipped. Wane never touched anyone. Ever. I didn't know why, or what had happened to him, but I knew touch triggered him into violent memories.

I was so stunned by the kiss that I missed him stepping back.

"Kai isn't going to hurt you," he said, eyes flickering with amusement. "He's more likely to push you to the ground and rut you."

My mouth fell open in shock as Wane went to stand with the others, that glimmer of amusement growing in his eyes. "Hey—"

I drew a knife when Kai grabbed me, but I was a little distracted when instead of pulling my hair or choking off my air, he thrust his hand inside my leather trousers and cupped my pussy.

"Ah—" I gasped, fingers white around the knife when he buried a finger inside me.

We were out in the open, on a dirt road surrounded by low hills. There were houses only a minute away. Anyone with sharp eyes and magic would be able to see where his hand was.

"Tell me I can call you Haley," Kai demanded, his face hard but a gleam of obsession in his crimson eyes. The ink wrapped around his body moved, restless.

"Fuck you," I breathed, and threw a scowl over his shoulder. "And fuck all of you for just watching."

Even Emlyn didn't intervene, his arms crossed over his chest and curiosity on his face. His blue eyes were a shade darker, hunger barely hidden there. Great, he was enjoying the show.[4]

"Who made this pussy wet, my rose?" Kai asked, stroking his finger in and out of me as much as he could with my trousers in the way. That was another thing—he kept calling me that. *My rose.* He hadn't explained why, and refused to stop even when I cut him a teeny, tiny bit with my knife. I'd given up trying.

"Like I said," I spat, my face hot and the heat spreading to the rest of me. My knife slid a little lower, less threatening. Dammit. *"Fuck you."*

Kai leaned into my personal space, his lips finding my neck—a spot he'd found through relentless study of my body these two months. "Was it Harvey? Wane? Or—was it both of them, together?"

I stifled a groan, my pussy clenching around his finger.

Kai laughed against my throat, grazing sharp teeth in a threat. My heartbeat jumped. "I felt that, *Haley.*"

"Fine," I gasped when he adjusted his angle. He loved the noise if his grin was anything to go by. "You can call me Haley."

"I know I can. That's old news." He wrenched my body into his with the finger he had inside me, putting pressure on a spot that made me moan. Loudly. "Let's talk about you wanting two cocks at once."

"Never said at once," I panted, glaring at his sharp, infuriating face.

Kai tilted his head, crimson hair spilling over one shoulder. "So you *don't* want your mates to fill your needy holes at the same time? To fuck you until all you can do is tremble and moan as we give you so much pleasure that you forget how to breathe?"

"Kai," I warned. Pleaded.

His finger curled inside me, moving faster. I wanted another, and like he could see the plea in my eyes or sensed it through the bond, he glided a second finger into me. My hips jerked into his, pushing them deeper.

"One in this needy, dripping pussy," he went on, putting his lips to my ear so every breath sent a shiver through me. "One in your filthy, swearing mouth. But that's only two— where should the others go?"

I was going to kill him.

"Make me come, or take your hand out of my fucking pants."

"Is that a threat, my rose?"

"Yes," I snarled, my whole body wound tight.

"Fuck, I love it when you threaten me," he groaned, dragging his mouth down my neck and nipping my throat. His fingers moved faster, and my face burned at the wet sounds his palm made when it ground against my clit.

I swore at the added stimulation, frantically sheathing my knife so I could clutch him with both hands. I hoped my fingernails drew blood; he deserved it.

Footsteps scuffed the ground and made me jump, but it was only Emlyn, Wane, and Harvey. Coming for a closer look. I groaned and dropped my head on Kai's shoulder, heat pounding through me.

"I think," Emlyn said, his deep voice making my inner muscles flutter, "our mate would like a cock in her pussy and another in her ass."

I shuddered hard, digging my nails into Kai's arms, my bottom lip caught between my teeth as his fingers drove into me faster.

"That was a big one, my rose," Kai purred. "Your pussy's gripping my fingers so tight. Is Emlyn right? Does your greedy ass need to be stretched around my cock while Em fills this dripping pussy, Harvey fucks your mouth, and Wane strokes himself, watching you be our pretty whore?"

I was a mercenary and a tough bitch; why was I whimpering?

I swallowed, nodding. My whole body was red hot under my clothes. I could only pant and cling to him as he fucked me with his fingers better than most men had with their dicks.

"Good girl for admitting it," Kai praised, kissing my neck and drawing back to look at me. I knew what he'd see; red-faced, wide-eyed, breathless desperation. His free hand curved over the back of my head as he laid another kiss on my cheek. "We'll give you everything. Won't we, guys?"

"Everything and more," Harvey promised, edging closer so he could touch me. Knuckles glided softly over my cheek and down my jaw, and I bit my lip to trap a whine, leaning into the touch.

"Everything you can dream of," Emlyn added, catching my eye as he walked around me, pressing his chest against my back. Broad, hot hands slid up my stomach to cup my breasts until my pussy throbbed wildly around Kai's fingers.

Kai flicked a glance to my left, and my heart lurched in my chest when I saw the hunger in Wane's expression. The angles of his bronze face were tighter, sharper, his silver gaze fixed on me. He stood a few paces from us, but his shadows had thinned enough that I saw the hands fisted at his sides and the way his stomach hollowed with a rough breath.

"There's nothing I don't want to do to you, Haley," he rasped, holding my gaze.

The heat in my belly coiled tighter, my toes curling in my boots. I didn't take my eyes off Wane, but it was Harvey who tipped me over the edge when his fingers shoved their way into my trousers and grazed my clit.

"Fuck," I cried, digging my fingernails into Kai's arms and holding on desperately as pleasure slammed into me like a hammer. The waves were so forceful and all-consuming that I

didn't stand a chance of holding in my moans. Anyone with their window open right now must have heard every breathy noise, and I did not care. It felt too incredible to stop.

"That's it," Kai breathed fiercely, stroking me through each spasm. "Come all over our fingers, Haley. This pussy knows who it belongs to; it's time you realised it, too."

That should not have made me come harder. Fuck, I was in trouble with these men.

It took a long, long minute for the shudders to die down. My head spun, strangely light. My lungs filled with blissful air.

"Beautiful," Emlyn sighed, his voice deep and rough as he wrapped both arms around my waist. "So beautiful."

I was a stab-happy, filthy-mouthed mercenary with a dark grey moral compass, but for the first time I felt feminine and desirable and—good. I felt really fucking *good*. I wanted to feel this more, and it wasn't just the orgasm. It was them, their words, the way they looked at me.

Harvey slid his fingers out of my pants first, licking my arousal from them instead of wiping them clean. The man was insane, or insatiable, or both. He groaned, eyes darker as they flicked to me. "I want more."

"Not now," Emlyn disagreed, stroking my stomach. "We're going to be late picking up the package; we don't have time for more."

He dropped a kiss on my head, almost like an apology. I never wanted to leave his arms. It was the safest I'd felt in months. Maybe years.

Who knew what I needed more than anything was for Kai to shove his hand down my pants and give me a grand awakening?

I'd been tolerating the mate bonds these two months, but possibilities opened up now, and they were endless. So many orgasms, so little time.

"Here," Kai huffed, stroking my pussy one last time before he withdrew his fingers. Harvey literally *skidded* across the ground to grab Kai's hand, sucking them clean.

My pussy throbbed again, more in curiosity than any pressing need. The sight intrigued me, too. These men had been together a long time before I found them. Had they ever been intimate with each other...? Gods, they'd be beautiful together.

"Shit!" Wane hissed so suddenly that I jumped.

I was still dazed and relaxed enough that I forgot to reach for a weapon, though. He threw himself at me, a whirlwind of shadows brushing my skin, wrapping around my body and feeling like *heaven* on my wings. Before his fingers could touch me, too, a solid cage of orange magic slammed down around us. It sizzled hot enough to tell me I'd blacken my fingers if I dared to touche it.

"Great!" Harvey snarled, pacing as much as he could in the cage, his tawny wings tense at his back. "Now we're fucking trapped!"

"I knew this was a bad idea," Emlyn growled, his softness gone and the gruffness back in his voice. He didn't let go of me, though, and Wane's shadows pressed up against me too.

"I wouldn't say *bad* idea," Kai disagreed, giving me an impish smile. "I'd say it's time for round two."

"Oh, no you don't," I argued, holding up my hands when Kai pressed his body back to mine.

"Oh, yes I *do,*" he countered, and kissed me hard, making any argument impossible.

His tongue made my head spin, my breathing non-existent, and my underwear soaked all the way through. Now I knew the pleasure he could offer, I wasn't opposed to more. I just liked bickering with him.

When his mouth dragged down my jaw, I looked at Harvey and Wane for backup. This was the worst time for sex, and an even worse time for an orgy. We needed to get out of the trap before the mercenaries found us. Or worse—*him*. Locke's favourite hunter whose intense stare chilled even my blood.

I should have known better than to expect sense from Harvey.

He already had his cock in his hand.

6

Ten years later

I couldn't say for sure what woke me up, but the four bonds wrapped around my soul were my number one suspect.

Wane was innocent—he was tucked against my chest, warm breaths puffing over my skin. His shadows were the thinnest I'd seen them in a while, only a light mist draped over his back. It was a sign of how safe he felt here with me.

It had been two years since the last attack, and I had to admit things were starting to feel steady and secure. I still slept with a knife on the bedside table like I did ten years ago, but at least I'd stopped putting it under my pillow. Mostly because Harvey nicked his ear on it one night and whinged about it for three weeks. It was no bigger than a papercut. Big baby.

I jumped when the dull smack of flesh meeting flesh came from downstairs, my wings ruffling in surprise—one splayed behind me and one draped over my mate, our feathers overlapping. Ink and blue-black merged into one.

"Zivai," I murmured to wake Wane, though if anyone ever witnessed me being so soft and calling him *my heart,* I'd firmly deny it.

A breath caught in his throat; his arms tightened around me and a velvety shadow caressed my cheek. "Is it morning?"

"Mm," I confirmed, enjoying the feeling of Wane holding me close. He was taller than I expected when he first dropped his shields for me to fully see him, but nestled so close to me he seemed worryingly small and fragile. I ran my fingers through the long, messy strands of his chestnut hair and was rewarded with him melting into me like he was made of liquid night instead of flesh and bone. "Someone's fighting downstairs."

He jerked like I had when I heard the noise, rubbing his eyes as he pulled away and smiling at my noise of complaint. "You don't sound worried."

"There's no panic in my bonds," I replied, sinking deep into my soul where the others were entwined around me. Emlyn was busy but distracted, and Harvey and Malakai thrummed with determination and satisfaction. No panic, no alarm, no stress.

"Come back here." I opened my arms, taking this rare chance to study Wane in all his beautiful glory.

A soft green shirt hung loose over his torso but it clung to the defined curves of his upper chest, and his long hair tumbled over his shoulders, mussed by sleep. A vein in his forearm caught my attention, and I wished I could trace it with my tongue. I wished I could kiss all the pale scars that made a callous canvas of his body.

But it was a miracle and a gift that he'd sleep in a bed with me, and let me *hold* him. As badly as I wanted more, wanted *everything,* I couldn't push him. The idea of hurting my mate, triggering him, made me sick.

"You're not wearing a shirt," he murmured, as if he'd forgotten during the night.

I waggled my eyebrows, stretching on the bed. "Enjoying the view?"

He laughed, silver eyes averted from my gaze but trailing the muscle, curves, and scars of my chest and stomach.

"Always, itzaia," he said, husky and sweet.

Itzaia—*my soul.*

When he was so adoring and lovely, could you blame me for being a complete sap in return?

He snuggled back against me, his hands tracing a raised slash on my lower belly. I ignored the way my gut squirmed, his fingers on my stomach reminding me of the emptiness inside it. We'd been together for ten years, safe for two, and trying for a baby for most of that time. And ... nothing.

Sensing the turn of my mood, Wane pulled me flush against him, his arms tight around me and shadows caressing me.

Another loud smack came from downstairs a minute later. Wane drew back with a frown.

His features were softer than Harvey's up close, his eyes the same quicksilver but heavier, more haunted. I knew some of his past now, knew he and his brother had been raised in true and total darkness and only saw light when they killed their jailor uncle and fled their abusive father. I couldn't imagine living my entire childhood in the dark, never seeing the sun for twenty years.

I kissed the curve of Wane's jaw as he frowned at the door, as if he could see what our family were up to through the wood.

"I bet they're trying the Devil's Tornado again," he mused, amusement in his soft, raspy voice.

I jolted back, eyebrows slamming down over my eyes.

"They better fucking *not* be. The last time they did that, they broke my good knife display and put a hole in the wall."

Wane laughed, and as gruff and annoyed as I was at the thought of our home suffering more idiotic destruction, my heart went all soft and squishy at the sound.

Before I climbed out of bed, I trailed my fingertips along his jaw and brought his face to mine for a quick kiss. It wasn't easy to judge how much contact he was okay with, so I tried to be as gentle as possible. But sometimes he surprised me, like now when a hot hand grasped my thigh and pulled it over his leg so he could fit closer, kissing me deeper, harder.

"Fuck," I groaned against Wane's lips, my hands tingling with the need to feel more of him, to sink my fingers into his hair, to hold his face as he kissed me like a starving man. But I held back, not wanting to ruin the moment. Heat and liquid built between my legs, my clit throbbing hard, and I arched into his body, desperate and flush and sensitive.

"Touch me," he rasped, his hands wandering down my bare back until I was shuddering and moaning into his mouth. His taste overwhelmed my senses with the sweetest wine until I was drunk on him, and I wasted no time in touching him.

I tangled fingers in his hair, and slid my other hand under his shirt and across sleep-flushed skin. Wane kissed me hard, rough with the same urgent passion I felt as I caressed his body, loving every single inch of him.[1]

We only drew apart when something crashed downstairs.

"Fuckers," I spat, but breathlessly. My head spun, need pulsing in my pussy and my skin on fucking *fire.*

"Should I kill them for you?" Wane asked, silver eyes bright with happiness.

"Depends what they broke," I muttered, stroking my fingers across his stomach. I drew them from under his shirt when he shuddered, and brushed his brown hair back into place before letting go. "I suppose we should go see the damage."

"Haley," he breathed when I climbed out of bed and hunted down a shirt.

"Mm?"

"I'm sorry I can't—"

I snapped upright, tunic in hand. "Fuck that. You're completely perfect. Don't *ever* think you're not. You give me *everything* I need." I waited for him to look at me, but he didn't. "Wane. *Zivai.*"

His breath hitched; he lifted his head and met my steady gaze. Kneeling on the bed, his wings slumped behind him, he looked like the broken man I met ten years ago. Sometimes, I thought I was still the snarling, broken woman they met, too. Healing took time.

"You give me everything I need," I said emphatically. "You are enough."

A corner of his mouth flicked up; he ran his hands down his face. "Ten years, and you're still telling me that."

"And I'll *keep* telling you," I replied, opening my arms and wings in an offer.

He scrambled off the bed and practically dove into my embrace, bending over so he could touch me everywhere. I wrapped him up in my arms, and bound my wings around him in a protective cocoon.

The distinct sound of someone being slammed into a wall echoed up the stairs, and I tilted my head back to yell, "Stop breaking my shit!"

"Get down here and stop us then!" Harvey shouted back.

I laughed, laid a kiss on the side of Wane's head, and let him put space between us. Through the bond, I felt the itchiness of his discomfort approaching. He'd almost reached his quota for touch this morning.

"Tea?" I asked, angling my head in a *follow me* gesture as I headed into the hall.

The guys planned this house long before we met, but I swore they'd looked into my head and built my dream house. It was everything I ever imagined, from the huge attic bedroom to the round windows on the landing to the bright, airy kitchen and living space downstairs.

I hoped there was still something left of my beloved kitchen, but I wasn't too optimistic.

"Alright, fuckers, what did you break?" I demanded, stalking into the open plan room on the ground floor, and scanning it with a keen eye.

My sofas were intact, and my replacement weapons cabinet was still standing. There were three logs scattered across the room, though, and in the kitchen ... *godsdammit.*

"Devil's tornado?" I demanded, watching Malakai and Harvey grapple with each other, circling so fast they'd be dizzy if they weren't so demonic.

It had been a shock to find out they weren't regular demons, but long-lived *arch*demons. They weren't as immortal as Lucifer and his inner circle, but they'd last a good five hundred years. As their mate, I still wasn't sure what that meant for me—being bound to them could extend my life, too.

"Two plates and a mug," Emlyn answered my question, nodding at a pile of shattered pottery that had been swept into the corner, likely by him. My other mates didn't clean up after themselves. Spoiled brats.

"I warned them they'd knock them off," he added, lifting a mug of coffee to his mouth and glancing at me over the top of a leather-bound book with a gold tree stamped in its centre. "Any chance you can rein in your brother, Wane?"

"Zero chance," Wane replied with a long-suffering huff that did little to cover up his fondness.

He approached the kitchen via the long route, avoiding the whirling mass of limbs to grab the coffee press and pour dark liquid into a mug.

I frowned, watching the floor so I didn't cut myself on any wayward shards of broken crockery as I approached. Wane didn't drink coffee; he'd gone through a phase of drinking herbal tea but was now firmly in his black tea era.

I swear, my entire body, heart, and *soul* softened when he added milk and honey, and I realised he'd made the coffee *for me.*

I let all my love show when he handed me the mug. My heart legitimately skipped when he bent to kiss my brow even though he was at his limit.

"Hey, you don't look at *me* like that," Harvey complained, tossing shaggy hair out of his face.

I took a drink of sweet, bitter coffee and smirked. "Stop smashing up my house, and I will."

"*Our* house," Malakai corrected, shoving wine-red hair off his forehead. Damn, he looked good all sweaty and worked up, his eyes gleaming with excitement and inked scripture swirling on his bare chest.

"*My* house," I corrected right back. "Em, whose house is it?"

Emlyn set down his book and steepled his big hands. "On paper, it's ours. But in reality? It's yours, Hales."

I stuck my tongue out at Malakai. A thrill made butterflies burst in my stomach when his red eyes flashed. I'd pay for that comment later, and enjoy every damn second of it.

"We need to go shopping," Wane murmured, opening cupboards with one shadow-wrapped hand while the other held a mug of steaming tea. I was pleased to know him, and his drink of choice, so well.

If I could go back in time and tell myself I'd be here, living in an amazing house, with four men I loved so much my heart exploded, in domestic fucking bliss? I'd check myself into an asylum for delusion.

"There are spiced cakes," Emlyn replied, stretching his arms over his head, either because his muscles were stiff or because he wanted my eyes on him. I trailed a hungry stare over every bit of bulging, tempting muscle, and the heat Wane had started upstairs pounded again in my pussy. "We can heat those up for breakfast, and later—hello, Halwen," he laughed when I plopped onto his lap, straddling him.

His arms settled around my back, reassuringly strong.

"Don't mind me," I murmured, resting my hands on his big shoulders. Em was still a man of few words, but his deep, rumbly voice was addictive as hell. Especially when I felt it vibrate on a certain area...

"Are you in heat?" Malakai asked with a laugh.

"Yes," I deadpanned, resting my head on Em's shoulder to give Kai a sulky look.

"I propose a change of plans," Harvey said, his voice lower, softer as he prowled around the table. I bit my lip. "Spiced cakes can wait; I know exactly what I want to eat for breakfast. Up on the table and spread your legs, sugarplum."

I laughed in surprise, but heat razed through my body and I swallowed. I looked from Emlyn to Harvey to Kai and Wane. If I hadn't glanced at Wane, I'd never have seen the shadowy figures in the garden outside the window—or the ball of fire streaking from the forest right at us.

"Wane!" I screamed and threw myself out of Emlyn's lap, slamming into my shadowy mate.

I knocked him away from the wall just as the unnatural fire hit our house and spread faster than a wildfire.

7

"*I*tzaia, *itzaia,*" Wane breathed, running panicked hands over my face and down my neck to my shoulders.

"Are you hurt?" I demanded, my head rattled but my instincts kicked in instantly. "Did the magic touch you?"

"No," he rasped, grabbing my waist and rolling us further into the kitchen. "I'm fine."

"Guys?" I demanded, my voice screeching.

"We're okay," Emlyn rumbled, loosening the knot in my chest.

"Apart from being under attack," Kai hissed.

Shadows blasted around me and Wane as he crawled to the couch where the others sheltered. "I'll kill them," he seethed.

"I'll fucking help," Harvey spat, looking remarkably like his brother when they were both raging with protectiveness. "It's him again."

The assassin we'd tried to kill six times and failed, the smug, evil bastard who taunted and gloated. He broke Em's arm the last time we fought.

"Neither of you are doing anything," Emlyn growled, nostrils flaring in his bearded face as he took charge. "Get out the back door. We're not fighting."

"Like *Hell* we're not," I spat, peering around the side of the sofa. Through the fire and smoke, I glimpsed shadows, figures. I knew which one was his—talk and commanding, his hair sleek and pretty. That beauty hid a deep, wicked ugliness. "They just sent a *fireball* at my house! I'm not letting them destroy what's left of it."

"The next one could hit *you*," Emlyn hissed right back, his teeth bared and sharp behind his beard. "Out—all of you. *Now!*"

I didn't argue, but I made my displeasure known with a glower as we crawled towards the back door, only faltering when the house shook as more magic hit it. Not fire this time. This was *him,* I knew it. All the fine hairs on my body stood on end, my stomach churning and soul flinching like he'd struck me and not the house.

I jumped when another fireball hit the front of the house, thrown by whatever merc Locke paid this time. Kai and Wane both had shields around the exterior, but the fire burned through them like cobwebs. Emlyn was right, as much as I didn't want to admit it. And I couldn't let one of my mates be burned next.

I gazed longingly at my weapons cabinet, but it was all the way across the room. Instinct wouldn't let me leave my mates' sides to arm myself.

"Wane," I breathed, glancing around for my mate. I could feel him beside me, and his heat met my side, but he'd vanished entirely. Not even his shadows were visible. "It's alright; no one's going to hurt you. I won't let them."

Fierceness bled into my voice with that promise. Harvey had grown up in the dark too, but he'd filled himself with light and humour in defiance of those horrors. Wane had taken the dark *into* himself. He'd been through worse, unspeakable nightmares. Even Harvey wouldn't tell me what had been done to him, but Wane's scars gave me a good guess.

Even years later, my bastard client, his monster of a *father,* was still hunting him. The man who abused his children and let his brother do the same, who made Wane into a terrified man—he would never let them live in peace.

Two fucking years, that's all we had. And now the tentative peace we built crashed and burned around us.

"Fuck!" Kai exploded, rage in his voice when the exterior wall in the kitchen came tumbling down. But there was pain there, too. This was our home, our sanctuary. We were *happy* here—and it was on fire. *"Shit!"*

"Keep it together," Emlyn growled as we crawled faster, the voice of reason. "Kai, go out first and take out anyone who's out there. Then Hales and Wane will follow. Me and Harvey will take the back. Defensive position."

My ears hunched by my shoulders at those two words. For years, I'd heard them every few months. In the beginning, I'd drilled and practised for hours every day until I learned the manoeuvre, until it was second nature.

We'd been *safe!* We were supposed to live happily ever after here. My throat burned. My eyes stung ruthlessly.

"Kai," I choked out when he reached the back door. He snapped his attention to me, his crimson eyes livid. "Don't do anything stupid. Please."

He blew out a hard breath at what I didn't say—*don't leave me*—and nodded. He was still shirtless from sparring, so nothing covered the thick lines of text wrapped around his chest as they began to spiral faster and faster.

"I'll stay safe if you will," he agreed.

I nodded, my throat too tight to speak.

We were supposed to be safe! I was terrified someone would get hurt, but equally terrified that any progress Wane had made these past two years would be lost. He worked so fucking hard, had healed *so much,* and it felt like I already lost him with the first blast.

"Hales," Emlyn murmured, and I dragged my eyes away from the door Kai disappeared through. I couldn't hear sounds of a struggle outside, but I felt the thrum of Kai's power and imagined invisible whips choking off our attackers' air. Snakes, every bit as alive as Kai. *"Breathe."*

"I'm fine," I dismissed. But there was a pit in my stomach, and I couldn't catch a breath, and I was going to be sick.

I didn't miss the look Emlyn shot at the space beside me, where heat wafted from Wane's body. Em could sense what was wrong, what I needed. I shook my head at my protective mate. I'd be fine as long as we all got out of this unhurt.

I noticed no one spoke about defending the house; we were abandoning it like we'd abandoned so many houses over the years. But this wasn't just a safe house; it was our home.

My bottom lip wobbled when a shadow wrapped around my wrist, the ends tying together so I wore a soft, velvety bracelet.

"We'll be okay," Wane murmured.

I nodded, and choked down the lump in my throat.

It was running and fighting time, not breakdown time. I needed to get my shit together.

A grunt came from outside, and I took that as my cue to jump to my feet and burst through the door.

There were seven people in our vegetable garden, most in the standard black uniform of all assassins and mercenaries, but one in dark crimson leather. Ah, shit, not an Islavian warrior. There were three of them in the mercenaries' guild and every single one of them hated me. There were even more who *weren't* part of the guild, and they hated me more.

"Traitor," the warrior woman spat, her saliva burning a hole in my lawn as I paused in the garden.

Angelfucker!

The air shimmied behind me, telling me Wane followed. Emlyn and Harvey wouldn't be too far behind us.

"Flavia," I greeted, subtly nudging Wane towards the mercs trampling my rose bushes. "Delightful to see you again. And look, you've made friends. I'm proud of you."

"Is now a good time to be taunting her?" Kai demanded from deeper in the garden, whipping his hands through the air at lightning speed. Mercenaries were struck down or knocked aside wherever his invisible power lashed.

I watched one man smirk as he brought a knife down on the power, cutting himself free. I snorted. Malakai's magic wasn't ropes or cord; he wielded *snakes*, and like the mythical Hydra, whenever one was cut, two grew back.

"Halwen," Flavia spat at me, abandoning her attempt to free one of her buddies to give me her full focus. Lucky me. She looked the same as ever, snotty and sneering, her tanned face and golden hair pretty but the rest of her dripping in hideousness. "I wondered where you crawled off to."

We'd been friends until we got into a minor disagreement about a shared job. The orders had been to kill a crime family, and I'd been completely on board until I found out that included a five-year-old boy. Flavia tried to assassinate the kid. I tried to assassinate *her.*

I tilted my head, circling her and aware that my two other mates crept into the garden, their panic and adrenaline thumping through my body like it was my own.

Blood roared in my ears, mine and that of everyone else here. Locke's favourite Hunter came leisurely closer, content to watch. His blood pounded the same rhythm as mine—fast and violent. *Bastard.*

I focused on Flavia, heat like a wall behind me as fire

raged. "Crawled off to? I've been living in the lap of luxury in a giant house, with my every need attended to by my servants."

"Mates," Kai bit out, grappling with a massive mercenary.

"Same thing. Where have *you* been, Flavia? Miserable and alone as usual? Last I checked, even rats ran from the sight of you."

She bared her teeth—needle-thin and silver—in a semblance of a grin, and drew her long, serrated knives. Those knives were a declaration of murder in themselves.

From the corner of my eye, I saw a giant, green-skinned fucker charge at Harvey. Without taking my attention from Flavia, the biggest threat, I lifted my hand and flicked my wrist. Most demons had elemental magic, or flight or strength—something normal. But I could feel the thump and flow of blood in someone's veins.

Right now, the blood leaking from someone Wane killed sang to me, and I felt the slowing heartbeat of whoever Kai was choking out. But it was the panicked thrum of my mates' pulses that called to me, that reminded me why everyone here had to die. The exhilaration in the mercs' blood just wound my fury to a fever pitch.

It was scarily easy to grab control of the green guy's bloodstream and give it a little tug. His heart seized; I felt it even across the garden and my own blood shuddered in response.

Flavia rushed at me, sensing what I was doing or just bored of waiting to fight.[1]

"Really, Sugarplum?" Harvey groaned when the green guy exploded, covering him in goop and gore. Ah, I might have tugged a little too forcefully.

"Sorry," I called, but my attention was fixed on Flavia as the golden woman hurtled at me, flickering light limning her red leathers in fiery orange. My poor, burning house.

Hurt and wrath fused inside me; I used them to launch across the lawn and slam into Flavia before she could gain the upper hand.

"I've had plenty of company, for your information," Flavia bragged, lethal teeth bared as she aimed her knives at my chest. I grabbed her wrists, digging my nails into her golden skin. "Thanks to you, I've been busy this last decade and paid handsomely for it."

"Happy to be of service," I replied, teeth gritted against the force of keeping her back, my biceps burning. Fuck, I'd forgotten how strong the Islavian warriors were. They trained in a volcano at the heart of Hell, for Lucifer's sake. *I'd* trained in a children's home in shitty Akstrang, and then in a war camp in even *shittier* Jinsevia. I was outmatched.

But I had more to lose.

Even all these years later, Cassander Locke was still trying to repair his fucked up reputation and get Wane to lie that his statement was false. I desperately wanted to know what was in that statement, and at the same time I was terrified of it.

"Cassander doesn't like you much," Flavia told me, pushing her knives closer until the tips touched my skin. Now would be a good time for me to grasp control of her blood and stop her heart, but like all the Islavian warriors, I couldn't touch her with magic.

"Yeah, I got that impression," I spat, slamming my knee between her legs and knocking her back an inch. "The feeling's mutual."

"He's set on your murder," Flavia taunted as if her vagina wasn't screaming in pain. She wrenched her arms back, and used my surprise at her surrender to swipe a blade across my stomach. *Son of a—*

"He's not killing *any* of us," I snarled, grabbing the blood of two of her buddies and melting their veins. They hit the lawn and collapsed into blood, the thick stuff running down the slope towards the forest that encircled our home.

We should have been safe here.

Rage made me faster, stronger. I might have been without a weapon, but I had my mates with me and I had power.

"He's paying anyone five times the usual amount if we bring him your head," she laughed, and something inside me froze, going very still.

"When you say Cassander wants 'you' dead, you mean me? Just me?"

"Mhmm." She snapped her needle teeth at my throat, laughing when I dove under her fist and spun around her back, my heart crashing when I saw the embers of our home. "Just you; you're special like that."

If he only wanted me dead, that meant he was trying to capture Wane *and* the others? Like fucking Hell he was taking a single one of them.

A woman screamed, but I couldn't take my eyes off Flavia to see which of my mates caused it. The sky grew darker, the sun disappearing as the moon came out—Wane's power, his control of the dark. And whether he realised it or not, he had power over light, too.

I shuddered as the warmth of the sun was replaced with burning, icy cold. The roar of the hunter's blood quickened. Even Flavia's eyes widened with fear when colour bleached out of the world. I could still see if I squinted, but the world was cast in greys and blacks.

"You're not killing my mate," a quiet, *furious* voice spat, and warmth heated my front as Wane stepped in front of me. He was visible now but only as a swarm of ink and shadows. "And you're not taking me back to *him.*"

Flavia snorted.

Rage blinded me. Power seethed like a battle in my blood; I grabbed the heart of every enemy and crushed them until they all collapsed. The hunter—was gone, out of reach like he knew what I planned. Thuds told me the rest of them hit the ground, but it wasn't enough. I speared my magic at Flavia's blood—and hit a brick wall. It jarred my magic, my soul, clanging through me like a punch.

"You think you can outrun him forever? He's practically a god," Flavia laughed, doing a good job of hiding her panic at Wane's darkness.

"He's a monster!" Wane shouted, louder than I ever heard his raspy, broken voice. "He's a monster, and a rapist, and a *fraud."* He quieted his voice, the darkness growing thicker around us. "I won't go back to him, and I won't lie for him. He can rot in the Damned Realm for all I care."

Flavia chuckled, diving at Wane, but all I could hear was one word on repeat in my head. All I could think about was my mate hiding in shadows most of his adult life, shut in the dark for his entire childhood, jumpy at sudden movements, triggered by touch, and unable to be intimate with his mate even though I felt the desperate need in him.

Locke ... he ... he raped my mate, my soul—my Wane?

Through the near-pitch darkness I saw Wane's shadows wrap around Flavia's throat. I saw her angle her knives up at his ribs, and my wings snapped out at my sides as a growl of lethal, unending rage shook my ribcage.

The thump of my mates' hearts filled my senses until I could almost taste blood, the pulse of their beats shivering over my skin. But it was *hers* I focused on, so furious, so *consumed* with my magic that I could finally sense it.

I clenched my fist, seizing control of her body, forcing her still for Wane to land the killing blow. Her death was *his*, not mine, and through whatever instincts came with our bond, I knew he *needed* it. He needed to reclaim the power, needed to be in control of himself instead of the fear that had taken over him.

Shadows shoved down her throat—not just to suffocate her I realised, as the thick tendril ripped out again, her heart in its clasp. Holy fuck. I'd never seen Wane like this before. He squeezed the organ in his power, his veins pumping faster, until her heart splattered into blood and matter.[2]

It took me too long to realise the darkness was now absolute, and I couldn't glimpse a single shape around me—because the fire had gone out. Our house—*fuck*. I almost didn't want Wane to pull his shadows back, didn't want to see what was left of it.

"He'll never stop hunting me," Wane rasped, so quiet I almost missed the words.

I stumbled towards the sound of his voice, but hesitantly. Touching would be out of the question right now. Even the sound of my voice could be like salt in a wound.

"He'll stop," I whispered. "I'll make him."

"So will I," Harvey swore, somewhere to my right.

"You know I will," Emlyn rumbled, sounding like a grizzly bear.

Malakai let out a soft hiss, the bond between us like a fierce current. "It's about time we eviscerated that bastard."

The darkness peeled back slowly, a glimmer of sunlight peeking through until I could make out the rough shape of my mates around me—there were Em's broad shoulders and big arms; there was Harvey raking his hands through his shaggy hair; there Malakai stalked closer, his figure tall and foreboding; and three feet in front of me, his head ducked and fists clenched at his side, faint light outlined Wane's body.

"The house ... it's gone," Em said in shock.

I didn't follow his line of sight, didn't want to see. "Where do we go now?"

"Back to Sailas," Harvey murmured.

Wane spun to face him with an explosive hiss. "We *can't!*"

"We need to kill him before he kills *us,*" Harvey snapped back.

I sucked in a surprised breath, cold all over. Harvey never shouted at his brother. Not once in the ten years I'd known them.

"He'll keep coming at us," Harvey went on, his tone harsh and fear in his silver eyes as he drew closer. "You said it yourself, Wane, he'll never stop hunting us. So we turn the fucking tables; we hunt *him.* We kill the bastard."

"It's so easy for you. You were his favourite; he didn't scar you."

"Didn't scar me?" Harvey laughed, something cruel and sharp in his voice, something—

Broken.

Oh god.

I covered my mouth with a bloody hand, backing up a step as I realised—not just Wane. Locke hadn't hurt one son; he'd hurt both. And not with fists and knives like I'd thought all this time.

My stomach roiled and heaved.

"Didn't *scar me?* I might not wear them on my body, but they're here." Harvey screwed his finger into his head. "You think I came out of that place unscathed after everything he did?"

Wane's throat bobbed; he didn't say anything. But I sensed the vicious edge of his fear turning to brittle, shaky misery.

"You think because I don't wake up screaming, covered in shadows, that I sleep *easy?* That I don't dream of the darkness, never knowing who moved within it, or if someone was going to grab me, throw me onto my stomach and—"

He heaved for breath, and with every word I watched them land like knives in Wane's chest.

Wane staggered back. His soul splintered with pain; I felt

it as clearly as I felt Harvey's mania, his deep-born terror.

I twisted aside as my stomach clenched, and vomit rushed up my throat, splattering what was left of the vegetable garden.

"He'll kill her," Harvey whispered, pain thick in his voice. "He'll kill our mate, Wane."

"I know," Wane breathed. The tears in his voice took a dagger and slammed it right into my heart.

"Stop," I rasped, wiping my mouth on the sleeve. "Just—stop. You've hurt each other enough. We need to get out of here before the hunter returns. Em, where's our closest safe house to Sailas?"

"I'm not going back there," Wane hissed.

"I know," I assured him. Kai's hand found the small of my back to support me. If I were him, I'd have kept my distance; I could easily throw up again. What Casander Locke did and allowed to be done by others to my mates, his own—his own *sons*—

I clenched my fists, fighting the cramp and roil of my gut.

"But Harvey's not wrong. We need to stop him." I held up a hand when Wane began to argue. "Let's get out of here and find somewhere safe for now."

I allowed myself one glance at the blackened rubble of our home.

We could search the ashes for anything salvageable ... but it hurt too much to even try, so I took a step towards the forest. It didn't have an official name, the forest that shielded and protected us for years. My mates jokingly called it the Forest of Halwen. It hurt to leave it behind.

"There's nothing left of the house," Kai realised, his voice tight and devastated.

"*We're* left," Emlyn disagreed. "That's all that matters."

I knew he was right, but it felt like we'd lost everything. And I didn't know what we were going to do now.

8

*T*he safe house was in a little village between Sailas and Iarlon—the home of Lucifer and his all-powerful inner circle. I preferred to stay away from this swath of Hell; too many power players. Too many guards and enforcers. Not a comfortable place for a criminal like me. But at least the villagers were sweet and welcoming cat-demons with badass spikes on their tails and ears that twitched.

The neighbours were the only silver lining as we moved in. Harvey went straight to the punching bag in the basement; Wane wrapped himself in his shadows and hid where we couldn't find him; Kai started opening and slamming cupboards, looking for food; and Emlyn hovered on the threshold, staring at the unfamiliar street.

My eyes stung as I tucked myself into his side, wrapping my arms around his big frame. I was exhausted and emotionally drained after the journey; I'd lost all my fight hours ago.

"We can build another home," I whispered, not brave enough to say the words any louder. "I'll take on more jobs; Kai can help, and you and the brothers can find work here in the village. We'll get it all back. I promise."

Emlyn's chest moved with a huge sigh. He settled his arms around me, his chin resting atop my head. "I hope so, Hales. But I can't see that future for us right now."

I was bullshitting and he knew it, because I felt the exact same way. We were back on the run. It was like two years ago, when we barely spent two months in a place before fleeing it for somewhere new, always outracing the endless mercs Locke sent after us. And that damned hunter—always him.

"We've got each other," Emlyn said eventually, watching two small kids playing down the street, their furry tails swishing through the air. I didn't look at them; it was just another reminder of how miserable our lives were.

Em kissed the side of my head and then guided me inside. "We'll be—*for fuck's sake,*" he spat.

My eyebrows shot into my hairline when I saw the state of the small, dated kitchen. All our safe houses were stocked with non-perishables and long-life food in case we needed to move in at a moment's notice, and I presumed those non-perishables had been *inside* the cupboard when we arrived. Now, tins, boxes, and jars were discarded all across the countertops and the kitchen table, and there were even lentils strewn on the floor.

"Malakai," Emlyn hissed, his nostrils flaring and shoulders rounding.

"Em," I said when he took a determined stride across the room. "Don't. He's stressed, we're all stressed. Just—don't start a fight. Please."

Emlyn huffed a breath through his nose like a raging bull, his hands flexing at his sides, but he nodded.

"I'll clean this up. Go—go check on Wane?"

"If I can find him," Em replied, but he stiffened when a crash came from downstairs—where Harvey was beating the shit out of a punching bag. "Leave the mess; you find Wane, and I'll check on Harvey."

I nodded, my heart tight and painful at my mates' suffering. Didn't we deserve to live in peace? Sure, I was a criminal and I'd killed people, and the guys were ruthless when it came to survival, leaving a string of bodies in their wake, but come on! It was *enough*. All these years, and now thinking we were safe only for our home to be razed to the ground...

I'd had enough.

I loved Wane more than life itself, but I had to go against his wishes this one time. Cassander Locke needed to die.

9

*I*t was easier than it should have been to sleep alone that night. Normally, all my mates piled into bed with me, but after a day like today, I told them I needed space and that wasn't a lie. I practically vibrated with rage about losing our home and the life we'd built there, and especially our peace of mind. It was easy to let the guys think I was pissed at them, too.

I'd apologise for it tomorrow, when Locke was dead. Or I'd never come home, and they'd believe I was angry with them for the rest of their lives. *Fuck!*

I raked a hand down my face, my conviction wavering as I stood in our temporary living room. The furniture was different here, and the whole place smelled of stale air and disuse, but there were already signs of my mates scattered around: a pint glass Em left on the coffee table and the jacket Harvey found in the drawers upstairs thrown across the sofa.

We couldn't keep doing this. A life on the run was no life at all, and I was *done*. Happily ever after or not at all.

So I dragged my stare from the house and left through the

back door, the hinges oiled earlier tonight to let me sneak out soundlessly.

I made it three streets away before hairs rose on the back of my neck and my skin prickled with warning. I was being followed.

I tucked my wings in tight, my body on high alert, senses sharpening. Thank Lucifer all our safe houses were stocked with weapons; I missed my beloved knives and daggers, but at least I had *something* to draw. The weight of iron in my hand was comforting. So was the whoosh and thump of my power when I reached for it.

Blood chugged sluggishly within the houses around me, but thrummed much faster in my stalker.

I sighed, my pale pink braid flying as I turned, scanning the darkness. I didn't see him—he was well hidden—but I knew he was there.

"What are you doing, Malakai?"

"What are *you* doing, my rose?" he threw back, his tone sharp. But the term of endearment told me he was in a good mood. Excitement and eagerness explained the fast rhythm of his heart. It was a welcome change from him trashing our new kitchen.

"You know what," I muttered, watching him peel away from the shadow of a house and cross the road to me, dressed head to toe in black with his red hair slicked back and a scarf pulled over his chin. He walked with a swagger and confidence that suited him too damn well, his crimson eyes pinned on me.

"I do know," he agreed, reaching me on the pavement. "Which is why I had these brought from my safe in Iarlon."

A furrow cut between my brows as he lifted his hands and I saw twin long daggers, both with viciously sharp tips and wavy shafts. Lovingly wrapped in pale pink, the handles beckoned me as Kai flipped them in a flash of a movement, gripping the blades as he held them out to me.

I took them in a daze, trailing my gaze over the etchings down the centre of each dagger. I didn't speak or read this particular Hell language, but I knew the whorls and loops by heart. Every year, on the anniversary of our meeting, Kai bought me flowers—small, white soulcaps from the forest around our home, picked by him personally—and hand-wrote a message that vowed *I will always be your shadow and light; you will always be my rose and life.* He wrote it in both his native dialect and mine.

I'd kept every note in a box in our room.

They were cinders now, I realised.

"Fuck, Kai," I choked out, swallowing down emotion. I was too raw for thoughtful gifts like this.

"They're forged from the first volcanic eruption of Hell."

"Just casually?" I laughed, thick with emotion. The eruption had shaped Hell into the landscape it was today. "How the hell did you do this?"

"It's our tenth anniversary in a month," he replied, sliding closer, his hand gliding possessively across my waist. "I've been planning this all year."

"Romantic bastard," I teased, leaning up to kiss his smooth jaw. "I love you."

"I love you, too," he replied, his voice serious and rough but a ripple of awe going through our bond. "I have since the day we met."

"When you tried to kill me?"

"Yes," he confirmed, red eyes flashing. "Since that exact moment."

I angled my new beloved knives down so he didn't spear himself on them—he was dumb and romantic enough to not care about bleeding out as long as he was close to me.

Kai's hand closed around my throat, a reassuring warmth

that *shouldn't* have relaxed the stress from my body but somehow did, and he slammed his mouth into mine. He kissed me with a rough, uncontrolled passion until we were both breathless and shaking.

It killed me not being able to touch him, but I was too attached to my knives to put them away just yet.

"Soft bastard," I breathed against his lips when he rested his forehead against mine.

His mouth flattened into a thin line. "Tell anyone that, and I'll mutilate every part of your body."

I snorted, drawing away. "Sure you will."

He narrowed his gaze, baring sharp teeth I usually glimpsed just before they sank into my skin to heighten my pleasure.

"I love you," I told him again, just to watch his viciousness melt.

His eyes grew bigger, lips softer, and a sigh left his now-smiling mouth. I never tired of seeing that effect on him, and he never tired of hearing *I love you.*

His fingers flexed around my neck; he leaned even closer until his words brushed my lips. "Who do you belong to?"

My pussy throbbed; my breath caught. "You."

"And who do I belong to?"

"Me," I whispered fiercely.

"Always," he swore, and kissed me before drawing back. "Now let's go use your pretty knives to behead a snake, shall we?"

I moved my weapons around until I could sheathe one of my gifts and held out my hand, confidence and determination filling me when Kai wrapped his fingers around mine.

"We need to find the fucker first," I said as we set off walking. "But I have an idea where to look."

10

*I*t took us three hours, but we finally found a hint to Cassander Locke's location. I'd never hated anyone as much as I did that bastard, so I didn't even baulk when a bald guy in a seedy pub told us he'd done a job for Locke in Iarlon. If that was where he was, that's where we'd go.

Kai and I borrowed a horse and sprinted for the capital, following the rough description Baldy gave us. Every time I came, I always expected there to be guards with swords and killer magic on the gates into Iarlon, but Hell was civilised in this part of the realm.

Here, people went about their daily business with a calm and ease I envied, not glancing over their shoulders or jumping at the sound of a cart rattling down the cobbled streets. Or a kamikaze horse bolting after we climbed off his back.

"We should move here," Malakai murmured, his eyes on a landlord closing the stained glass doors of a classy-looking inn, laughing with the last of his customers as they left. "It's a fucking paradise."

Everything was so well kept and *clean*; even the village

we'd moved to was a little unkempt and raw around the edges. Here, the cobbles shone and lush trees lined the streets; the houses were pristine and all the shops were inviting as we strolled past them, looking like two ne'er do goods scouting for trouble.

"We wouldn't fit in," I replied, looking at the flowers over-flowing from a pale fountain in the middle of the road. It was the prettiest damn roundabout I'd ever seen. My covetous heart wanted to steal it; the rest of me wanted to take a hammer and shatter it to pieces. After the dark ugliness of the day we had, it felt like salt in the wound.

"Good point," Kai murmured after a while, leading us past the fountain and down a pale street full of banks and busi-nesses. "Two weeks and Harvey would be chased out of the place for doing something dumb."

I slid a look at Kai. "Two *days,* and your smart mouth would get you thrown in a cell."

Sharp teeth flashed as he grinned. "You'd be right there with me."

Okay, he had me there. We were a troublesome duo. Emlyn had more grey hairs than ever, and as a near-immortal archdemon, that took a lot.

A shadow passed overhead, and without a word we flat-tened ourselves to the side of a pale newspaper printer. I held my breath, my head tipped up, eyes scouring the sky for—

"It's a pigeon," Kai groaned, dragging an ink-wrapped hand down his face.

Okay, so we were a little jumpy. But in our defence, someone had burned our house and tried to kill us. And the mastermind of that was right here in this city.

"On the plus side," Kai added, squeezing my arm as we set off again, "no one's followed us yet. We got farther than I expected."

I made a noise of agreement, spotting the steep golden

staircase Baldy had described. It was right where he said it would be, its stone columns and railings wrapped with ferns and evergreens. This place was so damn pretty. Who told a Hell city it could be pretty?

"I can't tell if the guys know we're gone," I told Kai as we headed side by side up the staircase, elegant streetlamps guiding our way. "We're all stressed already; I doubt I'd even notice the change."

The houses up here were grander, older. Definitely the sort of place Locke would live. He might have raised my mates in the dark, and hurt them unspeakably, but above the basement where they'd lived for twenty years had been a palatial manor house.

There were no words strong enough to describe how despicable he was.

"You'd notice it in Emlyn," Kai chuckled, gliding his hand up the railing. "He'll lose his absolute shit when he finds you gone."

I winced.

"He might even break my nose for helping you," Kai added, his red eyes scanning the street we emerged onto.

The roads were wider up here, with flagstones rather than cobbles, and pale brick arches joined both sides of the street overhead, strung with colourful lanterns to brighten the dark.

"There," I hissed, pointing at the biggest house at the end of the street and barely noticing the way Kai's jovial smirk fell. "That's the house Baldy told us about."

"Jesus, *look* at it," he breathed, staring at the arches, columns, and exterior staircases. It was like a mini castle, and it was pretentious as hell. Pretty, but pretentious.

Maybe we should liberate it; it fit my personality.

"How do we get in?" I murmured. "We should probably hide; we look suspicious."

"We *are* suspicious," Kai quipped, but I felt a ripple in the air—his magic was ready to play.[1] "There's an alcove there."

I hurried into it, glad to be hidden in the shadows as I squinted at the windows and doors of the palace. "That fence there could probably reach that window if I jumped."

And didn't fall six feet and crack my head open...

"Not a chance," Kai growled, his hand finding my hip and holding protectively. Like he thought I'd run off and attempt it now. If I was going to do that, I wouldn't have told him beforehand. I wasn't an amateur.

"You got a better idea?" I asked, raising an eyebrow.

His lips twisted to one side as he assessed the house, his clever eyes flickering. Fuck, he was handsome like this, all competent and devious. I leaned close, dragging my lips up his pale, inked throat to kiss his jaw.

"Either you stop that or I rail you right here in this alcove," he hissed, his hand flexing on my hip.

"Tempting," I murmured. But I couldn't hang onto a single good emotion today; it all came back to our house burning and Wane terrified and Harvey snapping because panic pushed him to breaking point. "But I think I'd rather kill that bastard and fuck you as a celebration."

"Good plan," Kai agreed, and proved he was perceptive as fuck because he laid a lingering kiss on my temple to soothe the raw edge of my hurt.

"I need him dead, and I need us to be safe," I confessed, my voice uneven.

"I know," he murmured, pulling me into a too-brief hug. "So let's go kill the bastard. And to answer your earlier question, my rose, I *do* have a better idea."

I gave him a questioning look.

He just jerked his chin at the gates, and my breath caught as his invisible power surged, filling the air with a charged ripple.

"Holy fuck," I breathed, almost reconsidering the alcove fuck when his snakes tore the gates completely off their hinges.

The quiet night was splintered by the loud grating of tearing metal, the shriek as the gates skidded across the ground even louder.

"Let's go," Kai ordered, serious-faced and all business as he flicked his hands, hauling open the big front door of the house. "I'll go first and take out any guards; the second you see Cassander, use your magic on him. Don't fuck about; we get in, we kill him, we get out."

I nodded, calm settling over me, clearing out all my emotions. It wasn't natural but this calm had been with me for years now. I used to get excited by jobs like this, but with my mates at stake, all the fun was gone.

I fell in behind Malakai as he stormed through the broken mouth of the gate, my mate blowing up the steps like a sandstorm. I drew one of my long daggers and reached for the blood around me as we crossed the threshold. There were three sluggish heartbeats, but none of them were Locke's particular rhythm.

"Fuck," I snarled, glaring at the pretty ivory foyer we found ourselves in. It smelled of roses and lilies, and I wanted to steal this house *so* badly. "He's not here. We'll have to wait until—"

"Until what?" a familiar—and highly unwelcome—voice growled.

"Ah," I breathed, turning to the door slowly, like I was facing a firing squad. "Hi, Em."

Emlyn's nostrils flared, colour high on his cheekbones and his salt-and-pepper hair wild. "Don't *hi, Em* me, Halwen Vakhara."

Oof, full name.

Okay, he was pissed all the way off.

Harvey followed him into the house, his stare jumping from the pale marble walls to the pots overflowing with greenery to the art hanging on the walls. I'd never seen his bronze face so wan, or his posture so tight and edgy. He looked around like he was waiting for his father to jump out and throw him back in the basement where he was raised, and bile hit my throat in a burning rush.

"You're not supposed to be here," I breathed, my voice tight as I took a step towards them. "You're supposed to be home, *safe*—"

"So are you!" Emlyn exploded, throwing up his big hands and stalking closer.

"Can we at least kill the fucker while we're here?" Kai muttered, his hands flexing at his sides.

"I told you," I huffed, giving him a glare he'd done nothing to deserve. "He's not here—"

But another heart beat thumped, unfamiliar and fast— exhilarated. Wane was beside me, close enough to touch but invisible to my eyes, but just beyond the front door there was another person.

Fury exploded through my blood. I grabbed hold of my magic and speared it towards his heart to collapse the rotten thing in his chest. But the second I touched my magic, the building rocked.

"What the fuck?" Harvey breathed, the whites of his eyes showing.

"Shields," Kai growled, teeth bared and his bands of ink coiling faster around his body. "Fuck!"

I grabbed Harvey's arm, and threw him behind me so I could shield him. "Wane, get behind me," I ordered, cold spreading through my whole body. "Em, Kai, beside me."

My tone must have told them how deadly serious I was because they moved instantly into formation as footsteps came up the front steps. We barely entered the massive house, so we could easily see the tall, slim, black-haired man who paused on the top step and assessed us. He wasn't what I'd pictured, but I should have known better; he was a politician, so of course he'd be slick and slimy and smug.

I could see my mates in his features and it sickened me, the reminder of what he'd done to them making me shake with rage.

The calm I slipped into was gone, replaced with bone-deep terror. *I'd* done this, brought them into a trap their abuser set.

"I'm sorry," I choked out. "I'm so fucking sorry."

No one spoke.

Cassander Locke assessed us with a smile, his hands in the pockets of his long, expensive coat. "I knew you'd fall into one of my traps eventually, but breaking into Lucifer's spare home?" He tsked.

My stomach crashed.

This was Lucifer's home—*the devil's* home? We'd blown the gates off and broken in. Fuck. *Fuck.*

I was going to be sick.

"Very naughty," Locke laughed.

Wane shook so hard the air shivered over me. I fumbled blindly and grabbed his wrist, squeezing tight.

"I'm going to cut you into pieces," I hissed at Locke, the sound coming from deep in my throat.

His mercury-silver eyes sparkled. "I doubt that. You're trapped in these shields, and until a member of Lucifer's guard comes to free you, you're going nowhere. I'll be long gone before that happens. But so will my treacherous son. The shields can't hold a shadow—so come here. *Wane,*" he barked, a clear order.

"Don't say a single word to him!" I hissed. I bet Locke looked respectable and trustworthy to anyone who didn't know the vile things he'd done, but all I could see was poison and ugliness, and *no* fucking way would I let him touch my mates again. "He's not taking you anywhere," I swore to Wane, to Harvey. "You're mine."

Locke snorted, toeing the solid barrier that apparently trapped us inside the house. The barrier he knew would come down. He must have paid Baldy to send anyone who came asking after him here. Motherfucker.

"You were idiots to fall for it," he taunted, bragging of his own cleverness. Piece of shit. "I knew as soon as you ran, you'd follow one of my trails. What was the plan? Kill me?"

I bared my teeth.

"Shut your fucking mouth," Emlyn growled, his hand thrown behind himself, resting on Harvey's arm. "Kai, get us out of here."

"I'm trying," Kai breathed, his panic a sharp spike in my chest. "Whoever put these shields up is stronger than me."

"A pity," Locke murmured. "Wane, *come here.*"

I tightened my hand around Wane's wrist.

"If you don't come here *right now*—" Locke began, spit flying from his mouth.

"You'll what?" a blunt voice asked—a new voice.

Clawed, lilac hands locked around Cassander's arms, and it was satisfying to see a tall, purple woman with short, dark hair slam that monster into the wall beside the door.

"These five criminals broke into Lucifer's home; I was just making sure they didn't escape before the guards got here," Locke lied.

I hissed. Em snarled.

"Shut it!" the woman barked, rattling Locke's body with shockingly strong hands. "I heard every word you said, so don't try to talk yourself out of it. From where I'm standing, six people broke into Lucifer's house; you were the ringleader."

"No!" Locke sputtered. "I'm a politician, not a criminal. Talk to the devil, I was the mayor of Jast."

"Fascinating," she deadpanned.

I jumped when Cassander threw something back into the woman's ribs, making her grunt. When they broke apart, I saw it was a knife shining with red blood. Fuck!

"Wanker!" the woman hissed.

"Kai, try something!" I breathed while they were both distracted.

Kai threw me a sharp look that said he'd tried fucking everything.

"No," Wane breathed beside me, going rigid. "He's going to—"

I snapped my attention back to the open door in time to see Locke bolt through the broken gates and disappear into the shadows of nearby buildings.

"Don't let him get away!" I screamed at the woman. "He's a *monster*; go get him, kill him, whatever—just *don't let him go!*"

The stranger straightened, her hand slapped over her bleeding side. It wasn't a deep wound, but it had been enough to distract her, and now Locke was gone.

"Don't go anywhere," she growled. "Lucifer will want to question you."

My stomach dropped, but Wane's wrist was still solid under my fingers and Harvey was still behind us. Locke hadn't touched them.

But it wasn't much of a victory.

11

*M*y knees slammed into the marble floor of Lucifer's throne room, flinching away from the terrifying demon on his dark throne above us. My whole body shook. His power pressed on me, and I had a sick feeling he wasn't even using his magic—he was just *that* powerful.

Renna, the purple woman whom Locke stabbed, wasn't an unlucky bystander or even a guard—she was one of Lucifer's inner circle.

No part of being carted into the palace—the *actual* palace, not just the giant house we broke into—by a woman who was besties *with the devil* was a positive experience.

Neither were the gold ropes wrapped around our wrists—binding even Wane. I scowled at the floor, not brave enough to show any attitude to the man on the throne.

"These are the people who broke into my home?" Lucifer asked Renna, his terror-inducing bestie.

"Found them trapped in your shields," she grunted, strong arms crossed over her chest as she lurked beside us. Like we'd try anything stupid with our hands bound and *the ruler of hell* watching us.

Although ... Kai might. I gave him a warning look. If we kept our mouths shut, we'd get thrown in a prison cell. If we gave Lucifer snark, we'd get ourselves killed.

"There was another guy," Renna added, giving Lucifer a significant look. "Slimy bastard, said he's the mayor of Jast."

"Former," Harvey spat, his chest rising and falling fast. I watched him, a knot of worry in my chest. "He hasn't been the mayor since everyone found out what he did."

I dared a glance at Lucifer, and tried not to get distracted by the fact he was actually kind of hot. Alright fine, he was drop-dead gorgeous and it was confusing. His long, black hair hung loose around his shoulders, his mouth pressed into a flat, serious line behind his beard, but there were smile lines around his red eyes, and the way he sat on his impressive throne, clothed in elegance and riches, *screamed* power.

I quickly glanced away. I didn't know what I'd been expecting but not ... that.

At least he didn't look murderous at Harvey speaking.

"I've heard of his crimes," Lucifer replied after a moment, distaste or disgust in his voice. "What did he want with my house?"

I jolted when four pairs of eyes fixed on me.[1] "What're you looking at *me* for?" I hissed at my mates.

Kai gave me a pointed look.

Oh goody, *I* was the mouthpiece. Shouldn't they have picked someone smarter and calmer? Shouldn't it have been Em?

I darted a glance at the shockingly handsome devil, and to the best of my ability, answered with respect and calm.

"He didn't want your house; he used it as a trap for us. He's been hunting us for ten years. Your house was a convenient cage for us."

Lucifer glanced at Renna, who nodded her dark head.

"I heard the bastard say something similar, bragging about how fucked they were. And then he stabbed me," she growled, staring at the blood still trickling from her.

"Where is he now?" Lucifer asked, a thread of emotion—anger, maybe—entering his even voice. I'd pictured him as emotionless and uncaring, but he was definitely a person and not a robot. That was a good sign for us, right?

"Bolted," Renna muttered. "I chased him as far as the river park, then lost the bastard."

Lucifer let out a slow breath, fingers flexing on the arms of his throne. "So Cassander Locke set a trap for you using my house, and he wanted you to be brought here. Why?"

"He wants us dead," I replied, losing all calm. My words were bitten off; rage poured through my whole body. "If you know what he's done, you know he's a monster who—"

I couldn't say it. The words wouldn't come out. I swallowed hard.

Lucifer shifted in his throne; I watched from the corner of my eye, waiting for him to smite us like he himself had been cast from heaven. "Who are you?"

I licked my bottom lip, my mouth dry. The marble grandeur of the throne room pressed on my chest until I could barely gasp. "I'm no one; Halwen Vakhara, orphan and nobody."

I glanced at my mates, trying to covertly ask if I should use their real names. Emlyn nodded, encouraging.

"This is Emlyn Johahn, Malakai Virex, and Harvey and Wane van Khama."

"It was—" Harvey added haltingly, his breathing splintered and rough. I reached my bound hands across and squeezed his, holding tight. His tawny wings sagged to the floor. "We changed our names, didn't want *anything* associated with that piece of shit. But it was—it used to be—"

He couldn't say it. My heart broke.

"Locke," Wane said from within his cocoon of shadows, the inky tendrils not visible but covering him entirely. My heart ruptured with pain; I expected it to collapse.

Lucifer sat back in his throne with a sharp inhale. "I see. Does he believe everyone would forget his crimes if you're dead?"

"If I tell everyone I lied," Wane breathed, so quietly I feared Lucifer wouldn't hear him.

But the devil nodded, rage crossing his tanned, bearded face for a moment before it was swept behind calm and patience.

"He wants the rest of us dead," I added, my eyes on my mates, frantic to help them, to heal them. But their wounds were inner, and there was nothing I could do. "We've been on the run for years, and we thought we were safe. This morning —he sent mercenaries to burn down our house. It was my last straw."

I looked Lucifer dead in the eye and ignored the squirm of my stomach. "I'm sick of running, sick of being terrified that bastard will find us and take my mate from me."

Lucifer inhaled so quickly I'd have called it a gasp on someone less terrifying. "Your mate."

I nodded, my throat swollen. I wanted my daggers, wanted the comfort of them in my hands, but they'd been confiscated.

"These are my mates. They're mine, all of them, and I—I couldn't let this happen again. We lost our fucking *home*," I spat, and wasn't calm enough to modulate my language even for the devil. "We lost everything we built for two years and— I decided to stop running. To go after *him* and take out the bastard. So if you're going to kill anyone—"

"No," Harvey choked out.

"It should be me," I finished, not daring to look at my

mates. "I was the idiot who thought I could hunt him down. *I* walked us into a trap. I broke into your home—but I thought it was Locke's. So don't ... don't hurt my mates. Please. It was all me."

"She's lying," Kai growled, straining against his ropes. "I went with her. I ripped off your gates."

I shook my head, tears building. I didn't want to leave them, but the thought of them being snuffed out of the world was unbearable. "That was all me." I blinked back tears, holding Lucifer's stare. "It was all me."

Lucifer sighed. Not a tiny wisp of a breath but a huge, heaving sigh. "I'm not killing anyone. You were obviously set up, and this is far more complicated than a normal break-in."

He rubbed his face, looking tired. I stared, confused where the terrifying leader had gone. He looked normal and human, and—real. This was weird. Why wasn't he ripping off wings and horns, throwing our innards to his terrifying bestie?

"I can't let this go unpunished, or everyone will get ideas about breaking into my home."

"The gate's wide open; no break-in necessary," Kai drawled.

Renna let out a guttural growl. I didn't speak *Terrifying Purple Woman From Hell,* but even I understood it was *keep your mouth shut.*

Emlyn knocked his hands against Kai's leg, echoing the order. They'd had to wrap the gold rope around Em's hands three times, they were so big and powerful. The ropes must have been soaked in magic; I couldn't feel a single heart pumping blood around me. Not even my mates'.

Renna cleared her throat and gave Lucifer a meaningful look. The devil sat back in his throne with a little smile that made me nervous.

"I have a proposition for you," he said, meeting each of

our eyes. Something in his face flickered when he looked at Wane, writhing in shadows, only parts of him now visible through the tendrils, but Lucifer didn't make a comment.

I stiffened. Proposition? This did not sound good.

"What kind of proposition, sir?" Emlyn asked as courteously as I'd ever heard him.

"Isn't the correct term of address, *your majesty?*" Kai whisper-hissed.

"I thought it was *your highness,*" Harvey added.

"Shut up," I barked at both of them. "He's the fucking devil; let the man speak."

For a moment, I wasn't waiting for an axe to fall, and it was just a normal moment of being exasperated by my mates —and so entirely in love with their nonsense.

"Thank you, Halwen," Lucifer drawled, almost amused, and I stiffened at *the devil* speaking my name. "The last custodian of the Damned Realm died five days ago."

"Sorry for your loss," Emlyn murmured.

If Kai had said those words, it would have had a snarky undertone, but Em genuinely meant them. I wanted him to wrap his arms around me and give me one of his signature bear hugs that made everything feel alright for a little while.

Lucifer nodded in acknowledgement, light catching the silver and gold embroidery on his fancy tunic. In comparison, mine was washed-out blue and had dirt crusted on the hem and sleeve. I didn't even know how it got there.

"If you agree to take on the role of custodians of the Damned Realm, I won't punish you for this crime. Even better—if you keep the souls there in line, I'll leave you alone. You'll never have to see me again in your whole lives."

My eyes shot to Em, then Harvey, Kai, and Wane. *I say we go for it.*

Kai widened his eyes emphatically. *But it's the fucking*

Damned Realm, *where the worst of humanity are sent to suffer when they die.*

Wane averted his eyes, but he nodded. He thought we should accept the offer.

"Hell no," Harvey hissed. "It's a place of misery and suffering."

"But Locke will never find us there," Em breathed, looking at all of us.

And that was a strong enough point that we couldn't argue against it.

I faced Lucifer, my stomach in knots, and said, "We'll do it. Proposition accepted."

12

There should have been a cautionary phrase about jumping to conclusions without any proof. You know, *be careful what you wish for,* but more along the lines of *be careful what you assume about the maniacal abuser determined to kidnap/kill you.* That would have come in really handy right now.

The move to the Damned Realm went without a hitch, if you ignored the fact we'd moved to a realm within Hell that was the home of misery, suffering, and nightmares come to life.

I didn't know where to start with being the custodian of this place and keeping the souls of the damned in line, but that was a problem for tomorrow. Now, they were nicely locked inside the realm, burning in their fiery pits or screaming from caves deep down in the rotten earth. So we ignored them and focused on scoping out the huge manor house that came with the job. The past custodian had left all their shit in it, so on the plus side it was furnished.[1]

"Home sweet home," I sighed, leaning against the admittedly gorgeous black island in the kitchen. For a second I forgot my mates were furious with me, but then I met Emlyn's gaze and flinched.

"What were you *thinking?*" he demanded, stalking across the cold grey tiles, seeming even bigger than usual with his muscles strained and arms crossed.

"I'm sorry," I replied in a small voice.

"We're lucky we were only sent to the Damned Realm—we could all have been *killed!*"

I wrapped my arms around my middle, my stomach knotted up tight. "I know."

"Of all the stupid things," he growled, grinding his teeth. "We're struggling to stay one step ahead of Locke, let alone surviving the bastard head-on!"

Sour saliva filled my mouth. I was going to throw up.

"Enough," a quiet voice rasped.

"You should have stayed in the safe house—" Em growled.

A tear burned in the corner of my eye. He was right—every single word. This was all because of me. I was a fuck-up.

"I said *enough!*" Wane yelled, his hoarse voice loud and forceful. He unravelled his thick blanket of shadows and stalked across the kitchen—but to *me,* not Em.

A cry caught in my throat when Wane pulled me into his arms, holding me so tight he might actually hold the broken bits together.

His lips skimmed my temple and quieter, gentler, he said, "Can't you see Haley already knows everything you're saying? You're hurting her. If you keep pushing, she's going to break."

I was already there, breaking into little pieces, but I didn't correct him.

"It's not like we set out to get ourselves killed *or* exiled to the Damned Realm," Kai muttered, the blood in his veins thumping fast with anger. Or, if I knew him, helplessness—his least favourite emotion. "We can't keep running. Running has one outcome: Wane and Harvey back in their own personal hell and the rest of us dead."

Wane tightened his arms until I grunted, and I wasn't sure if it was at the idea of him being at his father's mercy—or lack thereof—or at the thought of me dying.

"It was reckless," Em argued, but gentler, and I heard the exhaustion in his voice now. He was as scared as the rest of us, but masking it better.

"It was *desperate*," Kai corrected, his voice as sharp as the knives he'd gifted me.

The knives ... my bottom lip shook; my eyes burned and blurred. They'd been confiscated when we were marched into the palace in Iarlon, and Renna hadn't given them back.

My breath caught, broke, and emerged as a sob.

"You've made your point, Em," Harvey sighed, no sarcasm or smart remark on his tongue. "There's no going back now; it's done. Maybe they did us a favour sending us here. Kai's right—if that bastard finally caught us, there's only one way that would end."

"It's okay, my rose," Kai murmured, suddenly behind me. He wrapped himself around my back, hugging Wane in the process.

Safe between them both, I lost even more control of my emotions, and a rush of broken cries escaped my clenched teeth.

"My daggers," I gasped out, burying my face in Wane's soft shirt. "Kai, Renna *took* them."

His fingers ran through my hair in a slow, soothing stroke. "I can have more made."

A laugh strangled me. "Where are you going to find more volcanic metal?"

"Don't underestimate me, Haley," he murmured, kissing the top of my head. "I'm capable when I put my mind to it."

But they were gone—our tenth anniversary gift, the sign

of Kai's love and commitment. And Emlyn was angry at me. And we were stuck here for the rest of our lives, in the realm of eternal fucking suffering. And ... it was all my fault.

"I should have listened to you, Wane," I whispered, ignoring my sobs. "I'm so sorry."

"Shh, itzaia. You have no reason to apologise; you were trying to keep us safe." He said the last part in a sharper tone, his eyes fixed on someone over my head.

I swallowed the huge lump in my throat. My good intentions didn't seem to matter now.

"We'll be fine," Harvey input, muscling in on my right, his heat sinking into me. "If we've been fine in the thirty other hellholes we've stayed in, how's the Damned Realm gonna be different?"

"When did you get all sunshine-y and optimistic?" Kai drawled, tightening his arms possessively around me.

"Shut up," Harvey muttered, shoving him. "Asshole."

"Love you, too," Kai replied and made kissy faces.

A tiny smile curved my lips and some of the brutal heaviness lifted off my chest. They were acting normally, like this was any other day, and it made everything easier to bear.

Except for Em being angry. *Nothing* could make that bearable. I squeezed Wane, turned to kiss the angry line of Kai's jaw, and rested my forehead against Harvey's, giving him a deep, apologetic stare.

"Nothing to forgive, Sugarplum, so stop looking so pitiful," he said, quiet and just for me. "Or I might forget how vicious and stabby you really are."

It was a little easier to smile. A little. But it didn't make it easier to detach my body from their arms and force myself to meet Emlyn's stare.

"I'm sorry," I choked out, using up all my courage to face him. "I didn't—I didn't mean for this to happen. Worse case scenario, I thought I'd die killing the bastard and you'd be safe. I-I *hate* seeing you all scared, watching you j-jump at noises outside, feeling how tortured you are through the bonds. I just..."

I wanted to fix it. But now I saw how fucking stupid that idea had been. Cassander Locke wasn't the sort of man you caught off guard. He wasn't even the sort of man you survived.

"No," Emlyn breathed, and I froze as he rushed across the space between us. He caught my face in his warm hands and brushed the tears off my cheeks. "I made you cry."

"It's not all you," I replied, my voice thick. "I'm fine."[2]

I began to shake when Em pulled me against his body, hugging me tight.

"Fuck, I'm sorry I snapped, Hales," he murmured, guilt heavy in his deep voice. "The thought of you in danger drives me crazy. I keep thinking about what would have happened if we hadn't shown up, all the things he could have done to you."

Growls rose from behind me, one low and raspy—Wane. He knew first-hand all the vile things Cassander Locke could do to me. So did Harvey. I bit my lips together as they wobbled again.

"It's okay," Em murmured, tucking me closer with his hand on the back of my neck. "We're still alive, and we're together. We can figure everything else out."

"Quite the change of heart," Kai muttered.

"Don't," I sighed. "No more arguing today."

"Forgive me if the sight of my girl crying is a wakeup call," Em huffed at Kai. His voice was placating enough that I squeezed him tightly in gratitude.

But a chord of alarm spiked through my chest. A sharp intake of breath echoed the alarm, making cold race through my blood. It took me a second to realise it was Wane, and panic was spreading in our bond like ink through water.

"Wane?" I breathed, peeling away from Emlyn to watch my mate wrap himself in layer after layer of shadows, his terrified silver eyes the last thing to disappear.

"That's not my shadow," he rasped, gesturing with a tendril of darkness at a patch of shadow in the corner of the kitchen between the black cabinets and the wall. "It's not mine. *Harvey, it's not mine!*"

All the blood drained from Harvey's face, leaving him wan. He jumped in front of Wane, backing him up to the marble counter, and the rest of us reacted instinctively even if we had no idea what was going on.

"It's an inherited power," Harvey explained breathlessly, his eyes wild. When I pressed into his side, his whole body was shaking. "Wane's shadows—they're inherited."

And if that mass of shadow in the corner wasn't Wane's, and it certainly wasn't natural by the way it ebbed and flowed...

I bared my teeth, my voice deep and guttural. "Get the hell out of my house."

I was almost sick when the shadows peeled back, layer by layer, until the sleazy, smirking asshole within was revealed.

He looked too much like my mates for comfort, with his sharp, defined features, his hair the same chestnut brown. He resembled them even more closer up, not separated from us by a barrier of Lucifer's power. But he was a monster and an abuser, where my mates were caring, protectors through and through.

"You touch anyone," Kai hissed, throwing his hands out, "and you *die.*"

Cassander Locke laughed, a quiet murmur of sound. Quietly confident and sinister enough to send a chill down my spine. I reached back and grabbed Harvey's clammy hand, gripping tight.

"Actually," Locke replied casually, inky darkness pooled in his hand, "you're the ones who'll be dying."

We pushed tighter together, growls all around me. I waited for Locke to unleash the shadows in his hand; I realised too late that the darkness wasn't the threat, but *hiding* it.

I'd never seen a shotgun up close before, never heard the devastating sound of gunpowder exploding.

A piercing shriek filled my ears when it went off, ringing like a bell. When Emlyn fell, I didn't even hear my own scream.

13

*E*m hit the kitchen floor so hard his head bounced, a red stain spreading across his chest from the hole blown through his middle.

"No!" Malakai roared. I didn't hear the sound; numbly, I watched his lips form the words, watched devastation twist his pale face.

Harvey launched across the kitchen at his father, his tawny wings snapping with a vicious gust of air and his head ducked low to ram his horns at the bastard. Locke evaded the blow expertly, grabbing Harvey's spiralling horns to keep them out of his gut. Barely even exerting himself.

My ears kept ringing. My soul was frozen, numb, until my terrified stare dropped from the gun to my mate, bleeding on the floor.

"Em," I breathed, crashing to my knees and touching his face, his shoulders, his neck, avoiding the mess the gun made of his chest. He was still warm, but so frozen that I knew instantly, and denied it.

"Emlyn, come on, wake up."

I shook his shoulders, only making his hair flutter and

wings ruffle. Nothing else moved. Not his chest or his heart. It didn't pump at all because—because he was—

"No," I gasped at my own thoughts. He wasn't. He couldn't be. It made no sense; he'd been holding me a minute ago, warm and reassuring and *whole.*

But there was too much blood, and the shot hit at a close range. My whole body shuddered. The wound was smoking, but not with ordinary grey smoke—this was black.

Shadows.

Fuck—

No!

If the gun wasn't loaded with normal ammunition, the rules of human weapons didn't apply, and he didn't have to reload it—

"Harvey!" I screamed, throwing myself to my feet. *Too late, too late.* I reached my mate in time to catch him as shadows blasted into his chest and out through his back.

"It's okay, you're okay, it's okay," I babbled uselessly as we collapsed to the floor, hot blood soaking my hands when I pressed them against the wound. His wings splayed over my legs, heavy and drenched red.

"Sugar—plum," he choked out, silver eyes fluttering. His hand pressed weakly to mine—and fell limply away when his eyes turned dull, all the life gone from them.

Nonono. This wasn't happening. This wasn't *happening.*

"*Harvey!*" I screamed, my throat so raw I tasted blood. Or maybe some of Harvey's blood had splashed my face. I shouted his name, like I could bring him back if I was loud enough. "You can't—can't leave me. You can't!"

But he didn't move. He didn't smirk at me or make a smartass remark. He didn't even blink, his eyes open, still fixed on me, but empty.

"Harvey," I gasped, bowing over him, my chest cracking open from the inside. "Harvey, please."

A wail built, loud enough that I heard it even over the ringing in my ears. I sounded like a siren, a banshee. My mates were dead. Emlyn and Harvey were dead.

Shadows slammed down in front of me, and I no longer cared what Locke did to me. Harvey's blood covered my hands, his wings draped over me, but the blood that soaked into my pants was Emlyn's. My Em, my protector and safe space.

I keened louder, the sound coming from deep in my soul. I was close enough to wrap my shaking fingers around Emlyn's.

They were already cold.

The air shuddered, and I snapped my head up, horror closing off my air and silencing my wail. Kai—that was *Kai's* magic.

Oh gods, it wasn't Locke's shadows walling me in but Wane's; he'd wrapped himself around me, tears soaking the back of my shirt and his fingers knotted with Harvey's.

"Kai," I rasped, staring at the bubble of darkness, gasping in panic and shock. *"Kai!"*

Where was he? I couldn't see through the thick dome all around us. I needed to see. I needed him safe, *alive*. Em and Harvey were dead. Really dead. I choked down vomit. Kai was going to take on Locke alone. Kai would be ripped away from me, too. I struggled in Wane's arms, blood rolling down my hands as I reached for the dome.

"No one," Kai seethed, too close—to us *and* Locke. I couldn't see him but I felt the iron poker of his horror and fury like a brand on my skin. Another part of me broke as I struggled to reach him. "Fucking *no one* hurts my family."

"Let him in the dome," I gasped, frantic as I pawed at the shadows. "Wane, let him—"

A boom as loud as any explosion rocked the floor beneath us as Kai called up a snake bigger than any I'd felt before. I tried to scramble away from my dead mates to get to Kai, to pull him back, to protect him.

My magic—fuck, *my magic!* I seized the slow, steady blood pounding through Locke's body and sank inner claws into it, burning with the need to splatter him into a million pieces and—

No, I really *was* burning. Where my power met Locke, my magic *scalded.* I gritted my teeth, screaming, crying. Em and Harvey were dead. I would follow them soon; this pain was *nothing.*

But the longer I held on, the harder it became to sense Locke's blood. It scorched and slipped through my fingers. I lost my grip entirely when another gunshot blasted through the room.

I flinched so hard, Havey's wings slid off my legs.

Wane's whimper filled my ears, his arms wrapping around my waist and squeezing so tight, I couldn't draw enough air to scream.

The slam of a body hitting the ground was unmistakeable.

Kai, my Kai—my secret romantic, my steadfast friend, my heart and soul and—

I couldn't breathe, and I no longer *cared* about drawing breath. I laid Harvey gently on the ground and turned in Wane's arms.

I knew how this would end. We both did. I was too numb to fight. I didn't even want to.

I wrapped my arms around Wane's shoulders and gripped as tightly as numb arms would allow.

"I love you," I rasped, choking on air. "I love you so much. I'll never stop loving you, no matter what."

Tears streaked down Wane's face, shining as bright as his mercury eyes. He blinked and another rush of tears rolled down his cheeks. I leaned forward to kiss one away, then the other, and his bottom lip wobbled.

"You are every bit of light in my world, itzaia," he choked out, his arms shaking but viciously tight around me.

"And you're mine, zivai," I rasped, burying my face in his shoulder and holding him tight. "I want you to run. The second the dome comes down—"

But death came on the fifth gunshot, when Wane's shadows finally buckled. He didn't get a chance to run, or even scream. After that, there was nothing.

PART II - HUNTRESS

14

A hundred years later

There was nothing ... until there was *something*.

There was dirt on my face, pressing on my mouth, my nose. It was everywhere, penning me in like a cage. Its earthy scent was all I could smell, all I could taste. A wordless scream shook my throat as I clawed at the cold dirt above me, forcing my weak, trembling hand through, carving with my claws until I saw daylight.

Someone ... buried me.

I scrabbled more frantically, pushing the Earth away until I could breathe, until I could see more glimpses of light.

I sat up with a desperate gasp when I cleared enough space, pawing at the ground under me, the ground I'd been *buried* in.

Oh gods, oh gods.

I swivelled my head, sucking down air and tasting my own grave dirt as I searched frantically for Harvey, Em, and Kai.

My mates—*where were my mates?*

The marble floor had gone from under me. Instead, my fingers sank into loose dirt, cold and shocking as it crumbled.

"What...?" I rasped, my voice thick with disuse.

A panicked breath scraped up my throat. I wavered, nearly falling back to the ground when I saw massive, thick-trunked *trees* around me instead of the kitchen in the Damned Realm house.

What the fuck?

"Guys?" I choked out, crawling unsteadily to my feet. I had to grab a tree to stop myself face-planting the ground, and my wings snapped clumsily out at my sides. It was too dark to see much except the rough shape of trees and the cloying darkness around me. How did I get out here? And where even *was* here?

There wasn't a forest around the house in the Damned Realm. I'd never actually seen a forest this old; the trees were *massive*. They reminded me of the forest around our home before those bastard mercs razed it to the ground, but these were far taller. Far older.

One thing was for sure: I was on my own. No more shallow graves dug in the dirt. No mates in sight.

The last thing I remembered was darkness wrapping around me as gunshot after gunshot ricocheted through our new home. Light broke through after repeated shots, and then something slammed through my body—and that was it.

Locke *killed* me...

So where the hell was I? Human souls went to Hell after they died, but I was already a demon, and I was ashamed to admit I'd never really thought about where demons went after death. Nowhere. If anything, I thought we were snuffed out of existence and there was nothing left.

"Guess this is the afterlife," I groaned, finally finding my feet and taking a step without the tree's assistance. I scrubbed the muck off my face as much as I could, but I could still taste it.

Fuck, every part of me hurt. Walking was not a fun experience. But staying here was out of the question unless I wanted to live in the forest.

"This hurts too damn much to be the afterlife," I hissed, hardly daring to voice my suspicion. I felt *alive*—hot and pulsing with pain, not cold and numb.

I hesitated with my fingertips over my wrist, but forced myself to check for a pulse and—

Holy shit, I *was* alive.

I was so confused and relieved and stressed, I wanted to curl into a ball on the forest floor. Mostly, I wanted to find my mates, hunt down a bed, and snuggle with them for the world's longest sleep.

My chest tightened, pain rupturing through my soul. I brushed it tentatively, and hissed at the fractured mess, the frayed threads of each bond, greyed with death. They died— really, truly died.

But I was alive, I was back somehow. And if *I* was, they had to be, too. They *had* to be.

I could find them, wherever they were. No matter how long it took me.

But first, I'd hunt down Cassander Locke and make him wish he'd never been born.

15

J walked for hours, numbly putting one foot in front of the other until a cluster of lights flickered on the edge of the horizon. I groaned in relief, my whole body aching from dying, being reborn, and walking miles through forest and farmland. My wings dragged along the floor, my shoulders too weak to hold them up. When the lights became a village, I could have cried.

In the fading light, I finally dared to peer down at my body, noticing with a twist in my stomach, I still wore the clothes I'd been shot in. Blood was crusted all down my front, the crimson almost black, dirt muddied my trousers and —*what the fuck?*

I'd been a badass bitch before, but I'd never had ink on my arms. Now a tattoo spanned the length of my right forearm in a strange combination of lines, arrows, dots, and a half circle that looked like a crescent moon.

"Oh, *fuck* no," I hissed, clenching my teeth as I stared at my new tattoo. I'd seen something like this before, on a mercenary who'd picked up a curse from a mark in the south of Hell. This was a *curse* mark.

Some bastard buried me alive and cursed me.

I pawed at my clothes, pulling up my shirt, ripping my bloody pants down, twisting to see my back, bending to scan my legs. The good news was my legs were curse free. The bad news: a *massive* curse mark was inked up my stomach.

I had two curses. Someone fucking *cursed* me!

Anger fuelled the last of my journey down the hill into the village. I lifted my wings back into place and stormed right up to the first person I found—a farmer herding his cows into the pen for the night. The sun was setting behind the farm, crimson and blood-orange, an appropriately violent backdrop for my current situation.

"Hey," I called in my new scratchy voice. The farmer turned in surprise to see me, or maybe to see anyone out here on the edge of the village. "Weird question. What's this village called?"

"Wenthai," he replied in a brusque accent that reminded me of home. I faltered, the familiar accent unexpected. "Where did you come from?" he asked with faint amusement. "You're not local; I don't know your face."

"I came from that damn forest," I muttered, stabbing a finger at the trees I'd woken up surrounded by. Bastards had tripped me up at every opportunity with their roots, swung branches into my face, and filled the air with biting, irritating insects. Plus, the canopy was so thick that I couldn't risk flying.

"Ah," he said with a knowing smile on his ruddy face. "The Forest of Halwen's been known to swallow people and cough them up again. It's all the magic in it."

"The..." I stumbled back, emotion making my voice break. "What did you just say? The Forest of Halwen?"

"Yeah," he confirmed, giving me a strange look as he wiped sweat from his brow. "Where did you think you were?"

I shook my head. *The Forest of Halwen.* The name my

mates gave to the woods around our house. The house Cassander Locke's cronies burned down. My chest pulled tighter, but there was something fragile to the emotion now instead of anger. I wanted to burst into tears.

My mates were still alive. This was a message.

"Thanks," I said gruffly, and turned away from the farmer. I didn't need directions to the nearest city; this was my home. I knew the way like the back of my hand.

"Hey, are you in trouble?" he asked, hurrying after me. "Come inside, my husband can make you a spiced tea. We've got paper you can use to write a letter. No communication stones, I'm afraid."

"I'm fine," I replied, and cleared my throat when it came out thick and harsh. I turned to him and pasted on a smile. "Really. You're kind; that's pretty fucking rare and I appreciate it. But I'll be fine. I know where I'm going."

Back to the capital, to the mercenary guild headquarters. What else was I going to do? I had no home, no mates, and no money.

I needed a job.

16

"*Y*our name's not on the list; you're not coming in," the six-foot-three guard on the guild's double doors rumbled.

"What a cliché," I muttered, my eyes narrowed and sharp fangs bared. "Look, I'm a guild member. Check my name— Halwen Vakhara."

He crossed dark bronze arms over his considerable chest, leathery brown wings ruffling in irritation. "I checked. There's no one currently registered with that name, only an inactive membership that's been dormant for years. And I mean *years.*"

Well, how many years were we talking? Three? *Ten?*

I gnashed my teeth and spelled it out for him, slowly, "That's me. Haley Vakhara; how many damned Halwen Vakharas do you think there are in Hell?"

He shrugged, giving me a no-nonsense look with beetle-black eyes. I suppressed a growl of frustration.

"Someone killed me, which is why I haven't been an active member. Kinda hard to do jobs when you're six feet underground."

He snorted, shifting to stand clear in front of the big door, barring my entrance. "You don't look so dead to me."

"That's because I'm *not,*" I growled. "Look I understand it as much as you do, but I'm back from the dead and I need a damn job. I'm a registered member; you can't pull this shit with me."

When he said nothing, a stoic wall of leather and muscle, I threw my hands up in exasperation. He reacted to the movement like he would a threat, and I released a scream of rage when he grabbed my arm, spun me, and slammed me face-first into the wall beside the door.

In positive news, I was closer to the door than I'd been before. I could have done without the little stones biting into my cheek and the burly guard's hot breath fanning across the back of my neck, though.

I suffered the indignity of him patting down my body, searching my ragged, bloodstained clothes for weapons. He grunted in confusion when he came up empty.

"Like I said," I growled against the brick wall, "someone killed me, buried me, and now I'm reborn. No weapons, no fucking clue what's going on. So I need *a job.*"

He grunted again and flipped me around when I bucked in his hold. He released me with a little shove into the road. "You'll have to reapply for a position."

"I'm Haley Vakhara, you giant lump of stupidity! I *have* a position."

But I might as well have been talking to the guild's sturdy brick wall.[1]

"Fine," I growled, and gave him my meanest glare. "I hope a wasp stings your asshole."

"Just doing my job," he muttered, affronted.

I shrugged and pretended I looked badass and intimidating when I stormed away, and not like a once-buried corpse that had been dug up. Or rather like I'd punched my way out of my own damn grave.

Hatred and rage burned in my heart, but I curled my hands into fists and forced myself to calm as I walked down the steep road, no clear destination in mind.

Find a job first, buy weapons second, hunt Cassander Locke third.

I could steal knives, but people who owned their own personal armouries tended to be the people you wanted as friends, not enemies. Turn my back, and there'd be a dagger, a throwing star, a sword, *and* an axe buried between my shoulder blades.

I scanned the street as I walked, searching for somewhere that might accept me for a job, surprised at how gleaming and *new* everything looked. Had they rebuilt the city? A bakery was out of the question—Emlyn was the baker. If I tried anything in the kitchen, houses tended to burn down. The florists were a hard no. Not because I couldn't tend to flowers or make an arrangement; because they reminded me of the soulcaps Malakai picked every year on our anniversary.

How many anniversaries had I missed? I'd have to make it up to him when I found him again. I'd have to make it up to all of them—Kai, Harvey, *and* Emlyn.

An ache burned behind my ribs where my bonds used to live, but I gritted my teeth. My brain throbbed in my skull, along with the haunting sense that I'd forgotten something, but when I examined it more closely, a sharp bolt of pain made me stumble into the pretty iron fence of a café.

Fuck!

I clutched my head, waiting for the pain to pass, and eyed the sweet little café in front of me.

"I can't cook for shit, but I can move plates from the kitchen to tables and back again," I mused.

I'd take a pot washer's position, for Lucifer's sake.

Ugh, that phrase had a little more meaning thanks to actually *meeting* the guy. He hadn't been a total bastard, and I supposed he'd been fair, but still. Sending us to the Damned Realm? He couldn't have thrown us in a jail cell for a few years? Not that I thought we'd have been safe from Locke—or his hunters—there, either.

"Enough," I rasped, pain stabbing my chest, my head, and my soul. "Enough."

It was done. I couldn't go back and change it; I had to live with the consequences of my actions that night.

I reached for the gate to the café at the same time the glass-inlaid wooden door swung open, and I came face to face with a black-haired, purple-skinned woman I never thought I'd see again.

"You!" I snarled, and launched myself at Renna.

17

*S*he dodged my first blow, snapped up a gauntleted wrist to deflect the second, and caught my first on my third. Okay, so I was a little rusty.[1]

"Excuse me?" she snapped, her eyes hard. "Care to explain why you're trying to rearrange my face?"

I laughed, the sound coming from low in my chest and *oozing* with bitterness. I ripped my fist out of her lilac hand and bared sharp teeth.

"You don't remember me? You exiled me to the fucking Damned Realm, and you don't even *remember* me?"

I slammed my fist into her shoulder, pretty sure the blow only landed because shock bloomed across her sharp face and she stared at me with sudden comprehension.

"You're—but that's impossible. There are reports of your death. I've seen the sketches; you were blasted into three pieces."

I winced. "I could have lived without knowing that, thanks Renna."

She shook her head, her sharp black hair cutting through the air around her jaw. "You're supposed to be dead," she snapped. "What deal did you make to come back?"

"Don't you think I'd have asked to not die in the first place if I was going to make a deal?" I snapped right back.

"You broke into Lucifer's house; you're an imbecile."

"I didn't *know* it was his house," I threw back, shoving her shoulder.

She shoved my hand away hard enough that my wrist ached.

"Whatever is happening here," a soft voice put in, and both Renna and I jumped when a pink demon in a bonnet and pinafore peered through the doorway, "can you take it away from my café? You're terrifying my customers."

A glance through the door showed her customers were watching, looking more eager for a show than terrified, but she was right that this wasn't the right setting.[2]

I backed up, keeping an eye on the purple woman and waiting for her to draw one of the many knives on her person. I cursed myself for not swiping one when I had the chance, and then ground my teeth when the word 'cursed' proved too sensitive.

"How are you alive?" Renna barked, as sharp and curt as I remembered. Her whole body was sharp, from her figure to her features to her personality.

I swept my arms out at my sides and shrugged. "I don't know. I woke up in the Forest of Halwen last night. A name that no one should know, by the way, because it was a private name between me and my mates. But apparently everyone calls the forest my name now.

"Oh, and when I say 'woke up,' I really mean I dug myself out of a shallow grave and nearly choked on dirt. I don't know what happened, or how I'm alive, or where my mates were."

If knives could soften, Renna did just that. Her mouth pinched a little less, maybe. "They're not with you?"

She cast a look around the street, like Kai would sneak out of the shadows with his snakes poised to strike, Emlyn would creep along the rooftops and leap off, his feathery grey wings spread in flight, or Harvey would blind the street with his sunlight, a smirk on his face, or—

Or what? I gritted my teeth when pain exploded through my tender skull. Renna didn't miss it but she must have thought it was the pain of missing them.

"Come with me," she sighed, her eyes narrowed. "Lucifer will be able to figure out what happened."

A laugh bubbled up my throat. I rose to my full height. "You're not taking me to Lucifer."

The last time I saw the devil, he made us custodians of the Damned Realm. The realm of suffering and eternal misery. The last thing I wanted was to be sent back there, and this time without my mates at my side.

So I had to get sneaky and clever.

"Holy shit!" I exclaimed, my mouth falling open as I stared at something non-existent at the bottom of the road. "Look at that!"

"What?" Renna snarled, turning.

The second she moved, I spun and sprinted up the road, aiming for a snicket between the florist's shop and a three-story house with a weathervane on top, the metal bright silver against the purple Iarlon sky. Fuck, I was out of breath. I shouldn't be panting already.

I made it all of seven steps, barely reaching the little side street before Renna's fingers hooked in my tattered clothes and she yanked me back.

"It's for your own good," she huffed, and locked her arms around my struggling body.

My stomach dropped hard when I felt the disorienting pinch and tilt of transportation. Shit, she could sift?

This is not fucking happening.

I lost control of my breathing as the street vanished around us, replaced by an endless black void tinted the slightest violet.

When we flew out the other side, I managed a single glimpse of a formal reception room with a roaring fireplace, a desk full of papers and files, and a sofa that held two people —a pretty young scarred woman with soft brown hair and black wings, and Lucifer, the devil himself.

When Renna's magic released me, I collapsed to the floor, claws scraping a fine rug, and I could do nothing to stop myself throwing up bile all over the devil's expensive, black shoes.

18

I'm dead, I'm so dead.

"Renna, didn't we agree no more kidnapping people?" the pretty woman sighed, getting off the sofa to hand me a tissue. "Are you alright?"

"Me?" I groaned, wiping my mouth and darting a quick glance at Lucifer. He looked exactly like he had the last time I saw him, from the long black hair that flowed over his shoulders, the bearded, dark gold face, the fine clothes he wore, and the dark eyes that watched me with an intensity that made me squirm. I quickly glanced away. "I was fine before this madwoman abducted me."

Renna crossed her arms over her chest, and gave Lucifer a wry look. "You don't recognise her, either."

Lucifer, in the process of wiping my vomit off his shoes, glanced up in surprise. He looked from Renna's smirking face to me as I got to my feet, helped by the winged woman I was ninety percent sure was Lucifer's queen. He certainly hadn't had a queen the last time I was dragged here—by the same damn woman—but fond murmurs around the capital spoke of a queen who helped save everyone and end a war. Impressive. The Justice of Hell they called her.

I wanted my own fancy title, but that could come after I found my mates and killed anyone responsible for keeping them from me. Why bury *me* in the woods, but not them? *Where are they?*

Lucifer was still scrutinising me, no doubt noticing the tattered clothes, the blood visible underneath, and my general sorry state. I sketched a bow that was more ironic than respectful and said, "Halwen Vakhara. You might remember sending me and my mates to be custodians of the Damned Realm. Great idea, by the way, ten out of ten, definitely didn't get us murdered."

Lucifer shot to his feet, shock widening his dark crimson eyes and parting his mouth behind his beard. "But you're dead."

"That's what I said," Renna remarked, dropping into an armchair and stretching out her legs like she owned the place.

"I'm missing something," the queen said, glancing between the three of us. "She can't be dead if she's here. Luc?"

Damn, she called Lucifer *Luc*. The man was terrifying, and brimming with power; she was brave as fuck. No wonder the people loved her.

Lucifer didn't respond straight away; he narrowed his eyes and walked a circle around me, like he was waiting for my arms to decompose and drop off.

"This is weird," I muttered. I wanted to shout *boo!* but the shudder that went down my spine at his close inspection kept my tongue in check. "Hey!" I gasped when he snatched my arm, fingers pressed to my wrist.

"Luc," the queen repeated, her tone different—exasperated. A deep V cut between her eyebrows. "What are you doing?"

"Checking if I'm corpselike," I supplied when he stayed silent, focusing on my pulse. It was still there. I was still alive.[1]

Lucifer dropped my wrist, picked up my other, and gave it the same treatment.

"Nice to meet you," I said to the queen over the devil's bowed head. "I'm Halwen—Haley. I've only been in Iarlon a day, but I've heard a lot about you."

She ducked her head, blushing. Cute. "A lot of the stories are exaggerated," she replied, casting a sharp look at Renna, who innocently cleaned her fingernails with a sharp knife.

"But well-deserved, sweetheart," Lucifer replied, releasing me from his intimidating study to give his partner a sickeningly affectionate look.

My stomach whirled like a tornado, a fist squeezing my heart. I missed my mates so fucking much. I swallowed down my pain and asked, "So. Any ideas how I'm not dead, sir?"

I used my most respectful tone, and mentally patted myself on the back.

"None," he sighed.

"I was shot, probably multiple times. It ripped me apart; I definitely died. My—my mates died, too."

Don't cry, Haley, don't fucking cry.

"And they didn't wake up with you?" the queen asked, her brown eyes big with sympathy. I shook my head, my jaw clenched against a torrent of emotion, and she softened even further. "I can't imagine how much pain you're in. I'm so sorry."

"It's fine," I ground out, swallowing the lump in my throat. "Could be worse, right? I could be dead." I tried to laugh, but I sounded like a donkey braying. Awkward.

Even Renna was eyeing me with sympathy now. Fuck, I must have sounded *really* pathetic.

"Anyway, I'll get out of your seriously beautiful hair," I told Lucifer, heading towards the door beside the sofas. "I don't know why your stabby friend kidnapped me, but nice seeing you."

He stepped into my path, because of course he did. My stomach dropped, dread crawling up my spine like an insect.

"The only way you could come back from being dead is with a god's or goddess's power."

"Which is a non-issue," I said slowly, "because the gods have been gone for years." I laughed nervously when they all exchanged a look. "Right?"

"Not ... exactly," the queen replied, and bit her lip.

"They recently became more involved in our lives," Lucifer explained, and for a moment the terrifying aura around him dimmed, making him more mortal. "Angels and alpha demons conspired to end my reign, destroy most of Hell, and rebuild it as something far more horrific."

I winced. "Parts of it are horrific enough as it is."

Renna snorted.

"It's not out of the question that a god would be watching Hell and moving game pieces around, but why resurrect *you?*"

All my respect and fear flew out the window, and I snapped.

"First of all, that's incredibly rude, Lucy. Don't talk to me like I'm worthless; I'd be pretty damn useful to a god. Second, I am no one's damn game piece. *No one's.*"

"Lucy," Renna choked out, tapering into a deep, guttural laugh. "I like her; let's keep her."

"I'm not a pet, either," I snapped, teeth bared and wings ruffling in agitation.

Lucifer began to speak, but he paused when his queen—I really needed to learn her name—crossed to the far end of the room. With her back to us, I couldn't see what she was doing, but I took advantage of the distraction to edge a little closer to the door. It wasn't like I could elbow *the devil* in the gut and run, though. Anyone else, I'd have already done it, but this was Lucifer. The big bad, the guy who ran the whole realm, the King of Hell.

When the queen turned back to us, she was holding a glass with a decent amount of amber liquid in it. A woman after my own heart. Wait, she was crossing the room, holding it out—she'd made the drink *for me?*

Fuck, she was impressive *and* sweet. She reminded me of my mum, or what I could remember before we moved from Earth to Hell and I never saw her again. I had a faint memory of singing, fierce laughter, and feeling safe in her arms.

"Thanks," I rasped, accepting the drink and downing half of it in one go.

"We're not saying you're a pawn," she said kindly, "just that a god or goddess might want to use you as one. Do you have any new powers?"

I shook my head, the alcohol burning down my body. "None. I do have these, though."

I held my arm out, and twisted it into the light so they could see through the dried blood to the black inked curse on my arm.

"Shit," Renna hissed, flying to her feet.

"Yeah. Also this." I lifted my shirt, showing the biggest, nastiest curse down my middle. "I don't know what these curses do, but I can tell you I never had them before I died. Someone must have tattooed them after I died, and then buried me in the woods."

"But why bring you back now?" Lucifer growled under his breath, eyes narrowed on my curse marks. "After a hundred years?"

I laughed.

No one else laughed.

"After *how many* years?" I demanded, my voice a little high, a lot screechy. I threw back the rest of the drink, my breathing turning frantic. "A hundred years?"

"I thought you knew," Lucifer murmured, an apology in the look his red eyes settled on me.

"You couldn't have told me?" I snapped at Renna, ignoring the sympathy and confusion on her sharp, lilac face.

"How was I supposed to know you were so clueless?" she snapped right back.

I snarled, hating that she was right. "I thought it'd been a few years, ten tops. Not a fucking hundred. But that's—I don't even know—I—"

"Oh, Halwyn," the queen breathed, and shocked the fuck out of me by swallowing me into a floral-scented hug that worked wonders on my jagged emotions.[2]

When she let me go, I noticed Lucifer watching me with that apologetic look again. That's how you knew your life was depressing; the devil himself thought you were pitiful.

"You know it's Halwen, like *the Forest* of Halwen, right?" Renna drawled, watching me closely. "A forest that was named a hundred or so years ago."

I shot her a panicked look, my hands shaking where they still held the tumbler. *No.* Just ... no. "That's—that can't be right."

"Why not?" Lucifer asked, tilting his head in a preternatural way.

"It's what my mates called the forest around our home before Cassander Locke burned it down. I thought—maybe they told everyone to call it that as a message to me that they're back, too. But if it was named a hundred years ago—my mates have been back, alone, for a hundred years."

I covered my mouth, feeling sick.

"Someone kept you apart," the queen guessed angrily. "If your mates were reborn a hundred years ago, why wait until now to bring *you* back?"

"Good question," Lucifer muttered. "But not an easy one

to answer. Someone went to a lot of trouble to do this; they won't be easy to find."

"I don't care," I snarled, putting the glass down on a nearby surface a little too heavily. "I'm going to find them, rip their intestines up their throats, and choke them with them."

The queen's eyes blew wide. "That's ... graphic."

"I like it," Renna remarked. "I'll help; I've been bored lately."

"You will not," Lucifer disagreed sharply. "I have a job for you."

"Oh, goody," she replied flatly, and dropped back onto the sofa. The two of us were kindred sarcastic spirits; if she stopped kidnapping me and dragging me to Lucifer's palace, I might even become friends with Renna.

"What do you need, Halwen?" Lucifer asked abruptly, like he'd been keeping it inside for a while. "It's my fault you were taken to the Damned Realm. It might not be my fault you were killed, but—I share some of the blame."

"She did break into your house, boss," Renna pointed out.

I ignored her. "I need a job. Badly. I need money so I can find my mates. I'm good at tracking—I used to be a mercenary before I settled down with my mates—but getting information out of people costs a pretty penny."

Or a hefty pouch of gold crowns, the most valuable coin in Hell's currency. Every pouch I handed over broke my heart a little.

"Positions in my palace are few and far between," the devil said, sympathy in his red eyes. "There's one job, but everyone I've offered it to has turned it down. It's too dangerous—"

"Danger is my middle name," I cut in, my heart leaping, racing. Who cared how dangerous it was; if it paid, I could get everything I needed to track my mates. I knew it would be a long search, and it might take months, but the sooner I could get started, the sooner I found them.

"What's your real middle name?" the queen asked, a flicker of laughter curling her lips. Her brown eyes glimmered.

"Danger," I insisted.

"Bullshit," Renna spat, pointing her dagger at me. "Tell us your actual name, and I'll give you this knife."

"You just cleaned your nails with it; do I look like I want your nail cleaning dagger?"

"It's free," she pointed out.

"Siybella," I muttered, and snatched the dagger from her outstretched hand. I'd need to deep clean it, but at least it was sharp. I felt more like myself with a weapon in my hand; my panic settled. Renna smirked deeper, like she noticed. "So what's the job?"

"I need someone to track alphas, and infiltrate their community," Lucifer answered, almost ... tired? "Most of them were dealt with in the war, but there are some left, quietly stirring up trouble. The last thing Hell needs is another battle, so I want them found and brought in."

"Alphas," I repeated.

The biggest, baddest, most powerful and *feral* of demons. They were more animal than man, and impossible to reason with. Get on their wrong side, and they'd start tearing limbs off and ripping out eyes. I usually gave them a wide berth, and avoided jobs with them. Of course, no one told me the job to hunt—uh? Harvey?—would involve archdemons. They were practically alphas themselves, but with a *few* extra brain cells.

"How many alphas?"

"It's hard to say," Lucifer replied cagily.

"So you have no idea," I sighed, dragging my teeth over my bottom lip.

But it was paid work, and work I was good at—tracking, hunting. It would get me one step closer to Emlyn, Kai, and

Harvey, and while I was out hunting the alphas I could search for my mates, too.

"I'll take the job," I told him, ignoring the flare of surprise in his eyes. "Consider yourself the proud employer of a new tracker. I'll report to you in the morning, shall I? Or do you want me to start now?"

Please don't say now. I was so exhausted I could fall asleep sitting upright in the middle of a raucous bar.

The devil waved his hand, looking as knackered as I surely did. "The morning's fine."

"Where are you staying?" his queen asked, something unsettlingly knowing in her gaze.

I hesitated a moment too long.

"Right, you'll stay in the palace. No, no," she cut in when I tried to argue. "I'm not letting you sleep on the streets. I'll show you to the guest wing. Follow me."

I gave Renna a wide-eyed look. "Is your queen always this bossy?"

"Always," she confirmed.

Lucifer chuckled, watching his queen with sweet, sickly love. My chest pulled tight again. I missed that. I missed it so damn much, and I'd only been alive for a day and a half. The weeks or months it took me to find my mates were going to kill me.

But I had a job, and somewhere to sleep. That was more than I had this morning.

"This way," the queen called, leading the way down the bright, airy corridor outside. "I'm Lili, by the way. Lili Kazana."

"Nice to meet you, Lili Kazana," I replied, distracted by the architecture, art, and the sheer *size* of the palace around us.

"We'll figure out what the marks mean," she said gently, watching me as she led the way through a courtyard full of statues and wild greenery. "We've got the biggest library in

Hell; there must be something in there about curses like yours."

The smile she gave me was probably supposed to be comforting, but all it did was remind me of the curses inked on my body. What were they for? What if I was cursed to die again in a week? What if I was cursed to never find my mates?

For a moment, I felt optimistic that things were going to work out.

My mistake.

19

*I*t felt like yesterday when I slept in our bed in the house by the forest, before Locke's minions set it ablaze and forced us to a safe house. I hadn't slept in that bed; I snuck out before unconsciousness could take me. The difference between this huge, four-poster, cloud of a bed in Lucifer's palace and our worn, five-sleeper mattress at home was crazy. It was too comfortable, too soft, swallowing my body whole. Where were the springs digging into my back? Where were the dips caused by sleep-heavy bodies?

It took me hours to settle, to stop scanning the cream and gold walls of the room, or staring obsessively at the shadows playing on the wardrobe and chest of drawers. I kept waiting for those shadows to come to life and attack me, for Cassander Locke to appear.

"It's been a hundred years," I whispered to myself in the dark. But I climbed out of bed to tug the curtains open and let more silvery lilac moonlight flood the room. I gave the furniture and pale bed another sweep, my heart clanging when movement chased through the big mirror above the dressing table across from the bed.

"It's *you,* you daft bitch," I groaned at myself, and climbed back under the nebular covers. "And Locke's probably dead by now; he was already fifty when he killed you. No way did he live to a hundred and fifty."

Cassander was a slimy bastard, though. Maybe he prolonged his life somehow.

"Stop it," I hissed at myself pulling the covers over my head and poking a hole so I could breathe cool air.[1]

I finally drifted to sleep when the sky began to lighten and exhaustion took over my body, dragging me down.

It seemed like as soon as I closed my eyes, they were blinking open again. But there was no stress wrapped around me here, no fear tightening my chest, only a warm weight pressed to my back and a pleasant heaviness resting in the dip of my side.

I groaned a wordless question, and the arm tightened.

"Go back to sleep, Hales," Emlyn muttered, grazing his nose against my shoulder and inhaling a long breath.

I drifted off again, safe and comfortable.

But then Em startled, his whole body jolting, and I came awake in response, scanning the room for threats.

"Is this real?" he rasped, staring at me while I assessed our room—the room back at the house that had burned down. My beloved bedroom. "Tell me this is real."

"It's a dream," I realised, a furrow between my brows as Emlyn gathered me so close to him that I grunted, his arms squeezing me so hard.

"But you're here. You're here." He scattered kisses across my shoulders, throwing his leg over mine to—to kick Harvey awake. Harvey was here? A small, choked sound escaped me. "Wake up. Now!"

Kai flew awake too, a flurry of swear words on his tongue until he spotted me. My heart thumped when Kai stared at me. I waited for him to rant or laugh or kiss me. Instead, he burst into shaking, wretched tears, burying his face in inked palms.

"Fuck," Harvey breathed, staring at me with disbelieving silver eyes. "You don't look hazy like you normally do in my dreams."

"She's here," Emlyn grunted, and pulled me up until I was sitting.

Somehow we ended up in a giant cuddle pile, with Kai sobbing and clutching me tight, Emlyn kissing every bit of my skin he could reach, and Harvey staring at me like I was a star given life—a miracle he never expected to see.

I hugged them all close to me, and ignored the sharp twist of pain through my chest. I knew something was off, something was missing, but for now I had my mates in my arms and I didn't care about anything else.

20

I woke in pain, clutching at my chest. Unable to breathe. Unable to process the vicious sensation that sliced through my soul and radiated to every part of me. I threw back the unfamiliar covers and stumbled out of bed, scanning the airy white room as if I'd find them here. My mates. My whole, goddamn everything.

"W—" I choked out.

My fingers flew to my throat as it closed, strangling the word before I could utter it. A name? I tried to recall it, but pain exploded through my skull with sudden cruelty, and I staggered into the windowsill with a cry.

"Fucker," I whimpered, digging my nails into the wood of the sill and staring out the window as I panted to catch my breath. Pain burrowed through my ribs and made a home in my heart. I gasped for air, resting my head against the cold window pane and waiting for it to settle.

Something very, very bad happened to my mates. Worse, I thought, than me being buried and having to claw myself out of a grave in the forest.

"I'll find you," I swore to them, reaching through my chest

for the bonds that tied us and finding only tatters and shreds. "I swear. No matter who I have to blackmail, threaten, or kill, I'll find you."

But I didn't know where to start, and the thought of returning to the Damned Realm sent a shiver of warning down my spine. My instincts screamed never to return.

There was no point trying to sleep again despite the early hour and the fact I was normally dead to the world before noon. Or just dead if you considered anything before yesterday. I shuddered, crossing the room to grab my new coat. It was red velvet and fancy and *so* not me, but I wasn't about to complain to Lucifer and his queen when they'd been crazy enough to clothe me in the first place.

It wouldn't have hurt them to give me a suite with a bath, though. I had to walk halfway down the quiet, sun-filled corridor to a bathroom where I could do my morning ablutions and soak in the tub.

I hoped a bath would cleanse my panic and hurt, but nope, the remnants of the dream were still there when I was clean, dressed, and hunting down breakfast.

Had my mates really been there, like Emlyn said? I wanted to believe that was true, that we'd connected in a mystical, mate-ish way, but it was too good to be true.

I slumped into the dining room when I finally found it, feeling weird in my velvet coat. I wanted my leather back, but I didn't know what happened to the safe house when we got caught breaking into Lucifer's second home. It was probably stolen years ago. A *hundred* years ago.

Fuck, I'd been dead a hundred years. I wasn't just reborn; I was a relic.

There was a demon slumped over a table, snoring so loudly the quills all over her black-and-white body rattled. I smiled when I saw a few of them scattered on the floor around us, and my eyes lit up as an idea struck.

Careful not to wake her, I crept over and scooped up the four quills from the floor, sliding them into my hair and wrapping a few strands around them to hold them in place, sticking straight up. Hell yes! Porcupine quill tiara!

My mood was boosted, and I looked cool as fuck, but I was still drained.

"Thank fuck," I breathed when I spotted a carafe of coffee, but when I tilted it towards a cup, nothing came out. I shook the glass. Empty. Fucking typical. I growled and put it down on the table hard enough to knock the quills out of my hair. Nooo!

My mood plummeted.

A different, deeper growl answered me in a long rumble, and I startled, spinning around to see—holy shit, a red panda as big as an elephant, with black horns spiralling off their head and red smoke wafting dangerously from their fur. The porcupine demon shot up from her nap, took one look at the panda, and bolted.

I tried to back up, but the table stood in my way, and when I reached for a knife I came up empty.

The panda rumbled at me, their big jaw unhinged like they wanted to swallow me whole. A whimper caught in my throat and the panda—laughed? Mammoth teeth bared and their big, furry chest shook with a rumble of undeniable laughter.

I stared into their eyes, searching for murderous rage and—

"Wait a fucking second," I blurted, stumbling forward a step as my heart took off beating like a frantic bird. "Tali?"

Her giant, furry head bobbed, and a laugh of disbelief shot from me. I hadn't seen her in years—a hundred and twenty years thanks to being dead. We were friends when I was a kid and we lived next door to each other. After my mum abandoned us on Earth, and Dad and I came to Hell to escape the pain of her walking out on us, Tali got me out of that darkness. She gave me something good when everything else sucked.

We'd been inseparable. People struggled to understand her because she spoke in growls, purrs, and grunts, but I always understood her perfectly. And unless something dramatic had changed, she had one of the fiercest eye-rolls known to demonkind. It spoke far louder than any words.

She used to take a running jump and dive into my arms; she'd been roughly the size of a housecat, so catching her was easy. But when her big butt wiggled *now* and she launched across the room, I squeaked and threw up my hands.

"You can't jump up, you're bigger than a horse, Tal-Tal!"

But she didn't stop running, so I braced for impact—and shrieked when her head butted the entire side of my body and a giant, slobbery tongue covered me in drool.

"Tali," I shrieked.

Before I could process the pressure in my chest, it bubbled up as laughter and filled the whole dining room.

Fuck, it felt good to laugh. It felt good to have a friend, too. I was so alone, and even though I tried not to think about it last night, it was impossible to feel lonely this morning. I should have lived a long, happy life with my mates, but now I was here and they weren't.

But I had a friend. I had Tali.

"I'm so fucking happy to see you," I choked out, wrapping my arms as far as they'd go around her giant neck.[1]

She nudged me with her head, questions in her eyes even as she vibrated with happiness.

"You're probably wondering how I'm still alive, and how I'm as gorgeous, glamorous, and mind-bendingly beautiful as I ever was."

The flat look in her eye when she drew back assured me she was not.

"Let's sit down; I'll tell you everything," I said, turning to glare at the coffee pot. "But first, I need coffee. Please tell me you can—"

I jumped when a strange cube of metal began to steam, and slanted a look at Tali to see the red smoke on her fur fade. "Well, someone's learned a new trick."

And so had coffee. Why was it pouring out of a hole in a metal box? *Shit, I'm losing my coffee!* I scrambled to put a cup under the flow, and when it shut off, I added milk and I couldn't hold back a groan at how damn good it was.[2]

Holding my ambrosia protectively to my chest—and slightly mourning my quill tiara—I sank into a chair at one of the dining tables, and tried not to laugh at the sight of Tali shoving chairs aside so she could sit her giant, furry butt opposite me.

"It started when I was sent to hunt someone. Only it turned out my client was an abusive bastard, and my target was my mate."

"No," I argued when Tali jutted out her furry red chin and fixed me with a hard look.

I told her everything that happened since we last saw each other, finishing with my new hunter job. I knew that look on her face—*I'm going with you.*

"I'm doing this alone; I can hunt, Tali. I've been doing it for years."

The dry look she shot me said, *you've been dead a hundred years.*

"Yes, thank you, I know that."

She huffed through her nose. *I'm going with you, and nothing you can say will convince me otherwise.*

"Fine," I groaned, and drew out my winning card as I

sipped the last of my coffee.[3] "But you're asking Lucifer for permission."

And no way was the devil going to allow my friend to come with me on a secret mission because she was worried I'd get a little stabbed.

And yet ... the smug look she shot me made nerves tumble through my belly.

"Wait," I protested when she lumbered to her feet. "You can't just go ask Lucifer *now.*"

She made a throaty sound that assured me she could.

"But he's Lucifer!"

She shrugged and uttered a groan. *He's my friend, too.*

"Wait, *what?* Get back here and tell me your life story too, Tali!"

I sped into the hallway after her, empty coffee cup in hand, but she was already bounding down the corridor with huge strides. I groaned a curse. Even with wings, there was no chance I'd catch up with her.

"Halwen Vakhara?" someone grunted, their voice low and gravelly.

I froze between one step and the next, apprehension crawling down my spine.

Anyone knowing my name when I'd been gone a century was not a good omen.

21

I turned slowly to face the bald, muscular man who spoke. Fuck, he was tall; I had to tip my head back to meet his scowling gaze.

"Yes?" I asked as calmly as possible. He gave off unfriendly bulldog vibes, and I didn't want to be bitten.

"General Callahan is looking for you," he replied, his scowling expression telling me he'd rather be anywhere but here, talking to me. "I'll take you to him."

I laughed, crossing my arms over my chest, and didn't take a single step. "Sure, I'm just going to follow a strange man I don't know to an undisclosed location."

He already turned to guide me down the hall, but he paused— and growled as he faced me again. "I'm Bernard, *your commander*. But you won't get your orders from me unless they're extremely sensitive, so Callahan can deal with you. Follow me."

"You have a lovely way with words," I replied, probably foolishly given he was a powerful commander. But telling Tali everything that happened had raked up all my pain again, and I wasn't in the best mood.

"You met my girl. Lili."

My mouth dropped.

"Holy shit, *you're* one of her men? You?" I winced. "Sorry, that was rude. It's just ... she's all sweetness and sunshine and you're—growly," I finished when he bared his teeth.

"Do you want to die?" he asked casually.

"Actually, I was gonna ask for tips. My mates are missing, but one of them is a bright, optimistic fucker, too."

Talking about Harvey made my heart hurt, but I refused to stop talking about my mates. If I did, it'd be like they didn't exist. "I'm a growly bastard like you; how do you put up with it?"

Bernard snorted, some hostility leaving him. "Pretend it's annoying when it's actually your favourite thing."

"Genius," I breathed, shaking my head in awe.[1] "So who am I hunting? I'm guessing that's why this Callahan's after me? I've got a job."

Bernard gave me a stern look that didn't have as much impact as it had a minute ago. "He'll brief you on your roles. But there's one thing I wanted to talk to you about."

"You? Want to talk? You don't strike me as the type."

He barked an abrupt laugh. Hell yes, I was making friends everywhere in this palace.

"On paper, your job is to hunt and retrieve alphas." He lowered his voice and checked we were alone in the corridor. "But we only need one alpha from each group to mine for information."

"Cute way of saying interrogate and torture," I quipped. When his huge shoulders stiffened, I added, "No, I mean it. It's cute; I'm going to use that. And don't worry, on the moral scale I'm far closer to black than white. I'm a hunter, thief, and assassin. It's not the first time I've been sent to kill someone."

"These aren't ordinary jobs," Bernard replied, his brow furrowed. "These are alphas."

"How many alphas are we talking?" I asked, and followed him down the hallway.

"This first job is seven."

"Seven?" I demanded, my voice shrill. The man had lost his mind.

Seven alphas against one angel-demon hybrid?

Fuck, those were depressing odds.

22

*K*alador was a truly *beautiful* city, so sweet-smelling that it was like perfume on my senses, with blooming trees and delicate flowers dripping like diamonds from balconies—and children ran through the streets with tinkling laughter.[1]

At least, that's what Tali told me it was like fifty years ago.

Now, I sidestepped a bull demon with a beer gut, the man brandishing a cutlass as he charged after a teenager with a clearly-stolen bottle of ale in his hand and a grin on his face. Neither of them cared that they sloshed through a questionable brown puddle, splattering their worn shoes.

I jumped out of the path of the 'water' and slumped into the leaning wall of a grimy inn. Inside, people yelled and sang off-key. Honestly, it was nostalgic.

"I love cities like this," I sighed. I'd had so many amazing nights in places like Kalador, all of them fuzzy with both age and ale.

The look Tali shot my way said, *this is a town and you need your sanity tested.*

"I could do without the river," I added, leading Tali down a snicket to an even grimier pub. "That thing stinks."

Try having advanced panda senses. I can pick out the individual notes of piss, shit, and vomit.

I wrinkled my nose. "Delightful."

She chuffed a laugh through her nose.

Tali got a few looks as we jogged down the cobbled road and onto the riverside path where our targets were said to be staying. Callahan, my truly *charming* commander, received word of alphas staying at a halfway house called the Cock and Claws. I snorted, remembering his face as he told me the name.

Cock is the name of an ale, Tali said with an eye roll, bursting my amused bubble.

"I refuse to accept that," I replied, and spotted the three-storey brown structure down the road, its top floor hanging over the bottom two and black beams criss-crossing the stone walls. "Oh look, it's a brown cock. I have one of those."

Tali's expression flattened, her furry brow heavy over vivid eyes.

"He's called Harvey," I told her cheerfully, "and he's very talented with it. By *it* I mean his—"

Yes, thank you, Tali cut off with a deep sigh. *Got it. Dick puns galore.*

"You know me, Tal-Tal. I can't let a good dick pun go unspoken."

I wish you would.

"If wishes were horses, beggars would ride," I quipped, and leaned my shoulder into the heavy wooden door of the Cock and Balls.[2]

"Wait outside," I told Tali with a scratch under her chin. "I won't be long. That looks like a lovely alley, don't you think?"

She rolled her eyes again, and headed around the back of

the pub. We never hunted together[3] but even after all these years, there was a deep bond between us and she must know what I had planned. Or she'd been on these kinds of jobs with other people. I pushed down the friend-jealousy that rose, and strode through another heavy door into a cramped little tavern that smelled of beer and sharp cleaning solution. Well, at least it was clean.

Sadly, the same couldn't be said for some of the patrons. But I'd worn shredded clothes and smelled like death for two whole days, so I wasn't about to judge.

I scoped the place out as I strode to the bar, dismissing three clusters of men before I found a group of demons with bulging muscles and massive shoulders sitting at the back, involved in a card game with a pile of money on the table. A flash of excitement went through me, fluttering my belly.

Oh, hell yes.

"Pint," I said to the grey-haired purple man behind the bar.

"Pint, *what?*" he barked back, barely lifting his head from the clean glasses he was organising into straight lines."

"Pint, pretty please," I said sweetly, and fluttered my lashes.

He flicked a look at me, and grabbed a glass, pulling a pint. Callahan had given me an allowance; I gladly handed over someone else's money and sipped the foam of my beer. Huh, not bad. At least it was somewhat cool.

"Thanks," I told the barman, who vaguely grunted in my direction and went back to straightening his glasses.

I made a beeline for the alphas in the back. There were only five of them, three men and two women, not seven alphas like I'd been sent to track,[4] but something told me a ruckus would bring the other two running out of the woodwork.

"Hi," I said shyly, letting my gaze linger on each of the alphas, cataloguing their appearances. I kept the reason why I was doing this in the forefront of my mind, holding onto my mates' faces as I batted my lashes at a muscular woman with rich brown skin and tight curls of hair. "Can I join you? I haven't played stress in years."

A green man with long tusks snorted but made no comment. Two others stayed silent, the two of them like reflections—both as pale as ice with short hair and the same face despite their difference in sex. But a slim, winged man assessed me with a critical eye, and the woman I'd batted my lashes at leaned back in her chair to give me an appreciative glance.

"No amateurs," the winged man grunted, scowling.

"Oh, don't be so glum, Ken," the black woman teased, giving me a sultry look and patting her knee.

Please let my mates never find out about this, I whispered to the gods and climbed into the woman's lap, setting my pint on the table. She was annoyingly comfy. Maybe I should browse for a female mate, round out my little family with some softness. Not that destiny took requests.

I'd done my research this afternoon, cramming all the recent history I could into my head, memorising the events of the war that only ended five months ago. Alpha demons made an alliance with angels—demons' natural enemy, of which species I was half—in order to bring Lucifer down. They wanted to end his wicked ways of keeping Hell peaceful, preventing mass murder, punishing rapists with eternal suffering, and providing a safe, generally clean place to live with actual *houses* instead of huts made of shit and mud. *How dare he!*

Alphas felt their rights had been breached by Lucifer keeping the peace; like spoiled children, they threw a tantrum. But their tantrum killed hundreds, and brought war on two sides to Hell. If it hadn't been for alphas, Heaven would never have gained an inch here, let alone destroyed so much.

There was also a whole thing with corrupt angels and evil gods, but I skimmed that section since it wasn't relevant. I knew enough to give the brawny people around the table a knowing smile and murmur, "I haven't seen any alphas in months. Where did you guys all go? I missed seeing your pretty muscles."

I played the role a little too well, squeezing the powerful bicep of the woman whose lap I sat on. She let out a pleased growl, sending a rush of warning down my spine.

This woman could rip you in two and eat your innards, my instincts screamed.

But she was an easy target, and alphas' main weakness was flattery. I took a drink of beer to bolster my courage.

The two pale twins laughed in unison at my question, low cruel sounds that made my blood run cold. They'd be harder to find a weakness in; everything about them screamed *apex predator* and *total psychopath.*

"Curious, aren't you?" the pale woman asked, tracking my every movement.

"Too curious," her male counterpart added, snapping his cards on the table.

The woman under me laughed so hard she rattled my whole body.

"She's not a spy; she's an alpha chaser." She ran her hand up my right wing, and I shuddered, primal terror shooting through me. I played it off as arousal, forcing out a soft gasp. "Aren't you, pretty thing?"

I swallowed and glanced aside, faking embarrassment. The twins laughed, believing the act.

Their game of cards was forgotten in the face of something far more interesting.

The big, green man leaned forward, parting his mouth in a grin around his tusks. "You need some real demons to show you a good time?"

I swallowed, and purposely licked my lips. Gave a nod in reply. If Kai found out about any of this, he'd go on a murderous rampage and then spend hours, maybe days, reminding me who I really belonged to. And don't even get me started on Em's possessiveness, or what Harvey would do to me.[5]

"I don't even know your names," I pointed out, casting a curious glance at the winged, dark-haired man who'd called me an amateur. "I'm Acacia."

"Pretty name for a pretty girl," the black woman purred, and stroked my wing again to elicit another shudder. My stomach cramped, instinct warning me to fight, that I was vulnerable. "I'm Micola."

"Ronald," the green guy said, eyeing me with unveiled hunger.[6]

"Ken," the winged man muttered, but despite his gruffness, his eyes kept returning to me, trailing my body. If he wondered why a shy, curious girl like me was decked out in leather, he showed no sign of it.

"Nice to meet you," I said, forcing myself to lean back into Micola and relax like I wanted to be here. I glanced at them through heavy-lidded eyes. Sex eyes. Ugh.

"Bria," the pale woman introduced herself, baring rows of thin teeth. Fuck, those were sharp-looking teeth.

"Bevan," her brother murmured, looking at me less like he was thinking of fucking me than dissecting me.[7]

Micola petted my wing, close to where it connected with my back under my coat, and I shuddered hard.

"Shall we skip the *getting to know you*s and get straight to the part we all want?" she asked, her voice low and husky.

I swallowed, flicked a shy glance at the rest of the alphas, running quick calculations of how I'd take them all out. I had three small knives, concealed so they wouldn't be noticed, and I had my magic. I could take control of the alphas' blood and either slow it so they passed out, or quicken it so they exploded; I'd be fine. Why was I so nervous?

"Gods yes," I breathed, turning my head to give Micola a coy look. "Are you—sure you want me?"

"Oh, pretty thing," she purred, stroking her hand up my back. "The things I want to do to you will make your toes curl."

Promises, promises. Shame I was here to kill her; if I'd been single, I might have explored those promises. The rest of the bastards didn't interest me, but I didn't let that show as I hopped off Micola's lap and secretly ran through how I'd kill them in my head.

"Our rooms are upstairs," she told me, resting a proprietary hand on my back. I calmed myself by picturing how Malakai would react to her hands on me. First, he'd cut her hand off, then he'd unleash his snakes on her until she screamed and begged for mercy. He wouldn't give it, obviously, but that wouldn't stop her begging.

My heartbeat calmed, and I kept my shy, sensual persona in place as Micola led me away from my drink and towards a tight staircase at the back. *Farewell, beloved pint. May we meet again.*

Ken and Ronald—exceptional names—followed, while the twins gathered up the money from the table. I didn't miss that they pocketed it, despite not winning the game.

"Here, pretty thing," Micola said when we reached the top, pushing open a door on a surprisingly nice little room. Two single beds were pushed against opposite walls with a small window between them and matching bed-stands. The floor was clean, and the place smelled fresh, not sour with sweat. This was nicer than most places I'd stayed while hunting as a merc.

It was a shame to paint it with blood.

The second the door closed behind us, I slipped the knife from the slitted pocket in my leather trousers and spun, driving it into Ken's thick neck. Throwing more weight behind it, I dragged the blade until his throat split and the light left his eyes.

"What the fuck?" Micola exploded, a shock of betrayal on her face for a moment before she recovered.

I was already moving to counter Ronald, who threw himself at me with a roar, launching over his dead friend's body and raising massive green hands. Maybe to throw me back, maybe to break my face. The only problem with his plan was I'd placed myself in front of the little window, so when he came barrelling at me, I simply stepped aside and his momentum carried him through the glass.

It shattered on impact. He fell to the ground with a scream.

There you go, Tali. Don't say I never give you anything.

I didn't wait for the thud of collision below before I spun to deal with Micola and the twins.

Wait. Shit, where did they go?

"You deceitful bitch," Micola spat from the doorway. Well there *she* was, but where were Bria and Bevan?

"It's nothing personal, just a job," I said with a shrug, taking a step after her as she moved into the hall.

I slammed into a solid wall, rebounding back with a gasp. Pain slit my stomach, and I stared in surprise at the sudden stab wound on my stomach, blood soaking through my shirt.

"You deserve everything you get," Micola called from the corridor. "Kill her."

Shit. I wasn't alone in the room, even if it looked empty.

When another arc of pain slashed across my back, *just* missing my wing, I realised the psycho twins were still here. I just couldn't see them.

The door swung shut; the lock snapped into place with a clang. Trapping me in a room with two invisible threats with orders to kill me. And a dead body.

*W*hen locked in a room with two invisible people dead set on murdering you, my first tip is to run for the smashed window. *Ideally,* clear the path between you and the window, but if the assailants are invisible you might end up like me.

"Son of a five-titted bitch!" I swore, spinning blindly away and slamming my palm over another slash on my stomach. Blood soaked down my side, staining my clothes, but they were shallow cuts designed to inflict pain, not slow me down. The twins were definitely psychopaths.

"Come out, come out, psychos," I sang, turning, trying to sense a disturbance in the air at the same time I grasped my magic.

I expected to feel the heat and rush of blood in two bodies but instead I felt ... nothing. Not like when I was attacked by an invincible woman in my flat; I didn't hit a block, there was just nothing there.

The core where my magic normally sat was empty.

I was powerless.

Air puffed out of me in a shallow gasp, my chest tightening. How was I supposed to win a fight against two invisible attackers with no magic?

Don't, I reminded myself.

I spun to the window, slashing the space in front of myself as I moved, slamming my wings down to propel myself faster. Paranoia made my skin tingle as I waited for another blow.

A low laugh warned me of another blow. I dropped to the floor with a grunt, flattening myself to the bare floorboards. Air shifted above me, and I used it to place the twin who'd tried to stab me again. Rolling onto my back, wings pinned uncomfortably, I slammed my booted feet into a solid body. Ha! The air flickered, Bevan's body visible for a moment. I adjusted my angle and slammed my heavy soles into his dick, dropping him to the floor with a screech. Fun.

Bria could have been anywhere, hidden by her magic, watching me. The awareness made my breathing short as I shot to my feet and dove for the window.

My skin prickled, little hairs standing on end. I made it two feet, then four.

I slashed my knife in front of me, clearing my path. Five feet.

Bria didn't laugh like Bevan had. She hooked her arm around my neck with no warning, and I screamed in surprise and frustration as she pressed mercilessly on my windpipe.

"Dick," I choked out with my last remaining air.[1]

She had my throat pinned, but there was nothing to stop me driving my knife down into her thigh, so I did, over and over. The muffled scream she let out was satisfying, even if it was right by my ear and drowned my hearing in sharp ringing.

Her grip weakened. *Promising.* I slashed up in an awkward motion that strained my muscles, but I managed to carve my dagger through her forearm. I earned a splash of blood on my chin and a howl of rage in my ear.

I gritted my teeth and tore her forearm from my neck while she was distracted. The floorboards creaked as I twisted unsteadily on my feet, jamming my dagger into where I guessed her chest was. The blade met bone first, but I angled it upward and thrust it under her ribs and right into her heart.

Thank fuck for that. My head spun a little, and I was bleeding from two shallow wounds. The last thing I needed was a long, gruesome fight.

Bria sagged, suddenly visible, and crashed to the bare floorboards with a glassy look in her eye.

I wrinkled my nose and wiped the blood off my face, staring at her body.

Killing stopped leaving a stain on my soul years ago; it was a necessary thing when you were a young woman with no family or home, and survival was essential. The first kill haunted me, my second brought me nightmares, but by my twelfth I got used to the shaky rush of adrenaline and horror.

This was my job; it would allow me to find my mates. I did what I needed to do, and if I enjoyed the fight and the thrill, that was just a nice bonus.

I meant what I told Bernard; on a morally grey scale I was far closer to black. I didn't have a tragic backstory, didn't have murdered parents or a brutalised sibling to drive me to darkness. When my dad died when I was seventeen, I found my way to the streets and met darkness the usual way: in people. Spend enough time in the shadows and the shadows start to take form inside you.

A whole swarm of them lived in my soul now; sometimes I swore I felt them brushing against me in a cold, pained wave.[2] I sidestepped the pool of blood forming under Bria's body and swung my leg over the windowsill, casting a glance down at the alleyway.

Oh, lovely, there was a huge pile of trash at the end of the little path, perfuming the air with rotting food and shit. We were lucky Lucifer had introduced toilets; otherwise the streets would be full of *actual* shit like they used to be. Another reason the alphas hated him. He brought change and progress and *cleanliness*. The horror!

Hovering on the ledge of the window, and careful to avoid the jagged edges of broken glass, I peered down and saw the splayed form of Ronald, his green skin sickly and a pool of blood under him. Aww, his blood pool matched Bria's. Something told me Bevan would be so pissed off about that.

Wait, where *was* Bevan? I only kneed him in the dick; he shouldn't be dea—

Rough hands slammed into my back, propelling me off the window frame and into a fall so sudden I screamed.

Well, that answered the Bevan question.

Tali roared in panic from the alley below. I didn't dare look down to see if she was okay or under attack herself. I wasn't scared of heights[3] but falling was still terrifying.

Screaming at the top of my lungs, I snapped my wings out as much as I could in the cramped alleyway. I barely had enough space to flutter them enough to slow my fall, but in positive news I landed on the cobbles on my feet and not my face.

Halwen! Tali rumbled, bounding down the alley towards me. If she'd been anyone else, the sight would have been petrifying. A massive, six-foot-tall red panda with horns and smoking skin raced towards me with her jaw parted and sharp teeth showing. But I read the distress in her fast pants, and her green eyes overflowed with worry.

"I'm fine," I said breathlessly. "Someone thought it was a good idea to *throw a winged woman out of a window!*"

I yelled the last bit at the window and hoped Bevan heard.

Tali butted her head against me, dragging her raspy tongue over the slashes on my stomach.

Movement drew my eye to a shadow leaning out the window, checking if I was dead.

"Next time, pick someone who can't fly, you stupid fucker!" I yelled at Bevan, which was probably not smart but it was incredibly cathartic.

"I'm fine," I insisted again when Tali made a low, trilling rumble. I patted her big head and cracked a grin. "At least I still have my pretty face."

She huffed. *When did you get so confident? And sarcastic?*

"What can I say? I've made some improvements over the years. Did any alphas come out this way?"

She shook her head.

"Great. That means there are still four left. We need to take out three and capture one. Bernard said you'd know how to call him to come and collect them."

Tali bobbed her head, about to convey something with her big eyes when her attention shot behind me. She growled so low my ribcage shook.

I spun, lifting my hand and mildly surprised to see I still held my dagger. Nice. I hated losing my toys. I reached for my magic on instinct, my stomach sinking when it slipped away like a ghost instead of responding to me.

Fuck, what happened to my power? Had death done this? Or were one of the curses inked on my body to blame?

Micola stormed down the alleyway, her brown face twisted with rage. Fair enough, I'd seduced her and then killed her friends; I'd be pretty pissed off, too. She was flanked by two alphas I hadn't met, one in russet hellhound form with glowing yellow eyes, snarling jaws, and a body almost as big as Tali's. The other was horrifying, a type of demon I'd never seen before. They were seven-feet-tall, thinner than was natural, and completely naked, with pale, translucent skin on display for all to see. Oh, and they didn't have a face.[4]

I shot Tali a quick look. *Remember we need one alive.*

She dipped her head and charged at the three alphas. Nerves twisted me up at the sight of my only living friend charging at three powerful, murderous alphas. But I reminded myself she was giant, had sharp teeth, and her claws could probably gut them in a single swipe.

I futilely grabbed for my magic, but at least I drew another, longer knife at the same time. I was still totally powerless, and getting more frustrated about it with every second. I'd become too reliant on my magic over the past few years[5] when dealing with Locke's hunter and mercenaries. If I had my magic, I could have exploded all of these alphas right here and now.

Minus one for Bernard, obviously.

Instead of handling it quickly, I was forced to race after Tali and jump into the fray. When she dove for the slender, pale alpha with her maw open, I went for the hellhound.

It's not a real dog, I reminded myself as I arced my knife at its body. *It's a man in disguise.*

I was glad when the hound snarled and dove aside, evading the sharp edge of my blade. Less glad when he swiped out with his claws and raked a burning, fiery path across my thigh.

"Alright, puppy, *that's it!*" I snapped, kicking out with my heavy boots and landing a footprint on his ribs, knocking the hound back a few paces. Up close, he smelled of brimstone and weeds. His yellow eyes narrowed as he assessed me for weaknesses.[6]

Tali growled in sudden pain, but when the hellhound launched himself at me, I couldn't spare even a second to check on my friend. Shit. I had no choice but to drop my weapons when the hound collided with me hard and sent me to the ground.[7]

Cold bled through the cobblestones and into my body as the hound snapped his sharp jaws at my face, slobber dripping from his sharp teeth. A drop landed on my cheek. I wrinkled my nose at the feeling of cold fluid dripping down my face.

"Gross," I gasped as I fought to keep those jaws as far from my face as possible. I got the sense the hound wanted to rip my head off with his massive fangs.

Why couldn't I have got a nice, normal job and saved up for weapons the safe way?

Because you're not nice, normal, or safe, my inner voice responded. She had a point.

Heat from the hellhound's panting breaths fanned across my face, and I gritted my teeth, straining to keep his snarling head away from my throat. A knee rammed into his ribs did nothing to dislodge him. My arms ached, struggling to hold back his full weight. Ah, fuck. I'd have to do something stupid and desperate, like letting go so I could snatch up a knife. But the chances of me burying steel in his skull before he ripped my head off was pathetically slim.

My arms buckled. A breath expelled from my lungs in a panicked rush. *Now or never.*

I loosened my grip, but the hellhound was torn away from me before I could risk my neck to find my knives.

Tali, I thought, my heart soaring. Instead, my stomach plummeted when I watched *Bevan* tear the hellhound off me. He grabbed one side of the hound's jaws in each hand and wrenched them apart until there was a sickening crack and the light left his yellow eyes.

"You just ... killed your own friend," I breathed, cold drenching my whole body as I scrambled to my feet, frantically scanning the ground for my knives.

They were behind him. Of course they were.

"You killed my sister," Bevan replied in a glacial, utterly dead voice.

"Fair point. No need to take it out on your frien—"

I cut off with a shriek when Bevan came at me with his pale hands outstretched, claws as long as my fingers extended to slice me to ribbons. Well, I knew what cut me earlier. Not knives after all.

He didn't turn invisible. No, he wanted me to see him as he killed me. I knew that rage, and guilt twinged in my chest. I'd have tried to kill me in his position, too. But I had a job to do, and I didn't know how else to find Em, Kai, and Harvey.

"I'm going to bleed you dry, and make you scream during every second of it," he said in a cold, flat voice that sent shivers down my spine.

We circled each other, me keeping a distant eye on the silver sheen of my knives on the ground, Bevan's pale eyes fixed on me like he could kill me with a single stare.

"While we're chatting," I said airily, like I wasn't scared shit-less, "I'd like to know where you came from. Where are the remaining alphas? I know you're still planning Lucifer's death."

"You don't know anything," Bevan replied emptily and threw himself at me.

I had a split-second choice between fleeing down the empty end of the alley and isolating myself, or racing towards the strange, faceless man and Micola—and Tali. I had to hope my friend would be enough backup, and Micola didn't get her hands on me. I knew she'd be far worse than Bevan.

"Tali, I've got a slight issue," I called, and bolted in her direction. My heart slammed into my ribs in a fast rhythm as Bevan's wicked fingernails sliced my back. He missed causing serious damage, though. I pumped my legs, quickly assessing the situation.

The faceless man was dead on the ground, missing an arm and half his shoulder. Had Tali ... *eaten* him?[8]

Micola swiped at Tali with a rusty pole she got from gods knew where. My heart plummeted when my friend was only able to avoid the pole enough to lessen the damage, not escape the blow.

"Hey!" I shouted, because one murderous maniac wasn't enough, apparently I needed two. "Leave my friend alone, you bitch."

Micola turned to face me slowly enough that my blood ran cold, and all the hairs rose on the back of my neck when her attention snagged on something behind me. It gave me a split second warning, enough to throw myself to the right, thumping into the wall in time to watch Bevan thrust his clawed hands through the air.

He'd have ripped out my spine. *Fuck, fuck, fuck.*

Tali snarled in my direction. *Be careful, you stupid cow.*

"Be careful yourself," I snapped back, shoving off the wall and inhaling sharply when Bevan threw himself at me too fast for me to evade him.

With the wall at my back, Tali grappling with Micola on my left, and Bevan throwing himself at my right, there was nowhere to go. No escape.

I tried to duck, but Bevan's claws slammed into the brick on either side of my shoulders, pinning me. A slow grin twisted his sharp face. His prey was caught. He knew I was dead.

I tried the old faithful and kneed him in the balls, but he was ready for me now and evaded my knee. *Fuck a duck, I'm dead.*

"You'll die slowly for what you did to my sister," he swore, mania in his sharp eyes.

"That makes no sense," I replied, because I was scared and

physically *could not* shut up. "I killed her quickly. It should be tit for tat."

His eyes drifted to my chest. He heaved his right hand from the wall, claws loosening mortar. *Not that tit, not that tit!*

Panic stole my breath. I threw up my hands, sacrificing my hands to protect my chest, my heart drumming my ribs.

Pain didn't slash across my palms, and a surprised breath froze in my lungs when Bevan tore his other hand from the wall and stumbled away from me. When I lowered my hands enough to see him, he was even paler than before, his black eyes wide and mouth parted as he stared at me. No, at my arms, where the ink on my forearm *glowed.*

The tattoo was black, but the power that glowed from it was eldritch and red. *What the fuck?*

"Cursed One," he gasped, stumbling back, horror shortening his breaths.

I was lost, reeling, baffled when in the next moment he pissed himself, a dark stain bleeding through his trousers. He couldn't take his eyes off me.

Cursed One. Great, now I had a title? I wanted to be a princess or a lady, not a *cursed one.* Life was so unfair.

At least Bevan wasn't attacking me now. I took advantage of it and demanded, "Where are the other alphas?"

I expected resistance and cold, icy rage. Instead he blurted, "A border town that was abandoned in the war. It's near the Bend of Boraven in the river."

"Why there?" I pressed, wondering if he'd snap out of this fear if I went for one of my knives. I didn't risk it. I'd come here for information and to kill alphas, and I wasn't going to pass up this chance.

"There's a collector, Lord Wynvail. He lures us there and traps us with magic and binding vows."

Well, shit. All the people I just killed might have been acting against their will. Murder didn't leave a sour taste in my mouth, but this did. Regret burned in my belly and tasted like guilt.

"Collector," I echoed, watching the pale alpha for any signs of deceit. He looked terrified; he shook so hard his claws rattled, his eyes glued to my curse mark. "What is he collecting them for?"

Bevan's throat bobbed. "I'm not supposed to say." But he must have been more scared of me than this Lord Wynvail because he whispered, "I don't know for sure, but I've heard whispers he's collecting us for someone else. Someone more powerful, who gave him the magic to bind us."

Fuck. That was just what I needed—a Lord and someone even *more* powerful. Queen Lili's gang of boyfriends would want to know all about this.

"Is he collecting them to kill Lucifer?" I pressed, casting a quick look Tali's way when there was a sudden movement. She swiped a big, furry paw through the air and knocked the pole from Micola's hand, snapping her jaws around the woman's hand in the next moment and crunching down. Gross. She was definitely eating them.

"No," Bevan gasped, breathless and shaking, his eyes never leaving me even as Tali tucked into her four course meal.[9] "I'm loyal to Lucifer. I swear!"

"And your Lord? Is he loyal?"

"I don't know," Bevan breathed. "Please spare me, Cursed One."

I glanced around the alley. Everyone else was dead.

"It's your lucky day, Bevan, I'm feeling merciful. You can live."

When Bevan collapsed to his knees and uttered endless thanks, I decided to leave out the part about Bernard torturing him.

J was exhausted when we got back to the palace, and my thighs ached like crazy from my bumpy ride home.[1] Cuts still stung across my body, gradually healing, and all I wanted was a hot bath to ease the aches. The last thing I wanted was Renna storming down the pale gold hallway, barking out my name.

"Not now," I groaned, my shoulders slumped and feet dragging on the floor.

"You'll want to come with me," she replied in a steely tone, her lilac face giving nothing away.

Did I have another job? Had she decided I was too annoying and she was going to murder me? Was she leading me to a thank you banquet as a reward for catching the alphas? Or rather, catching *one* while the others fought us and 'ran off.'[2]

"Fine," I groaned, salivating at the thought of a banquet. If it *wasn't* a banquet, I might kill this woman.

Renna seized my arm before I could second guess my decision, and hauled me bodily down the hall. Her legs were longer than mine; she practically dragged me across the castle while my boots skidded. Anyone who saw us must've had a right laugh.

"Damn woman, what were you in your past life? A debt collector?"

Renna snorted, not slowing her pace. "If I let go, you might face-plant the floor. You look awful."

"Please tell me you're leading me to a bed," I groaned, using all my focus to keep my feet under me, the palace passing in a blur.

Renna gave me an arch glance, her black eyebrows raised. "You're not my type. And I'm married."

I gave her the middle finger. I'd already fake-flirted with a woman today; I didn't have the energy left to do it again.

But I still had enough self respect to protest, "I'm everyone's type."

Her snort was dismissive. "Sure, sweetheart."

If I had any strength in my arms, I'd have elbowed her in the ribs. Instead they flop-shimmied at my sides, and I gave up after two attempts.

"Here," she said, pushing open a heavy gold door that flickered with black magic in response to her touch. Nice shields. Very nice.

Inside were three more doors, each sealed.

I groaned. "This is overkill."

"You won't think that when you see what's inside," she replied knowingly, digging out a key to unlock the fourth door and swinging it open on—

Heaven. Pure, steel heaven.

I let out a tiny whimper. "It's beautiful."

Renna shot me a look that questioned my judgement, and drawled, "It's an armoury."

"I want it," I said dreamily.

"Well, you can't have it," she shot down instantly, flicking sharp black hair out of her face as she led me to a specific area of the armoury.

Swords of all shapes and sizes hung from the walls, yet more rested in velvet-inlaid boxes on tables. I wanted everything. With this, I'd be strong enough to obliterate Cassander Locke. These weren't piddly little knives like I'd taken on the last job with me; these were *real* weapons. Even without magic, I could hold my own with these, and I wouldn't have to rely on my cursed marks scaring the shit out of my assailant next time.

They'd stopped glowing now, and looked like ordinary tattoos, but it was ingrained in my memory. Tali had been just as baffled to see them glow. Neither of us had a clue what had happened.

"Here," Renna grunted and held a closed wooden box out to me. My heart raced. It was big enough to contain a short sword. "I wanted to make sure I could find it before I said anything, in case the box had been lost during the destruction and rebuild."

The builders had done such a good job, I kept forgetting the whole city had been levelled a year ago.

"If you were trying to bag yourself another wife," I breathed, accepting the mahogany box, "this is definitely the way to do it."

Renna laughed coarsely, shaking her dark head. "Just open it."

I used my weak arms to lift the lid on the box, not prepared, nowhere remotely *near* prepared, for the contents. When I saw the two long, wavy daggers inside, the inscription still carved on the fuller of the blade, I burst into horrible, gut-wrenching tears.

My volcanic blades. My anniversary gift from Kai. I hadn't lost them.

"I love you," I choked out to Renna, cradling the wooden

box to my chest as tears veiled my vision. "We're friends forever now."

"Calm down." She looked disturbed at the thought.

But she'd given me a priceless treasure, and I would never forget it or stop being grateful.

I sniffled, and said, "You're stuck with me. Just accept it."

"Gods save me," she groaned.

25

I tossed and turned in bed, my daggers clutched to my chest. I'd never let them out of my sight again. I don't know how long it took me to fall asleep, but the day's events played through my head over and over, keeping me restless. I kept returning to the name Bevan had called me— Cursed One. It was a strange name even if he'd seen the curse mark on my arm. Cursed One suggested a title, a reputation.

How the fuck did I have a reputation when I'd been dead for a hundred years?

I'd either been mistaken for someone else, *or* someone knew I'd been reborn and told assholes like Bevan about it.

I needed to go to that Bend of Boraven and find out who else knew about this title. Someone might know what curses I actually had, and might know how to break them.

There was another possibility, but I wasn't brave enough to admit that was why I wanted to go to the alphas' town. Someone remembered me, and named the Forest of Halwen after me. What if that same someone created this Cursed One reputation so people would be too afraid of me to hurt me?

"You're thinking too hard, my rose," a soft voice murmured, a warm breath fanning across my cheek.

My heart jolted, tripping into my ribs, and I whipped my head back to stare—at Malakai, his tall body stretched out on the bed beside me, *here*.

My eyes burned, but I didn't take my eyes off him for a moment. He looked so damn good, with his dark red hair mussed by the pillow and his sharp, elegant face softened by sleep. Even the texts that wound around his body scrolled sluggishly, lulled to sleep too. He wore no shirt, every bit of flesh and ink on his toned body exposed, and my heart skipped.

My Malakai, my night, *here*.

"I'm dreaming," I breathed, and was surprised to find my voice scratchy with sleep.

Warm fingers brushed my cheek and traced the shape of my face. "Who cares if we're asleep or awake? I'm back where I belong."

Before I could reply, he rolled closer and stole my breath in a kiss. It wasn't a forceful or demanding kiss, but the passion in it made me weak. It had been so damned long since we'd been together. It didn't feel like a hundred years, but my body had experienced every minute of distance between us, and it reacted with a fierce need that made me gasp against his lips.

A hundred years—that's how long it had been since we last kissed, in the middle of the road in a town on the edge of Iarlon.

When his hot mouth dragged down my jaw to my throat, his forked tongue flicking over my skin, I groaned.

"Renna kept my knives. She gave them back to me. I didn't lose them, Kai."

"Knives," he huffed against my skin, raising goosebumps.

"Knives don't matter. *You* matter. Us being here, together, matters."

"They matter to me," I replied defensively, trailing my fingers through his long hair to grab a fistful of the wine-red strands. "You spent a lot of time, thought, and money getting them made for me."

"I told you I would get you more," he murmured, scraping his teeth down my throat and making my body flash hot.

"And did you?" I'd been gone a hundred years, but how long had Kai been?

"I ... don't know," he replied, pausing between kisses. "I only remember my dreams."

"Dreams?" I pushed on his shoulders, getting him to lean back so I could see his face, beautiful and deadly and sharp. "What dreams?"

"Like this one," he said, peering up at me with ruby eyes full of softness. "But you're not normally so ... here."

I blinked, processing that. "How long have you been dreaming of me, Kai?"

He shrugged, climbing up my body to kiss my cheek. "As long as I can remember."

"A year?"

He shook his head with a wry laugh. "Far, far longer."

My stomach dropped, a lump closing off my throat. Fuck. I reached for him, wrapping him up in my arms. "I think you were brought back before me. *Long* before me."

"Brought back?"

"We died, Kai. Cassander Locke killed us all. I dug myself out of a shallow grave four days ago, but I don't know where you guys are."

"Here," he said, pulling back a few inches to meet my gaze, something sad and longing in his expression. "We're right here, always waiting for you."

Fuck. My throat swelled with a bigger knot, my bottom lip suddenly weak.

We're right here, always waiting for you.

Fuck. *Fuck.*

"Sometimes we're together, sometimes I'm alone. Sometimes you're here, but never like this. I can feel the texture of your skin now; I can taste you when we kiss."

As if to reassure himself of that fact, he surged down over me and claimed my mouth in a rough, demanding kiss, forcing a gasp so he could taste me. A groan filled his throat as his forked tongue stroked mine, vibrating through his chest into my body, and he pressed his fingers into the softness of my thigh, curving my leg around his waist.

"I can call them sometimes," he said against my lips, pressing his body down into mine and devouring the expression on my face with hungry eyes. "I should call them now, but I want to be selfish and keep you to myself. When I wake up ... all of this is gone, I think. It only exists here, in my dreams."

I licked my bottom lip, my lower belly tightening with hunger at the look on his pale face. "Call them after."

"Yess," he hissed, almost snakelike as he returned to my lips with a fierceness that made my stomach jump. The air tingled with his power, as if he was right on the edge of control, and I arched up into him in response, giving up my own control.

"I missed you so fucking much," I groaned into his mouth, a soft moan escaping when he sucked my bottom lip, grazing with his teeth, a constant edge of danger and pain. "I love you."

Kai shuddered, a catch in his breath, and he kissed me so hard my head spun and I forgot how to breathe. Need pounded hot and fast through my pussy, and I rolled my hips up into his, the hardness there only encouraging my feverish desire.

Nights and mornings like this flashed through my head, sometimes in bed, sometimes on the sofa or the kitchen table or against a wall down a quiet alley, too needy and desperate to wait until we got home. Sometimes we were alone, sometimes my other mates watched, sometimes they were all involved. Every time, Kai was almost feral with need, his control over my body and pleasure was both obsessive and ruthless, and I came so hard I saw stars.

"Who do you belong to?" he asked, panting as his fingers climbed my thigh, slipping under the soft shirt I slept in and brushing the sensitive seam between hip and leg.

I pulsed with hot need, my hips unable to stay still, bucking with a pointed suggestion to Kai's warm, teasing fingers. "You."

"Fuck yes, you do," he groaned, his red eyes almost black with desire as he drew back and slid down my body. He pushed my shirt up so he could kiss my belly, then my ribs, and then fasten his hot mouth around a nipple, teasing with his tongue.

I threw my hand over my mouth and bit my palm, my body so neglected it was oversensitive. Or maybe it was just the dream heightening everything. This was both real and not. He was here, but somewhere else too. He could have been anywhere, could have been on Earth or Heaven, wasting away in the too-pure atmosphere.

He caught my nipple between his teeth and pulled until an electric sensation shot straight to my clit, making it throb wildly. I breathed shakily when he released my nipple and gave the same treatment to my other breast before asking, "And who do I belong to?"

"Me," I hissed, twisting my fingers in his hair as he kissed, licked, and bit his way down my body. My nipples throbbed, wanting him back. "You're fucking mine."

"Always, my rose," Kai groaned against my stomach, his breathing a wrecked mix of panting and gasps. Cold rushed into the places his kisses left empty, but he always found a new bit of skin to lavish with attention. My whole body tingled and buzzed. "I'm yours for life, death, and whatever else there is."

"My night," I promised, biting back a groan when he widened my thighs and sank lower over me.

"Fuck, you smell like I remember. I can taste your pussy on the air, too. This is real."

"It's real." I softened my grip on his hair, stroking strands back from his face, brushing gentle touches over the ridges of his sensitive horns.

I gasped when his hands slid under me and wrenched me possessively closer, adjusting the angle of my hips so he could stare at me. A growl built in his throat.

"Beautiful. Just as beautiful as I remember."[1]

I shuddered at the soft, careful touches he drifted around my pussy, his eyes rapt on me as I throbbed, dripping wetness.

"Mine," he snarled, and darted forward to lick up the drop, his forked tongue stroking from my ass all the way to my clit, both ends wrapping around it. "This pussy is mine."

His magic crackled through the air, invisible but so damn powerful, and I jumped at the tentative brush of something velvety and soft over my calf. For a delirious moment I thought it was his power touching me, but when it stroked higher, I laughed in surprise.

"Holy shit, I forgot you had a tail."

He grunted against my pussy, his tongue making rigid circles around my clit, teasing, heightening my need so I dripped for him and his greedy mouth. He sucked up every drop with a satisfied rumble.

"It's going to get you nice and ready for me," he said in a guttural voice, his tail gripping my leg when I rubbed my thumb over the grooves in his right horn—the more sensitive one.

"I'm ready *now.*"

Kai's ruby stare flicked up to me with enough warning to fill my belly with butterflies. "I decide when you're ready."

"Yes, my night," I groaned, and watched satisfaction flare in his eyes.

"Beautiful," he murmured again, but stared at my face, not my pussy, this time. The compliment hit deep and bloomed with warmth, comforting a broken place inside me.

His tail grazed my upper thigh, and I tightened in anticipation, my blood boiling with a need that was so familiar to me but strangely new too. My mind knew it was only days since I'd been with Kai, but my body insisted differently.

When Kai swirled his tongue around my clit and his tail brushed a soft stroke over my throbbing entrance, I twisted my head and sank my teeth into my shoulder, needing something to ground me.

"Does that feel good, my rose?" Kai asked with a casual flick to my clit.

I could only whine in response as his tail thrust into me, not as thick as his cock but certainly big enough to stretch me. I wrapped my fingers around his horn and gripped until the grooves bit into my palm. Kai snarled, teeth bared.

When his tail glided deeper, overwhelming my senses with the sudden fullness, my other hand fluttered, desperately searching, needing a tether while my body was overwrought with sensation. Kai's fingers entwined with mine, squeezing tight, the gesture sweet. But he smirked and drove his tail deeper, wrenching a tight, whining sound from me when it curled back on itself inside me, the head now twice as fat.

"Too much?" he asked, and kissed my clit.

"Yes," I cried.

"Good," he snarled, and drew his tail out a few inches, fucking me with it until my whole body shuddered. I was so overwhelmed with pleasure and fullness, I didn't know *what* I felt. "I want to consume every one of your senses. I want to own every single part of you. When I'm finished, there'll be no part of you that won't be aching for me, throbbing, begging for more."

I gripped his hand so tightly it must have hurt, wet sounds filling the room—our old room? I couldn't tell—as his tail drove its bulbous end into me, gathering speed until my body twitched with every thrust.

"I missed you so much," Kai said tightly, moving his tail faster until I struggled to speak, to find meaning for the words he uttered. "I missed your voice and your laugh and the feel of your hand in mine. I missed the way your cunt grips my tail so perfectly, and the way you throb around me, desperate for more but too afraid to admit it."

I shook my head fast. No more. Too much.

"Oh, I should *stop?*" he asked, and uncurled his tail inside me, gliding out quickly.

The unbearable sensation slipped away, but I cried out. No, I—I needed it back. It was too big and too much, but I *needed* it.

"Malakai," I pleaded, my eyelids heavy over my eyes as I gave him a desperate look.

"Hmm?" He smirked and ducked his head, tracing a maddening circle around my clit with his tongue, making my throb harder, so swollen it ached.

"Please. Give me your tail again."

"I thought it was too much," he replied, flicking an arched, amused glance at me as he pressed a feather-soft kiss to my clit. A loud cry tore from my lips, the touch making my need worse and offering no relief.

"Kai," I snarled, the sound a pure command this time.

"Yes, my rose?" he asked casually, his tail grazing my inner thigh, taunting me with my own arousal slicking the velvety skin.

Need pounded through me like a drum. I wanted his tail to overwhelm me with sensation again. My pussy was achy and so damn wet I felt it drip out of me.

"You're lucky I love you," I told him, the decree half a threat. "Give me your tail or give me your cock. Please, I'm empty." I gave him a sulky look, sure I was pouting. "A *good* mate would fuck me sensel—"

I didn't finish the question. His tail drove inside me, stroking every taut, sensitive spot until I was sighing in relief.

"You're going to come for me," Kai said in a hard voice. scraping his teeth over my thigh. "And you're going to scream my name. *Then,* I'll give you my cock."

I nodded fast, heat rushing to my face as his tail broadened at the tip and stretched me until the ache was pleasant, fulfilling instead of frantic. When he withdrew and slammed back inside me, setting a punishing pace, my eyes rolled back and my legs shook.

He fastened his mouth to my clit in slow, sucking pulses, and pleasure blasted through me like an explosion, my mouth hanging open on a cry. I forgot to scream his name, forgot what his name even was as he pounded pleasure through me, hitting the spot he knew would undo me.

Stars burst around me, my eyes rolled all the way back, and I trembled as wave after wave of pleasure hit me, unmade me, and left my soul in tatters.

I barely felt when his tail uncurled and withdrew, but my body hummed with every soft, loving kiss Malakai placed on my thighs, my stomach, my breasts, and finally my lips.

"You are my life," he breathed against my lips, his voice reverent.

I blinked my eyes into focus, a smile curving my mouth at the awed look on his handsome face. I lifted my fingers to trace the sharp lines of his cheekbones, the curved edges of his eyes, all the way up to his horns. His hips jerked where they rested between mine, somehow naked when I knew he'd been wearing loose sleep pants before.

"You'll always be my night and light," I breathed, reciting the words he said to me every year on our anniversary, the words etched down the centre of my swords.

His whole face softened, red eyes wide, blinking fast. "You'll always be my rose and life," he finished, his voice thick.

I tugged him to me, kissing him slowly, letting the emotion bursting from my chest soar through the kiss, hoping he could feel it in my soul even in the dream. We were still unnervingly distant in the bond, souls still in tatters. Maybe it'd be that way until we found our way to each other outside these dreams, too.

"Haley," he sighed against my lips, a soft expulsion of air that spoke of relief and weakness.

"I'm here. Really here."

"Never leave me again," he hissed, and reached between us, grasping his cock and slamming into me so suddenly, my back arched. "I want to stay like this forever. You're not allowed to leave."

A soft puff of laughter left me, and I kissed him. "You can't live with your cock inside me."

He bared his teeth. "I can."

He punctuated the statement with a rough thrust, making me gasp. I was already so sensitive thanks to his tail, but feeling his cock inside me was fulfilling on both physical and soul levels. I threw my arms around him, digging my nails into his back. My skin buzzed as the scrolling ink moved on his skin, power thrumming just under the surface.

I knew he wanted to set a slow pace and make love to me, but we were both too desperate for that, and emotions ran high. He crushed his mouth to mine in a brutal kiss and fucked me so fast we both gasped, moans filling my mouth and his, tongues gliding and forceful.

"My rose. Mine."

"My night," I groaned, wrapping my legs around him and rolling my hips up to meet each demanding thrust. Pleasure built fast and suddenly, and judging by the tension in Kai's back and the low, menacing snarl he let out, he wasn't far behind.

His power finally erupted, brushing me everywhere, curling around my wrists, squeezing my thighs, brushing my nipples. Making good of his promise to make me feel him everywhere.

"Kai," I gasped into his mouth, slamming my eyes shut as my release built, my body already clenching, trembling. "Oh, shit."

"Mine," he replied in a growl, echoing the word with every slam of his hips to my inner thighs. "Mine. Mine. *Mine.*"

Fuck. I sank my fingers into his hair and gripped tight, arching up into him, my breathing fast and sharp. My pussy gripped him tightly, clasping his cock so possessively that every thrust touched my most sensitive spots and made my toes curl.

"Kai," I choked out, legs locked around him, a guttural whine tearing up my throat and making his eyes flash.

"Yes," he hissed, his hands finding my hips and pressing marks into my skin as he watched me fall apart, never once letting up his feral pace. "Look at me, see exactly who owns this body." He brushed his lips across mine, soft and sweet, a

complete contrast to his thrusts. "Give me your climax, my rose. Let me taste it, feel it. I want to be consumed by you."

I moaned, burying my face in his shoulder, and stiffened when my release tore through me with the force of a burning sun. I choked out his name, my breath throttled in my throat and eyes blown wide as pleasure charged through me like fire and lightning.

"Take me," Kai gasped, his hands trembling on my hips. "Take all of me, my rose. Every part of me is yours."

My pussy gripped him in a brutal fist, demanding he find release too, and Kai grunted and came hard, jolting madly inside me. Heat spilled through me, filling me with every drop of him, and I gasped at the deep throbs of his cock against sensitive inner flesh, wringing more pleasure from me.

"Haley," he groaned, shudders moving through him as he clung to me. "Haley."

I held him as I came down from the high, deep pleasure making me limp and satisfied. When I ran my fingers through his long red hair, he shuddered and relaxed atop me, nestling his face against my neck.

"Don't leave," he whispered.

"I won't. I'll stay as long as I can."

If I could have never woken up, I'd have stayed there forever, holding him, ignoring the fractures in our bond to pretend we were whole again.

"My whole life," he murmured, his breathing deepening.

I waited until he was asleep to let my heavy eyelids close, knowing if I slept here, I'd wake up in the palace.

I resisted as much as I could, luxuriating in the feel of his skin under my fingertips, the weight of him pressing me into the bed. But finally exhaustion tugged my eyes shut, and I woke up, heartbroken and alone.

26

For two days, nothing of consequence happened and it was fucking weird. No one had attacked me, Callahan hadn't got a new job for me, and even Renna didn't turn up to bark orders at me. I didn't like it.

I'd spent a few hours with Tali yesterday, catching up after years spent apart, getting to know each other as adults.[1] But when Tali had to leave the city, I was left with nothing to do. Restless. Bored.

The devil and his inner circle were busy organising a new batch of souls who'd come from a mass shooting on Earth. I shut down my thoughts at the mention of guns, my own death and my mates' murders rearing like a cruel vision around me until I could almost taste the gunpowder.

Alone, I had no distraction from missing my mates. Nothing to keep me busy so I didn't stress about not dreaming last night. What stopped me connecting with my mates in my sleep? Where were Em and Harvey? Did Kai hate me for waking up and leaving him alone in his dream?

I also couldn't shake the feeling of darkness wrapped

around me. The sensation was so vivid, cold but nowhere near threatening—soothing.

I shuddered, pain lancing through my chest. My hand shot up and I clutched the painful spot, a frown tugging my brows together. I obsessed over the strange sensation for hours, but I couldn't sit still and let my own thoughts torture me.

So I hauled myself out of my room and went in search of the library Queen Lili mentioned. The pain in my chest followed.

The library was bigger than I'd been expecting, although maybe I was naïve for not realising *Lucifer's palace* would have a magnificent, three-level library filled with pale bookshelves, gilded edges, warm lighting, and *thousands* of books bound in soft brown leather. I paused in the doorway, my mouth hanging open.

I might have been in Hell, but this was something straight out of Heaven.

I'd only been to Heaven once, to the beautiful garden-like city of Wisteria where my mother was born. The bastards who lived there had taken one look at my black wings—the mark of a demon or Fallen angel—and bullied me out of the place. Funny, demons who knew I was an angel-demon hybrid had never made me feel any less for having an angelic side.

"Either come in and shut the door, or piss off and close it behind you," a low, female voice barked, snapping my attention to a grand, golden desk to my right where a woman with shining onyx skin and soft brown ringlets sat, glaring daggers at me.

I met her scowling stare, held eye contact, and slowly closed the door. "Happy?"

"Thrilled."

I smirked, strolling over to the gilt desk, lilac light filtering through a huge window on the far wall to give the whole room a dreamy cast. The fifty-something, narrow-lipped woman scowling at me was far from dreamy though, even if she did wear a soft beige gown and was beautiful enough to be the heroine of a legend.

"Since you're so sweet and willing to help," I said, giving her a troublemaker's grin, "can you direct me to a book on curses?"

The librarian looked down her nose at me—impressive, given she sat below me. "So you can curse me and Lucifer's whole empire? I think not."

I glanced at the wooden block on her desk that pronounced her AGATHA AVONLEA, CHIEF LIBRARIAN. "Why would I curse the empire when I live here, Agatha?"

"Aggie," she corrected through gritted teeth.

"I want a book on curses so I can figure out what the hell *this* means," I replied in the same tight tone, shoving up the sleeve of the violently pink dress I'd found in the wardrobe in my room.[2] "Any ideas, Aggie?"

Aggie rolled her thin lips into a flat line, the dark skin on her cheeks pulling taut. "That's a nasty looking curse."

"I had no idea," I drawled, shoving my sleeve back into place. "Your insight is truly mind-boggling."

"Try in that corner," she replied, picking up a book she'd left page-down on her desk, and not sparing me another glance as she waved towards the left of the big window.

"Thank you *so much* for your help. You've been delightful, Aggie."

She shot me a flat look over the top of her book. "It's nine a.m. on a Monday. Sorry I'm not bubbly and chipper."

"Try being dead for a hundred years, and see how chipper you are then," I huffed, and strode away from the woman. Showing impressive restraint by disappearing into the stacks instead of biting her head off.[3]

It took me a good half hour to find the section darling Aggie directed me to, but the sun was warm on my back and at least I wasn't thinking about the pain in my chest or lack of mates in my dreams. I was in no hurry, so I sat cross-legged on the polished floorboards and leisurely browsed the bottom shelf, picking out books with *curse* in the title and perusing their pages.

I wasn't surprised that none of the designs matched my marks, and that nothing referenced being killed and brought back to life. Of course it couldn't have been that easy.[4]

But at least I'd spent the morning distracted. A few hours later, I climbed to my feet and stretched out my arms, muscles dully aching from being in one position. I turned to pick up the last book and return it to the shelf—and shrieked at the dark face too close to mine, eyes bright gold and eerie as fuck.

"Holy *shit,* Aggie," I cried, slamming my hand over my racing heart. "You nearly scared me back to death."

"You've been here for five hours," she huffed, making me jolt in surprise. Fuck, had it been that long? "Idiot girl, you're probably starving."

She thrust a warm, buttery bread roll stuffed with bacon at me and stalked away before I could recover from the gesture. With a shrug, I replaced the book and bit into my bread roll, groaning at the explosion of flavour on my tongue.

I waited for Harvey to warn me against making noises like that unless I wanted to be bent over the breakfast table. My heart plummeted fast when I caught the reflexive thought. Harvey was gone, lost to me. But I refused to think he was dead. My mates had to be alive and resurrected like me. My dreams were *real,* not just trauma-fuelled delusions.

"I'll find them," I whispered to the watchful books around me, making the vow real by giving it a voice.

I finished the warm roll and left the library—and the

enchanting Aggie—to head out of the palace, my beloved daggers slapping my thighs as I walked swiftly. I expected a guard to step into my path and haul me back to General Callahan or maybe even Lucifer himself, but no one batted an eyelid as I strode out the main doors and down the pale gold steps into the city.

I shouldn't torture myself, but I couldn't fight the compulsion to return to the scene of the crime. Or rather, the house we'd broken into and been trapped in by Locke. The house that had made us custodians of the Damned Realm, ultimately murdered by the abusive bastard.

It took me three hours walking around the city, searching every corner for the steps that had led Malakai and I up to Lucifer's second home, to realise it was no longer here. It must have been destroyed during the angelic attack on Iarlon.

Like my mates, there was nothing left in the city to show it had ever existed.

The pain in my chest grew, festering into anger and a foul mood.

"The fuck are you looking at?" I demanded of a [bald,] red-skinned demon with a forked tail and a naked penis swinging around. I tried not to look, but it was *right there,* whirling like a windmill.

"My eyes are up here, darlin'," he replied with a warm laugh. But he winced when a furious man roared, "Get back here, Travis, I'm not done yelling at you!"

"Arguing with the husband," the red guy laughed with me, quickening his steps as his husband's voice grew louder. "You know how it is."

"Actually, my mates are probably dead," I replied flatly.

It was hard to hold onto hope right now, even if I'd kick myself for saying that later.

Ugh, his red face turned all sympathetic. It made my skin itchy and stomach even tighter.

"Good luck with the husband," I told him and quickened my footsteps.

When I reached a high ledge, I snapped my wings out and dove off the edge, air slicing at me as I took a wide arc around the capital. Seeing what remained and what was new.

From the air, it looked almost entirely different. The angels had really done a number on the city. Probably to weaken Lucifer so he'd be an easier target. Obviously that didn't work—he was every bit as intimidating and powerful as I remembered him.

I tried not to remember that day we became custodians of the Damned Realm, kneeling on the cold marble floor of the throne room beside my mates, terrified we were about to be sentenced to a gruesome, grisly death. The memory was blurry in places, but I remembered the panic in Em's eyes, the sharp fear in Harvey's voice, and the tension gripping Kai's body.

I angled my wings, catching a gust of wind and flying around the golden dome of an elegant, intricately carved building. A park encircled it, perfumed with honeysuckle. I got a strange memory of Wisteria, my mother's homeplace. Had someone built a piece of Heaven here in Hell? Two, if the library was angelic like I suspected. Weird.

I shook off the strange feeling crawling down my spine and followed the arch of the river, the water gleaming silver-lilac. The bird part of me wanted to freefall into the water and ruffle my wings in the world's largest bath, but I squashed the impulse and kept flying. I had no direction or plan, only an aimless urge to escape my past. As if murder and grief was something I could outpace.

I flew high to avoid a tall cluster of trees around a monument, and for a moment it wasn't a cushion of air that wrapped around me, caressing my wings, but shadows.

I jolted so hard I nearly fell from the sky, my heart slamming in my ribs. I could still feel the phantom touch of shadows wrapped around me, not strangling or threatening but almost ... protective.

I saw Cassander Locke's cruel, slimy face down the barrel of a gun and suddenly those shadows were all I could feel.

I doubled over, my stomach twisting violently, and I plummeted towards the trees fast, struggling to draw a sharp breath into my lungs. I flapped my wings like a madwoman to slow my descent, but the second my feet touched the golden flagstones under the trees, I dropped to my knees and vomited.

My throat burned and stomach cramped, and even as I was sick, I didn't know *why*.

I'd ... forgotten something. I couldn't shake the sense that something had been taken from me, and that was true of my mates, but there was more, I knew it. I just didn't know *what*.

I didn't know why there was a crack in my chest, why I felt deeply, irreparably heartbroken.

I spat the taste of vomit from my mouth and dove into my memories of the day I died. That was the trigger somehow, thinking about that day. It was as blurry as when we knelt before Lucifer, but brilliantly sharp in places—Emlyn's cry when he was shot, Kai throwing himself at Locke with his magic shuddering through the air, Harvey's blood soaking into my trousers.

But when I tried to focus on myself, my screams, my fear, it was covered in an opaque haze like someone had thrown a veil over it. I eyed the curse mark on my forearm as I pushed up to my feet. Something important had happened that day, and all the other blurry days, too. And if one of these marks was why I'd forgotten it, those memories had been *taken* from me.

"Fucking curses," I snarled, and stalked around the tall monument for the demons lost in the war. Flying was out of the question with my stomach sloshing like a ship on a stormy sea, so I got my anger out by slamming my boots to the ground with dirty stomping step through the park.

I riffled through my memories as I trekked through the city's clean, leafy streets towards the palace. In every memory from the last ten years I was alive, there was a sheen obscuring something. Whatever I'd been cursed to forget, it was entwined with every one of my memories since I met the guys.

I needed to find my mates, right the hell now.

*C*allahan was busy in a meeting with Cerny, Lucifer's spymaster, and the rest of their team. At least the ones high up enough to warrant an invite.[1] I tried to hunt down Bernard, but a scowling, grey-bearded soldier warned me not to bother him and Queen Lili during their date night. I gnashed my teeth, bristling with impatience and panic and the need to *do something,* but I took the man's advice.

I needed a job, needed a new place to search for my mates. I'd gone around every inn and pub in the last town, but I'd come up empty.

I'd spent too much time doing nothing these past two days while I waited for Cerny or whoever else to interrogate Bevan. We needed to know what we were up against, to formulate a plan for maximum impact, but the longer it took the less I cared about waiting.

I was a mercenary; I wasn't known for tact and patience.

Restless, I stalked to the training room. The shadow of my empty memories followed me there, moving around the high-ceilinged room like a spectre, haunting pieces of metal and padded cushions that were as alien to me as the little

black phones everyone was using. Tali had given me hers—
she didn't have the opposable thumbs to work it anyway—
but I had no clue how to use it.

Ugh, I was out of date. And old.

I approached a rack of weights along the side of the
room because at least I knew what a weight was, and
grabbed a small one while I stretched out the tension in my
arms and legs. I watched what the three other people in the
room did with the equipment, pretending I was admiring
their form instead of completely hopeless. When a man
with huge bull's horns spotted me staring, I gave him a
thumbs up.

"Great job, man."

He snorted and glanced away, but I imagined he was
pleased by the compliment. Even surly bull demons loved
compliments.

After another voyeuristic minute, I'd got the hang of how
the apparatus worked, so I approached an empty seat and
plopped down onto it, grabbing the padded bars on either
side of my head. I grunted at the pull in my muscles, but I'd
once carried a small pony on my back, so this was nothing.[2]

Fifteen minutes later, I was aching all over, drenched in
sweat, but my head would *not* shut up thinking and the
phantom grief in my chest had transformed into a living,
endless rage. Something that belonged to me had been
stolen. Someone had cursed me, went into my head and
rearranged my memories. They were *my* memories.

I left the weights and approached a punching bag
hanging from the ceiling, not pausing to wrap my knuckles
before I slammed my fist into it. Impact vibrated up my arm,
and I caught my breath. *Yes.* This was what I needed; pure
violence and messy rage unleashed on an unsuspecting
punch bag.

These things had changed since I'd last used one, sturdier

and stiffer, but it absorbed punch after punch without tearing off the chain it hung by, so I had no complaints.

Copper filled the air, the scent wrapping around my taste buds, but I didn't stop hammering blows on the bag, my hands throbbing and my breathing shot apart.

Memories flashed—the scent of gunpowder, the blistering heat of gunshots, the visceral, lancing fear of watching my mates crash to the floor of our new kitchen. Locke's smirk; the satisfaction and revenge in his eyes.

Why? Why did he hate us so much? He was Harvey's father, and I knew he was an abusive piece of shit, but when I reached for the memory of *why* Locke hunted us, I hit another hazy wall. Whatever lay beyond was firmly hidden.

"Fuck," I hissed, driving my bleeding knuckles into the bag again, my stomach hollowing with rough breaths, my whole body starting to shake.

"Woah, woah, stop before you do serious damage to yourself," a warm, honeyed voice called, swift footsteps rushing in my direction.

Soft hands caught my wrists and pulled me away from the punching bag. Curved eyes widened in a pretty, freckled face when I bared my teeth in a snarl.

"Get fucked," I spat at the pretty man, registering a tight outfit on a long, slim body and long red hair, scanning him for weapons and finding none—only white wings. Shit, how did he have *white* wings in Hell? They were pearly and untainted by a Fall.

"Halwen, I presume?" he asked, releasing me instantly and taking a step back like I was feral. Smart man.

"You're like me," I blurted, my rage faltering for a moment, "aren't you? You'd wither in Hell otherwise. You're part angel."

"I am," he agreed, his red brows tugging into a furrow. "I didn't realise you were."

I shrugged, pulling my black wings tighter to my back. "I know I don't look it, but my mother was an angel."

He smiled, like the threat had passed.[3] "Lili's like us, too. She mentioned meeting you."

I blinked—and then realisation hit. "You're not another of Queen Lili's harem, are you?"

How many did she *have?*

The pretty man gave me a crooked smile. "I certainly am. Speaking of, Cerny's looking for you. He sent me to find you; he has a job for you."

All the tension drained from me, and I let out a rough breath. "Thank *fuck* for that."

Right now I'd take any distraction. Even if it didn't lead me to my mates, hunting alphas was a perfect distraction. I couldn't think about the aching absence in my soul if I was fighting for my life against a city full of violent, brutish demons.[4]

"*C*overt," I breathed to myself as I flew through the darkening night along the river. "Subtle."

Those were Cerny's words—the *spymaster's* words. Riding into the alpha city on the back of a giant red panda wasn't going to cut it for this job. I had to pose as a rogue demon myself; I had to seem as unhinged and vicious as possible, and I needed to go alone.

I was fine with everything except the alone part. Alone, my thoughts ran wild, returning to those vacant spots in my memory, poking them like broken teeth and waiting for the throb of pain. It came every time, lancing through my head and chest.

"Leave it," I snapped at myself, keeping my gaze fixed down on the river, searching for a cluster of buildings. I'd already investigated three ordinary villages and an empty town demolished by the war, and found no alphas in either. Bevan had only given Cerny's team a twenty-mile area, not a specific location, so I'd been flying along the Bend of Boraven, circling in search of a city *all day*.

I was ready to land, find a tree to sleep in, and admit

defeat for tonight. Bevan might have been 'mined for information' but there was no telling he'd been honest. Maybe if *the Cursed One* had been present to scare him shitless, he might have been more open. So far, there'd been nothing along the river to show an alpha city was nearby. It was quiet, peaceful—and grating to my prickly soul.

I reached up to check the bone pin securing my pink hair into a knot on my head, releasing a quick breath when I found it still in place—and letting go quickly when its power lit my veins on fire.

"To pose as an alpha," Cerny said, his rugged face ultra serious as he watched me from the other side of his heavy desk. The office behind him was full of weapons, paintings, books, and a small topiary bush carved into a shocking likeness of the queen. "You need power."

"I had power," I muttered, scowling at the curse on my arm as I dropped into the green leather chair opposite the spymaster. "I used to be able to boil the blood in anyone's veins. Make their whole body explode."

Cerny blinked bright topaz eyes, the only sign of his surprise. "That would be useful."

"But since I died, it's gone," I muttered, and then gave Cerny a canny look. "You have a plan for that, though, don't you?"

"I do," he agreed, sliding open a drawer beside him and producing a small velvet jewellery box.

"I'm spoken for," I protested before he could open the box.

"So am I," he replied, the expression on his tanned face flattening. With his soft golden colouring, he looked more angelic than demonic, but that grumpy disposition was a hundred percent hellborn. "Very spoken for. Open the box, Halwen. And just know, the second you touch it, you'll experience a severe reaction."

I scowled, sliding the box towards me. "This better not kill me. I have a pretty good track record with coming back to life, and the second I do, I'm coming right for you."

"It won't kill you; it'll give you power. A lot of power."

"So I can pose as an alpha," I surmised, and snapped the box open, spying not a ring inside but a hair pin. The end was made of bone and sharp enough to draw blood, but the head caught my eye and made my heart pull tight. There were small, white enamel flowers decorating it, so similar to the flowers around our home—the ones Kai picked a bunch of every anniversary.

I reached out to brush my finger over those enamel flowers—and my whole body locked. My eyes flew wide, my mouth open on a scream of surprise as fire and ice filled my body.

My hair lifted off my shoulders, floating around my face, and my wings snapped wide, knocking things off the shelves of Cerny's office. I waited for the thud of them hitting the rug, but it never came. Oh fuck, everything was floating—from books on the bookcase by the window, to the knives and strange, unfamiliar weapons on the walls, to the knickknacks and objects decorating the room. Even the little topiary hovered.

"Help," I croaked to Cerny, my head thrown back as more power rampaged through me. I could taste the sparks on my tongue, sharp and bitter. My nose stung; my eyes streamed, stinging like I had needles embedded in them.

Glass cases rattled to my left, bookshelves lost their books on my right, and the room filled with the acidic bite of magic. Even Cerny reacted, a strange red mist hovering around his shoulders for a second before the whole thing cut out and I sank back into the chair, heaving for breath as things fell back into their places.

My head spun. I felt weird in my body, my limbs unwieldy.

"Good," Cerny rasped. "We know it works. Put it in your hair; only touch it if you need it."

"You," I panted, gripping the table's edge, "are completely insane."

The spymaster straightened the papers on his desk while I snapped the velvet case closed and shoved it away. "How do you feel?"

"*Like I got struck by lightning,*" I spat, scrubbing tears off my face. *My heart raced too fast, my skin tingling all over.*

"*Any pain?*" *he asked, lifting his gaze to give me a worried look.*

I paused to answer that and—I didn't hurt at all. Actually all my aches had gone from the trek through the city and from throwing up earlier, not to mention beating the shit out of a dummy. If I ignored the ever-present pain in my soul, I felt good.

"*No. That's weird.*"

Cerny smiled, a cunning thing that made me nervous. "*This will work. And if you're lucky, this new power might unlock your old magic.*"

Now, that sounded too good to be true.

I dropped my fingers swiftly from the bone pin when power burned through me, coating my tongue with sharp magic, filling my veins with freezing lightning and scorching lava. A steady current of air was the only thing keeping me airborne for a moment as my wings locked.

Fuck, that thing was potent. There'd be no mistaking me as anything but an alpha if I drew on its magic. I panted, my whole body pounding with the remnants of its ferocity, and—

"What was that?" I breathed, excitement making my heart leap.

A cluster of lights flickered as I angled my body to the left, but when I veered back, they were hidden. No wonder I'd missed them all afternoon; the city was camouflaged.

Now, I was focusing, there were scents of alphas on the air, and power thrummed like a static charge through this valley. A few trees had been felled, probably in an alpha rampage. I grinned, my heart beating faster, full of sharp magic as I swooped and landed on the road below.

"Found you."

I laid on my belly in the grass, using the tree cover to hide me as I scoped out the city that was cleverly hidden—unless you were looking for it, like I'd been. A sign driven into the ground proclaimed it Alphaven. That took a lot of thinking about; alpha haven.[1]

There wasn't a wall or iron fence ringing it to ward off outsiders; the whole thing was open. But I had no doubt if I waltzed into the city, someone would know my every movement.

I was counting on it.

My plan wasn't elegant, but it would work. I had insane power with the pin, enough that there'd be no doubt I was an alpha with extreme power. *Far* more than any regular demon. Alphas tended to get overwhelmed by their power and go on mad, destructive rampages. That was my whole plan: go on a rampage, draw attention to myself, and get snapped up by this lord who collected alphas.

It didn't need to be fancy; I was supposed to be an intellectually challenged alpha after all. Alphas lived to feed, fight, and fuck, and little else. I could play that role. Hell, back in my mercenary guild days, most of my allies lived for those three things. I knew the type of person I had to become.

I watched for another twenty minutes, looking for a guard patrol, sussing out the houses at the edge of the city. If this was anything like other cities, the better houses would be in its heart and the outer edges would be for the people struggling to feed themselves. I'd lived on the edges for most of my life, my dad doing his best to keep us alive.

Sometimes it pissed me off that we were in Hell, we were *demons,* and here we were working and acting like humans. But it was thinking like that that made rebels start an uprising against Lucifer.

I wasn't a fan of working, but I *did* like not pissing in a bucket, and clothes were nice. So was food that wasn't a leg ripped off another demon and roasted over a fire.

I glanced at the tattoo on my arm, letting it fan the flames of my rage, and watched the road ahead for another few minutes. Only a few people were about, but they'd be good enough witnesses to an alpha outburst.

"Let's do this," I breathed, and pushed off the ground.

The back of my neck tingled as I pulled the pin out of my hair—catching my breath at the power that electrified me—and slid it up the sleeve of my jacket so it had full contact with my skin.

Fuuuuck.

My tongue burned, my eyes prickling viciously, and for a moment I thought my body was going to explode at the sheer power that erupted through my system, frazzling everything from my eyelashes to my toenails.

I'd swallowed a star, my body lit up and frantic, and for a moment I was so consumed with magic that I didn't realise there was a big, clawed hand wrapped around the back of my neck and someone was shaking my body.

"Get the fuck off," I growled, my voice deeper and more resonant, echoing off the tall trees I'd used as cover.

I threw my elbow back and whoever had grabbed me howled with pain like I'd stabbed them.

"Don't know—what the fuck she is," a man croaked, my hearing as sharp as a razor. He released me and staggered back.

I spun, inhaling a sharp breath at the sight of four big, burly fuckers—three older men and a silver-haired woman around my age. Their clothes were made of leather and aged, dirty, all in shades of brown.

The woman's face split in a grin. "Looks like we'll be eating like kings tonight, boys. Wynvail will reward us for this capture."

Capture? *Son of a bitch.* I couldn't get captured for some Wynvail guy when I needed to get taken to the lord's collection.

"Back off," I warned, my deep voice making me jump. I held my hands in front of myself and blinked when long, bone fingernails grew from mine, my wings itching too. A quick glance showed my feathers were now tipped in bone. I gave the raiders a slow grin. *Come at me, fuckers. See what happens.*

I'd heard of raiders—they;d been around when I'd last been alive. They were a poorer, meaner version of bounty hunters and mercs, and would grab anyone and anything for a price. It wasn't far off what I'd done by going to grab—

Who did I go to grab?

My head flashed with pain as I tried to remember, and my knees buckled.

In that split second of weakness, the raiders swarmed in around me. I growled when someone slammed a hand over my mouth, crammed my wings tight to my back, and took my hands in a tight, restrictive grip.

"Dead—all of you," I threatened, ignoring the sweaty hand pressed to my face, muffling my voice. "You're all fucking *dead.*"

The silver-haired woman snorted, two of her cohorts echoing it. "You shouldn't have come so close to Alphaven, darling. Anyone stupid enough to wander out here is fair gain."

I snapped my teeth, the only thing I could move on my body. "I came here because I heard it was a safe place for alphas. My mistake."

"Big mistake," a huge, half-naked man agreed, something bullish about his face. "You'll wish you'd never been born in this city."

"Talking from experience?" I asked sweetly. "Because I can make things so much better for you, no problem at all."

The woman snorted, her muscles bulging as she slapped the guy on his shoulder. "Think she just offered to be your whore, Jhonna."

"She offered to kill you, imbeciles," the biggest alpha snapped, his long, pretty black hair flowing as he stalked towards me. Huge *and* intelligent? Someone call Iarlon's reporters; I had a ground-breaking story for their newspaper. "And I'll have to decline on his behalf."

"Pity," I replied, and tried to kick off the ground so I could use my legs to attack them. The second my legs swung up, someone kicked them from under me and I tipped back into the bastards holding me, utterly at their mercy, not even my feet on the ground.[2]

"You'll regret this," I growled through the hand muzzling me. "By the time I'm done with you—"

"Someone shut her up," the big, clever bastard barked, and a fist slammed into my skull.

Everything went scarily black.[3]

30

I jerked awake with a yell, metal rattling and my arms stretched above my head. I tilted my head back with a groan, my stomach already cramping with dread, knowing what I'd see. Yup, my hands were chained to the wall above me. An experimental kick proved my legs were chained, too.[1]

I squinted at the room I was in, surprised to find a dusty attic with short, sloped walls instead of a grimy basement. Huh, guess times were changing. It was nice to mix things up a little.

"Pretty," I murmured, watching fat dust motes float through a beam of sunlight before falling into the shadowy parts of the room. I was the only person up here, but there were chains on two other walls, so clearly this was a regular occurrence. I admired the set-up, but I'd admire it a whole lot more if I wasn't chained to a wall with my shoulders pounding from the awkward position.

I tilted my head against my shoulder, watching more dust spin through the air, the sun beginning to set beyond the short, angled window opposite me. It was the nicest place I'd ever been strung up, honestly. I couldn't complain about the view; I could see all the way across the flat rooftops of Alphaven to the rolling hills and the forest I'd hidden in earlier. There was a fire burning in the heart of the city, in the middle of an open-top building, the flames so high they almost touched the sky.

I watched the fire dance, curious to know if it would catch and spread to the buildings on either side, but steady footsteps on wooden stairs drew my attention back to the attic. Panic caught in my chest, but adrenaline raged faster, drowning out my nerves. The magic that burned through me from the hair pin up my sleeve seemed to pulse higher, fiercer, and I gasped as my bone nails lengthened, my body jolting, rattling the chains.

I couldn't see the staircase from where I was chained to the wall, but the pin's magic made every sense razor sharp. I knew it was a single set of footsteps, a single person, not heavy-set but strong. Normally I'd say male, but with alphas it was hard to tell. A woman could just as easily break my ribs as any man here. They weren't breathing heavily despite the climb to the attic so they must be fit. None of which were good signs for me getting out of this place and finding the damn lord.

"Hello again, Halwen," a low, cultured voice said, the steps reaching the top of the staircase, echoing into the attic.

Again. Hello *again*.

I bared my teeth. The only people I'd met in a hundred years were Lucifer's circle, which meant this bastard was a traitor in the palace.

"I don't know why you're stupid enough to come here and spy on me," the voice went on, echoing steps carrying him into my line of sight.

Every thought fell out of my head. The magic in my

system rampaged, making my fingers twitch, my tongue burn cold like I'd swallowed ice.

"I know you," I breathed, staring at the handsome, cruel bastard when he came to stand in front of me, his mahogany hair short and his sculpted face full of sickening satisfaction. He wasn't a traitor to Lucifer. I didn't know him from the palace. He'd tried to kill me—a hundred years ago.

He hunted us from safe house to safe house. He burned our house down. He should be dead. But here he stood, gloating at having me chained in his attic.

"I should hope you know me, Halwen," the hunter laughed, coming closer and raking a slow stare down my chained body. "I'm your mate."

31

J jerked away from the hunter when he reached a bronze hand toward me, my chains rattling violently in the empty attic.

"No," I hissed, not even contemplating it.

No fucking way. I'd remember him if—but there were gaping holes in my memories.

No.

This was a lie. My body shook, terror and rage meeting the bone pin's blistering magic in me, burning all the way to the tips of my canine teeth.

"Of course you don't remember me," he said smoothly, something in the way he looked at me making my stomach churn. "The last time we met was so traumatic, your poor mind must have blocked it out."

"You," I snarled, breathing faster, "are not my mate."

I'd know; I'd feel it. All I felt were the tatters of my broken soul, *nothing* that linked me to this creep.

"It'll take some time to remember me," the hunter told me, mild and smug as if I wasn't snarling at him. He stroked the backs of his fingers down my cheek, and my stomach revolted. Serves him right if I threw up on his face. "But we have all the time in the world now I've found you."

I spat in his face.

He reared back, nostrils flaring, his true, cruel face showing for a moment before he hid it behind a veneer of smug calm.

"You tried to kill me and my mates; you're not one of them."

He wiped the spit from his face with an unsettling calm. "You think that because someone tampered with your memories. I'm Wynvail. Your mate."

I shook my head, but those hazy spots in my memories taunted me. "I remember you perfectly. You hunted us, you hurt my Emlyn."

"That's the curse playing with your mind," he murmured, reaching out to stroke my face and ignoring the way I recoiled. "Your mates are Emlyn, Malakai, Harvey, and me. Harvey and I are brothers, remember?"

I shook my head. Ignored the catch in my breath. His touch burned, disgusted me. But it felt so *right*.

"You have two Locke brothers as your mates," he went on, a strange light in his eyes. "Both of us."

I wanted to snarl in his face, but I froze. He was right. I couldn't explain how I knew, but he was right. I ... I did have two brothers as my mates. Harvey and—this asshole?

"Then who cursed me?" I demanded, pulling on my chains.

"I don't know, honey," he replied, his cruelly handsome face trying to be soft, and failing.

"Don't call me that," I snapped.

Mercury eyes glowed at my defiance, and a quiet, animal part of me squeaked in terror. "Behave, or I'll leave you chained here all night."

"Why chain me at all if I'm your mate?" I challenged, my heart pounding.

Wynvail laughed, a corner of his mouth curved into a wicked slash. "I know you, Halwen. At the first chance, you'd bury a knife in my throat and run."

He had a point.

He brushed my cheek with a thumb, and I tried to push down my nausea at the soft touch. He couldn't be my mate. No fucking way. But I couldn't deny that what he told me made sense, and it felt right. Everything fit.

"Prove it," I growled at him, hiding the way my hands shook. Had I found them? Had I really found my mates? "If you're my soulmate, prove it."

He was an asshole, and a creep, and I wanted to break his nose, but I'd wanted to break Kai's nose in the beginning, too. Hope strangled me until I couldn't breathe.

"Look at me, Halwen," Wynvail murmured, his voice dropping as he came closer, his face so near to mine. His scent overwhelmed every sense, cloves and sugar and blood.

I swallowed and looked into his eyes, my heart skipping because—I *knew* those eyes. Memories tried to break out, to push through the drugged haze over my mind, and I flinched with a cry as pain pierced my head from all directions. It burrowed deep until I was sure my skull would burst.

"Stop!" Wynvail commanded, genuine panic in his voice. "Stop, or you'll break your mind, Halwen."

I bared my teeth, but he was right. I reluctantly retreated from those memories, panting, the pin's magic rising like fire and ice in my veins until my eyelashes tingled and I couldn't feel my face.

"Careful," he murmured, his cool hand cupping my cheek.

I remembered days like this, cool skin on mine, softness and care. My bottom lip wobbled. "Whoever made me forget you will die. Horribly."

"I'll make sure of it," he promised, and reached up to unhook my chains from the ceiling.

He was my mate; he really ought to have known I would wrap the chain around his throat and strangle him the second my arms were down. My muscles screamed, weak and painful from hanging above me, but the pin's sharp power erupted through me and gave me strength.

Wynvail laughed, the sound chilling, and reached up to— to snap the chains apart with a flash of white light before I could choke him.

What? How did he do that?

I shook my head at the pain that cracked my skull when I tried to remember his magic. I thought ... part of me had been waiting for shadows, like the darkness I remembered cushioning me when Locke killed me.

"I warned you to behave," Wynvail rasped, rubbing his throat as we stared at each other across the attic.

I shrugged, panting and pained. "Where's the fun in behaving?"

He grinned, a sudden flash of something in his eyes. Interest.

I held up my hands in warning as he edged closer, my claws long and made of viciously sharp bone. Power slashed through the chains around my ankles, the magic in the pin horrifically intuitive, and I took a step towards the staircase.

"You *know* me, Halwen, you just can't remember," Wynvail urged.

"Where are the others?" I asked, my stomach knotting at the thought of seeing them again, of all of us being together. *Please, please.*

But part of me was so scared it would never happen, and my throat closed up.

"Breathe, honey," Wynvail murmured, sliding closer to stroke my cheek. I shuddered, and couldn't tell if it was in relief or revulsion. I needed to get these curses broken as soon as fucking possible; I hated feeling disgusted a my own mate's touch.

I know those eyes, I thought again as I stared up at him, my heart thumping fast. He was so damned tall, I was going to develop a crick in my head looking up at him.

"I'll take you to them," he offered, and reached for my hand before remembering my huge claws. He grasped my wrist instead, his fingers cool and calming.

I laughed, fluttering my fingers. "Not a fan of the killer claws?"

"I don't remember them," he replied, guiding me to the staircase and down a tight, narrow hallway to the floor below. The house smelled of pine cleaning solution and coffee, an unpleasant combination. The decor wasn't much better. "Something new?"

"I woke up with them," I lied, unable to explain why I did. "What—what happened when you were reborn? Where were you?"

Wynvail's thumb stroked my pulse, making my heart beat faster as he led me to the bottom floor of the house. It was in pretty good condition, not falling apart like I'd expected the alpha city to be. To say these alphas wanted civilisation destroyed, they lived pretty comfortably.

"I resurrected ninety years ago, not too far from here. I've been trying to figure out what happened ever since." His silver gaze slid to me and lingered. "Trying to find you."

"I only just—came back," I replied, pain tightening my chest. They'd been back so much longer than me. "I'm sorry, Wyn."

The name came naturally—a fluke or a memory?

He pulled me closer when we reached a landing on the bottom floor, laying a kiss on my temple. My throat swelled, a strange blend of unease and comfort buzzing through me. "You have nothing to apologise for Halwen."

I elbowed him lightly, pushing off my pain. "I'm going by Haley now. Halwen's weird since there's a whole forest by the same name."

"You're welcome," he replied dryly, and I jolted, staring at him. This smug, attractive bastard with his perfect hair and straight teeth and expensive clothes.

"You..."

The mate who'd left me a message to say they were all still alive. The mate who never forgot me, who named a whole damn forest after me. Wynvail Locke.

"Me," he agreed, and squeezed my wrist, tugging me towards an open door that led into darkness. "Your mates are this way. The tunnel leads across the city."

My heart soared even as I felt like I'd throw up. I dredged up a smile for the mate who never forgot me and said, "Lead the way, Wyn."

32

*W*hen Wynvail said the tunnel led across the city, he meant it. We'd been walking for twenty minutes before any light flickered in the tight space. If it wasn't for Wynvail's soft breaths and his fingers on my wrist, I'd think I was alone down here. Being guided to my death.

"What *is* this place?" I whispered when the flickers of light broadened, casting a glow over arches carved into the walls ahead, and limning the bars across them gold. They were cells, but for who?

"The city was built over fifty tunnels like this," Wynvail replied, his voice low. "They were used to hold prisoners centuries ago. Now, they're for our most volatile alphas. The ones who can't follow rules."

I shot him a look, apprehension tight in my belly. "That sounds ominous."

He smirked. "It should. It's the only thing that keeps a lot of these beasts in line."

Beasts. But wasn't he a beast too? Wasn't I? We were both demons but a little bit *more*. I could sense it in him—the heavy throb of power, the dominance.[1]

"Fresh meat," a raspy voice whispered from somewhere to my right, and I flinched into Wynvail. The fingers he'd locked around my wrist felt far more protective than restrictive now there was a new threat. "Come closer, you smell so clean, so sweet."

"Back off," Wynvail growled, so much power and wrath in his voice that the man skittered away. He tucked me closer against him, his body as tense as iron,

"Sorry, Lord, sorry, Lord," the man whispered.

I swallowed the words on the tip of my tongue, resisting the urge to stare at Wynvail.

Lord? Fucking Lord? So *he* was the psycho collecting alphas?

Also, I'd killed six of my mate's minions...

Ugh, why could my life never run smooth?

I'd been sent to infiltrate the alphas so I could feed information about *my mate* to Lucifer's spymaster. I resisted the urge to bang my head against the bars of the next cell. When I looked into it, green eyes glowed back at me, and I inhaled sharply.

"They won't hurt you," Wynvail promised, watching me.

"Because they're scared to death of you," I replied dryly, but—warmly. This didn't scare me; the rest of my mates were maniacs too. "I'm jealous; I want people to be scared of *me.*"

Wynvail lifted my wrist and kissed the back of my hand. "All you have to do is slaughter everyone who tries to hurt you, and they will be."

I laughed. "I'll try."

Wynvail didn't laugh, didn't even smile. He gasped, a shudder moving through his body, and—and I realised he'd kissed my hand to distract me while he removed the hair pin from my sleeve.

"Give that back!" I snapped, reaching for it.

He held it above my head, a gleam of insanity in his silver eyes. Covetousness. Greed.

I growled in frustration, cursing myself for not being a six foot Amazon. I jumped, trying to snatch the pin from his aloft hand.

"Seriously, Wynvail, I need that."

"Why?" he laughed, an eyebrow raised on his sculpted face. He shuddered with a groan, the power razing his body from within. "So you can pretend to be an alpha? We both know you're not, honey."

"Yeah, well, I'm a reborn hybrid, so I'm probably more powerful than an alpha."

He grinned abruptly, and my heart skipped. He was completely and truly mad, wasn't he? "I wonder if you're more powerful than three."

"What?"

"You can survive," he murmured, his eyes smoky when they trailed down my body. "You're my mate, after all."

I hissed and dove at him when he tore away from me, stealing my pin, but a metal grate slammed down from the ceiling and I jumped back with a gasp, narrowly avoiding being impaled.

"You're insane!" I cried, staring at my bastard mate. Thief and lunatic. *Sexy, sexy lunatic.*

He tipped his brown head in acknowledgement and tucked my bone pin into his pocket. "Just like you, Halwen."

"What are you playing at?" I screeched, riling up the alphas in the cells along the tunnel, and momentarily deafened by growls and snarls. Why did solid bars separate us? What the fuck was he doing?

Wynvail gave me a long, scorching look. "Make me proud."

I bared my teeth, wrapping my fingers around the grate

that refused to budge even an inch. My stomach dropped when I saw my claws were normal, not bone. The power had left me entirely—Wynvail had it all.

"I'll make you pay for this, you sick bastard," I threatened, but when I looked up from my claws, he was gone.

PART III - MATE

33

A sudden roar of stone had me spinning, breath catching and dying in my throat when I saw the solid rock door behind me was sliding open. Dread shuddered down my spine; I stared at the door, reaching for my weapons—and coming up empty.

Fuck. He'd disarmed me before he strung me up in his attic.

My mate was a goddamn psychopath. If I didn't know better, I'd say he wanted me dead. And I'd lost my volcanic blades again. I was going to stab Wynvail after this, mate or not.

I faced the archway that had opened, taking a tentative step towards it and squinting at the space beyond. It took me a moment to place the bright orange glow and when I did, I cursed violently. There was an enormous fire burning in the centre of the rectangular arena, and rows upon rows of seats were arranged around the edges, the roof open to the night.

It was a godsdamned fighting pit, and I had no interest in fighting alphas—let alone three like Wynvail suggested.

But the bars behind me wouldn't budge, and ahead the

audience of alphas roared, a sudden rise of sound that made my heart jolt into my throat. *Oh gods, why are they cheering?*

It didn't take me long to spot why, or hear the grate of stone on stone as three more doorways rolled open, one on each side of the arena. Wynvail wanted me to fight, but why?

And if he'd stolen my pin, did he want me to lose?

I took a tentative step into the ring, the concrete cold even through my boots as I scoped out my competition. The crowd roared louder, not excitement so much as hunger—for blood, for violence. I hated places like these. The pit already smelled of blood, probably from the last suckers to be forced into the ring.

How many people had died here? More than a few, I'd bet.

I wasn't about to be the latest smear of blood on the concrete. I hadn't risen from the dead just to die again. Besides, Wynvail wouldn't let me be hurt too badly. His instincts wouldn't let him.

I patted down my body again, searching for *any* weapon, even a clam shucking knife, and hissed in victory when I found a tiny, thin blade tucked into a pocket in my leather trousers. So slim, it would have been missed. I drew it out and held it like it was precious, ignoring the pathetic size of it. It was meant for throwing, not grappling with massive, instinct-driven alphas, but beggars couldn't be choosers.

Another yell went through the audience hulking in their seats around me, and I gritted my teeth as I peered around the doorway to see what caused it: a huge shadow stalked out of one of the other archways.

For a moment, a memory surged to the surface and stabbed my brain with agony. Indistinct but sharp and brutal. I knew it wasn't real, but the flicker of flames in a fireplace filled my ears, and someone turned a page in an old book. I gasped, clutching the wall, blinking until my eyes focused on the fighting ring, grinding my jaw as I absorbed the pain.

This was the worst timing for a memory to try to resurface, especially as the huge alpha took a step.

My heart jolted violently in my chest. There was something about that gait, something about the way they moved. I took a step into the arena without thinking about it, an uproarious chant going through the crowd.

Kill her! Kill her! Kill her!

"Fuck you very much," I yelled at them, but only succeeded in drawing the attention of the hulking alpha. Oh gods, he was *huge,* his shoulders twice the breadth of mine and his thighs as thick as tree trunks.

I caught my breath when he came at me, faster than I expected for a man of his size. I didn't know how I knew he was male when he was still in shadow, the only lights coming from the stands above. As if Wynvail wanted us to be even more unsettled, in the dimness. Psycho bastard.

I didn't stand around gawping at the alpha. I sprinted around the edge of the fighting pit, angling my tiny knife for maximum damage and assessed the way the alpha ran towards me, hoping he had a cock because my knife was going straight in his crown jewels. The closer he came, scarily fast even as I dodged out of his path, the more familiarity and alarm blared in my head. It throbbed like a broken tooth, pain in each pulse.

The crowd kept up their cheery, supportive chant,[1] and I did the smart thing by not taking my attention off the alpha to give them my middle finger. But it was a battle.

The alpha didn't talk, didn't taunt or threaten; he just growled like he was feral and hurtled at me. He was bigger and more muscular than me, but I ought to have been faster. I ought to have been able to outrun him, but I could feel his breath on the back of my neck, lifting all my fine hairs and sending a rush of chills down my back.

"Shit," I gasped out when the growl grew loud enough to block out the crowd's jeers.

I pushed my legs harder, racing aimlessly away from the alpha, nowhere to escape except back into the tunnel I'd come from. And no way in hell was I trapping myself between an alpha brute and the metal grate. I was stupid but not *that* stupid.

The scent of leather and old books hit my senses, the only warning I had before a massive, scalding body slammed into mine, tackling me to the ground.

My front slammed into the concrete, pain crashing through my hip and making me cry out. The growl became a deep, throaty sound that made me tremble.

That scent dominated my senses, raking up so many memories that I couldn't breathe. Even as I waited for the alpha to tear out my throat with his sharp teeth, even as my hip screamed, memories drowned out everything.

Lazy mornings waking up to Emlyn tracing his fingertips over my ribs. Hectic afternoons watching him run around making us dinner while I planned a hunt, the scent of roasting meat and buttery bread filling the kitchen. Sumptuous nights where Em would lay me out in our bed and cover every bit of space on my body in kisses, rolling me onto my front so he could lavish my back in kisses too, only stopping when he reached my pussy, unable to resist tasting the arousal pooled there.

I jerked back to the present with a gasp, bucking suddenly enough that the alpha gave me enough space to flip onto my back.

The beast looming over me was a stranger, his salt-and-pepper hair long and grizzled, his beard so thick it consumed most of his face; the only parts I could see were golden and scarred. The scars were unfamiliar, the feral rage in his eyes was new and terrifying, but the eyes themselves, sharp and blue—I knew those eyes.

Even as a hand wrapped around my throat, lifting my head only to slam it into the unyielding ground, I reached up and brushed my fingers over his beard.

"Em. Emlyn, it's me, it's Haley." But I could see in his eyes my words meant nothing to him. Maybe words altogether meant nothing. I surged for him through the bond, reaching out my soul and—touching nothing but wind-blown tatters. He was right here, but he might as well have been miles away.

"It's Halwen, your Hales, remember?" I rasped, my throat in his too-tight grip, threatening to buckle. My heart collapsed, too.

I stared up at him, my mate, and knew I was a stranger to him. All I saw in his eyes was murder. Nothing to suggest Em was in there at all. He wasn't just an alpha—he was an animal.

"Emlyn," I rasped, holding his gaze. My heart jumped when his mouth parted, hoping he'd say my name. But he snarled, sharp teeth bared, and didn't speak a word. "Emlyn Johahn!"

Kill her! Kill her! the crowd chanted. Did they know he was my mate? Did they know Wynvail had sent me here to—to kill them? What the fuck was his game?

My heart soared when Em tore away suddenly, his hand ripped from my throat. He remembered. He—

"No," I whimpered, my voice so small. I shook my head over and over, crawling backwards until my spine hit the stone wall beneath the arena seats. "No."

Em hadn't had a sudden awakening; he'd been wrenched away from me so another alpha could take his place. They snarled and hissed, fighting over who got to kill me. Emlyn didn't shift into his giant, feathered form. Did he even remember he could fly?

I couldn't take my eyes off the second alpha even as I fell apart. He wasn't as big or physically intimidating as Emlyn, but I knew every bit of cruelty and violence he was capable of. I'd stood beside him while we dealt that violence to our enemies, revelled in watching him unleash that crazed darkness to protect me.

But when Kai shoved Emlyn aside and prowled towards me, I knew I'd receive the full brunt of his madness today.

I scrambled to my feet, my hand shaking around the pathetic little knife I had to defend myself.

"Kai," I breathed, my voice hitching, collapsing.

Unlike Em, he looked exactly the same. His dark red hair was flawless, flowing down his back, maybe a little longer, and his neck was inked with flowing, tiny scrolls of text that carried on down his body, brutality etched into the sharp lines on his face as he stalked me.

"This isn't you," I rasped, shaking too hard to properly defend myself, my soul shattering in my chest all over again. I'd watched him die, and now he would kill me. It was breaking me, severing my soul in even more places. "Kai. Look at me, listen. It's Haley, your rose."

His eyes flashed, and hope choked off my air. He remembered the name, he would remember me—no, he'd just seen the knife in my hand. Fuck. A sob choked off the rest of my air. I needed to fight; they didn't really want to hurt me, not deep down. It would ruin them if they woke up and realised what they'd done. But I wasn't sure I was strong enough to fight them.

Not when just the sight of them made me want to curl up into a hall and sob.

I kept my back to the wall, moving in tiny steps to put space between us, and this time I recognised the flare of light in his eyes—the pleasure of the hunt.

Goddammit, I am not your prey, Malakai Virex.

My heart pounded in my throat as his crimson eyes tracked me. *Please don't let me die for this.* I shut down every survival instinct and forced myself to stop moving. I wouldn't let him chase me. If I engaged Kai's hunter instincts, there'd be no hope for me.

"Why are you doing this?" I screamed at the stands above my head, knowing Wynvail sat in the seats above this wall. What kind of man threw their mate into a fighting arena with three unhinged alphas who were also her mates? There were only two explanations—he wanted me to kill them, or he wanted *them* to kill me.

You can survive. You're my mate, after all.

He was unhinged. If I survived, I'd kill *him.*

"Malakai," I snarled when invisible magic slammed me into the wall, bruising my already tender skull and dragging my attention back to him. "You love me, for fuck's sake."

More like he was obsessed with me, and completely and utterly devoted. He'd *never* hurt me like this. That was proof more than anything that there was nothing left of my mates.

His snakes coiled around my upper arms, dragging a cry from my lips at the sudden pain, and my vision wavered when fangs grazed my skin. Kai was a tall, dark-clad blur as he stalked closer, his tail lashing the air behind him. I remembered the loving way he'd looked at me in my dreams, and my eyes burned with tears.

I knew I couldn't get through to him, knew he was too animalistic to hear what I said, but it still *killed* me. It tainted my soul a little darker to lift my arm as far as I could while pinned and flick my fingers to send the knife flying.

It buried in his shoulder, drawing a grunt of pain from the man I loved with all my fucked up heart.

My tears overflowed at the sound, pain splintering through my chest as more cracks formed in my soul. After this, I'd be lucky if there was anything left of me to put back together.

When Kai grabbed the knife and drew it out, hissing with renewed pain, I threw myself against the cage of his invisible snakes and stumbled free.

I didn't look back; I ran as fast as my shaky legs would carry me, firing straight across the arena, my lungs burning as I gasped for air. A dozen places ached and screamed on my body, slowing me down.

I wanted to yell more obscenities at Wynvail, wanted to denounce him as my mate, but I didn't have the breath to spare.

Air hit me from below, and I gasped, pushing myself faster, harder. Kai chased me, sending his snakes to capture me again. Only this time, I knew I wouldn't get free.

"Shit," I cried when my knee buckled and I slammed into the concrete on my side, momentum throwing across the arena like a twisted bowling ball.

A roar of noise swallowed my senses, making me cry— the crowd screaming, frantic.

A massive clawed hand grabbed the back of my neck and flipped me mercilessly onto my back, snarling in my face when a crack of pain made me scream.

I cried, staring at the monster looming over me in pure terror. My blood ran cold. The beast was death incarnate, a thing of shadows, nightmares, and fangs. My whole body rattled, shaking uncontrollably. My lips parted to plead for my life but I couldn't breathe, couldn't make a single sound as huge jaws parted and he roared in my face.

My heart skipped when I saw the beast's face. I didn't know the dark fur, didn't recognise the darkness that bled from bright silver eyes, or the clawed paws that crushed my chest. He smelled like brimstone, not sun-warmed earth. But

I knew it was Harvey. His black, spiralling horns were the same, his molten eyes the same metallic shade.

But my Harvey was pure sunlight—merciless and bright but *warm*. This monster of shadows and teeth held no light.

I knew without being told that this was the Harveil whose name drew base terror, who destroyed a whole city when he and—when he and his brother fled their father. *Wynvail*. No wonder he was fucked up enough to send me into a fighting pit with my mates; Cassander Locke was an abusive, evil piece of shit. I didn't want to think about the things he'd done to him. Wynvail was a black spot in my memory, but Harvey —I *knew* everything that monster had done to my sunshine mate.

Locked in the dark, shut away for his whole life, never seeing the sun, never breathing clear air. Hidden in a basement beneath a glittering, socialite house like a dark secret.

"It's okay," I breathed, inhaling sharply at the pain in my ribs as I reached up to sink my fingers into Harvey's fur. I shuddered as I stroked the heated skin underneath, my heart breaking. "It's okay, my Buttercup. Everything's going to be okay."

But his silver eyes bled darkness. And I tasted magic in the air before power charged through my body strong enough to black out the entire arena.

My scream drowned out the crowd's feral cries, and for a moment all that existed was the empty rage in Harvey's silver eyes—

And then my back arched as the pain crescendoed, swallowing my awareness of the arena, the crowd, and my mates. It shattered me into nothing but agony, and I screamed until my voice gave out.

34

Harvey

*T*he doll's screams grated my ears, sounding like suffering instead of the usual victory. It didn't stop me pressing my clawed paw to her ribs and letting the destructive force of my magic burn through her.

Above, in the stands, my captor and master watched with a frown on his face. He always frowned when I killed. Never smiled. But if I performed well, he'd throw a whole leg of meat into my cell and the guards wouldn't shove their torture sticks into my body, lighting me up with pain.

I always performed well. His pet monster.

I didn't know who he was, didn't know when I got here or who I was. It didn't matter. Drawing blood and ending lives mattered; they bought me food and a reprieve from the pain.

So I pressed harder on the fragile creature under me, not looking too closely at her face. She didn't look like an alpha, but some of them didn't. Some of them were like pretty dolls —too breakable for a place like this.

Noise roared. The watchers, screaming as the doll's death neared. I felt it, brushing my side like a familiar friend, and wished it would come to claim me, instead. To end this.

I didn't know how long I'd been here. How long I'd been killing. I only knew it never ended.

The doll gasped something, a word that had no meaning. I only knew the ones my master taught me; everything else was gibberish.

I looked at her and wished I hadn't, a blade of horror slicing through my chest. I tore my gaze away, my heart pounding. It didn't matter what she said or how she looked at me; she had to die. If she didn't, I would.

Her defiant gasps reached my ears, her lungs fighting for breath. It would be soon—her death.

Ruddy light flared along her pale arm, coming from dark marks tattooed on her forearm, but the crimson glow died in the next moment. I caught my breath. What *was* that? The light had touched my paw; had she infected me with venom?

"Enough," my master shouted, and I whipped my head around to growl at him. Enough? She was still alive. *"Enough,"* he repeated firmly. It was one of the few words I knew. "Back down, *all* of you."

I lifted my foot off the doll's chest, not sure why panic gripped my chest when she lay still. She didn't rise to fight me, didn't even roll her head to the side to look at me with that unnatural stare again—like she saw me and wasn't afraid. She should have been afraid; she was stupid not to be.

I flexed the paw her crimson light had touched, claws extending and retracting, and was surprised to find my fur and flesh the same. I was unhurt. What kind of alpha was she, to not fight at all? Her light should have crucified me. Instead, the pads of my paw tingled.

"Return," my master called, ignoring the disappointed noise from the watchers. I wanted to kill all of them, but I'd tried that nine times before and each one ended with me in my cell, the guards jabbing sticks into my body until magic erupted and I screamed.

So I only bared my teeth at them as I dragged myself back to the doorway and through it into my cell. My paw still tingling, I curled up on the pallet on the floor and waited for the next fight.

Maybe this one would finally put me out of my misery.

35

Halwen

a soft touch on my forehead roused me, and I jerked upright with a cry, remembering the emptiness in Emlyn's eyes, the pure murder on Kai's face, and Harvey—I didn't know what happened to him. What had *been done* to him.

"Get the fuck away from me," I snarled at Wynvail, my heartless mate leaning over me, brushing hair from my eyes.

"How do you feel?" he asked as if I hadn't spoken.

"Like I was just almost killed by my mates."

He sighed, sadness in his molten eyes, cut into his bronze face. I curled my aching hand into a fist and slammed it into that face, breaking his nose with a crunch of cartilage.

"How *dare* you?" I seethed, crawling off the bed and refusing to admit how wrecked and weak I was. "What's your game, Wynvail? Kill me and get rid of a mate you can't stand, or kill all my mates so their deaths break me? Enlighten me; I can't *wait* to hear this explanation."

A muscle ticked in his jaw, but he didn't rise from where he perched on the edge of the mattress I'd slept on, his short hair mussed and expression tight. Tired. "I thought—they'd see you and recover."

He dragged his hands through his hair, but they were a little too steady. His voice was a little too fake in its tremor.

"They're beasts; you *saw* them. There's nothing left of the men we knew. Nothing left of our family."

The words arrowed into my heart and carved a piece out. I bled, where no one could see. But I shook my head, a cruel smirk on my face, mostly encouraged by the pain ravaging my ribs and shoulder. I'd healed while I was passed out, enough to walk around without screaming in agony, but not much.

"The only issue with that, Wynvail," I replied tightly, my eyes glued to him, "is I don't buy it. Cut the crap. Tell me the truth; I'm a big girl, and I assure you I can handle it."

After being trampled by Harvey, choked by Em, and bruised by Kai in the fighting pit, there was nothing I couldn't handle.

Wynvail pinched the bridge of his nose to stem the flow of blood and cut a glare at me. "You can't even *pretend* to believe I have noble intentions?"

"No."

"Fine," he muttered, licking blood off his lips. "I hate them, and the feeling is mutual. I hated them a hundred years ago, and now they're mindless beasts? They're a nuisance. They're in the way of what I want."

My stomach plummeted when his gaze dragged to me. "They're my mates," I breathed, wanting to wrap my hands around his throat and suffocate him.

"Not if they're dead," he replied, tilting his head to watch me when I snarled. "Then, you'd be all mine."

"You're insane," I laughed, shaking my head and ignoring the flash of dizziness. "Killing them will kill me."

"Not necessarily," he disagreed. "You already died once; there's no telling the effect their deaths could have on you."

"So you thought you'd experiment with my life and sanity by throwing me into *a fighting pit* with them."

He shrugged. "I knew you'd be fine. I was watching you the whole time."

"There's something broken in you," I said, my lip curling in a sneer.

For a moment, something real slashed across Wynvail's face, like I'd hit a nerve.

"No doubt there is," he replied flippantly, the moment over.

"You shouldn't be able to tolerate seeing your mate hurt." I spat, my throat sore thanks to screaming as Harvey brutalised me with magic. Fuck, he'd never forgive himself when he realised what he'd done. "But you're fine with me being beaten as long as they die and you get to win? Am I even your mate, or your prized toy?"

He tilted his head, considering that. "Can't you be both?"

"I'm out of here," I hissed, heading for the open gate in the cell. Oh, how nice of him. He'd locked me up with the rest of the beasts down here.

"If you want them to survive," he called, halting me on the threshold, "you'll have to offer me something I want with equal measure."

A low, burning laugh caught in my throat as I turned back to him. Here we finally had the crux of the matter. I wasn't what he wanted; I was just a pawn, leverage to be used.

"Go on, then," I laughed, empty and joyless. "I'm sure you're dying to tell me what it is you really want."

Wynvail rose, his movements calculated and elegant but hiding so much power that, for a moment, it rippled through the tunnels and robbed my breath. I held still as he crossed the cell to me, brushing a knuckle over my jaw.

"Archdemons are harder to kill than regular demons, you know that."

I nodded tightly.

"They can be killed an infinite number of times, in many different ways, and as long as there's a tether to bring them back, they never truly die."

"Why are you telling me this?" I demanded, baring my teeth and tucking my black wings tight to my back. Instincts screamed that I was in danger, that I needed to *run*.

"It's incentive to return," he replied mildly, and I froze as he leant closer to kiss my cheek, his lips burning hot. "They've survived so much, your mates, but I know the ways they can be really, *truly* killed."

I inhaled sharply and jerked away. "Keep threatening my mates, and I'll find a way to really, truly kill *you*, asshole."

He grinned, true pleasure in his silver eyes. "I welcome the attempt."

"Just tell me what you want," I said through gritted teeth, retreating into the tunnel to escape the power and desire surrounding him like a dark miasma, threatening to pull me under.

"There's a tiara in the bowels of Lucifer's palace. It belonged to an ancient goddess and holds untold power."

"Forgive me if I don't want to give a total maniac untold power," I drawled, my heart pounding fast as I scanned the tunnel, weighing my chances of successfully escaping.

But I'd be leaving my mates here. To fuck knows how many more deaths. To unspeakable suffering. To whatever made Harvey a bestial shell of himself.

Wynvail shrugged and leant against the bars of my cell, looking like an arrogant, repugnant prince with his short chestnut hair and that cruel, devastating face. "It's your choice, of course. Just know you'll be leaving your mates with *a total maniac*. And I have very little patience and mercy."

"No shit," I said under my breath. My skin itched, the feeling of a trap closing around me. "What's this tiara look like?"

"Like a tiara," he replied flatly. "Pretty, with white and red gemstones, intricate silverwork—I'm sure you know what a tiara looks like."

"I'm sure the palace has more than one tiara," I threw back in the same heartless tone.

He sighed, but there was no hiding the heat of obsession on his face when he looked at me. "Most tiaras will be powerless; you'll know it when you find it."

Speaking of powerless...

With a tight smile I pointed out, "It'll look suspicious when I return without my bone pin."

Wynvail didn't miss a beat. "You're a resourceful woman. I'm sure you can come up with a clever explanation."

"I'll have to tell them everything I know about Alphaven," I told him, the conversation like a battle. The whole tunnel was silent, like the demons were afraid the apex predators would notice them. "I'm sure you understand."

"Of course. As long as you understand whoever comes to breach the city will die painfully." He gave me a faux-sad smile. "Their deaths will be on your head, honey."

My wings ruffled, giving away my anger. "If I get caught stealing from Lucifer, my death will be on *your* head."

"He'll exile you to the Damned Realm. Home sweet home."

I jerked toward him with a snarl, wrapping both hands around his throat and squeezing tight. Wynvail grinned, grabbing my waist and wrenching me close, our hips brushing so I could feel the hardness under his trousers.

Ugh, he loved this. I let go of him like I'd been burned.

"I'll get your tiara, but I have conditions."

"Don't murder your mates?" he asked dryly, reaching down to readjust himself in his pants.

"Don't hurt them *at all,*" I corrected, my voice biting. "If I find out anyone has touched them, I'll keep your damned tiara for myself."

He shrugged. "Then I'll keep your mates."

Bastard. I snapped my teeth at him. "Second condition. Whatever the fuck you did to them, undo it. Whatever made them..."

"Beasts?" he supplied.

"Yes," I spat.

"You did that, honey," Wynvail said, watching my face like he was delighted by my horror. "With you dead, and your mates returned to life so long before you—a mere five months after being shot—they went mad. Poor creatures. It must have been torture to know you were dead and they were returned to life. To feel the absence of you in their soul every day. To know you'd never come back because you're not an archdemon like them."

I wanted to carve Wynvail's heart out of his chest with my claws. But I was going to be sick, and suddenly all my anger drained, leaving something weak behind.

They were like that—mindless and feral—because I died?

"How do I fix them?" I asked, my voice raw.

Wynvail sighed and crossed the tunnel to me, sliding his hand along my jaw in a soft caress. But his voice was as sharp as a sword when he answered, "You can't. They're gone."

"You're lying," I snapped and shoved him away, not caring that his sharp fingernails opened lines of fire on my cheek. "You just want me to think that because you want them out of the picture."

"If that's what you need to think, honey," he agreed,

licking my blood off his claws. "Are those all your conditions?"

"When I bring you this tiara, you let us all go. Em, Kai, Harvey and me."

His silver eyes flashed, his expression tightening. "That was not our deal."

I knew he'd argue, but I had a quick response thought out already. "And here I thought you'd enjoy the hunt of finding me again."

A low sound rumbled in his chest. "And what prize do I get when I catch you again?"

"Your teeth punched out of your face."

He laughed abruptly, his head tipped back and the rich sound filling the tunnel.

"I'm serious," I growled.

"I hope so," he replied, dropping his head to stare at me. "You're delicious, Halwen, and even more so for being deadly and poisonous."

He took a predatory step towards me but I evaded him. "I don't think so. I want your promise—your word."

"My word counts for very little, as I'm sure you've realised."

I swallowed. I knew what I had to do, I just really, *really* didn't want to do it. But I couldn't see another way to make sure he didn't kill my other mates while I was gone. I needed a guarantee. So I surprised Wynvail by sliding closer to him, laying my hands flat on his stomach before I glided them down to his hips.

That low rumbling sound came from his chest again and he grabbed my ass, squeezing and grinding my hips into his as his mouth slammed down on mine.

Pretend, I ordered myself. *Make it convincing.*

But when he bit my bottom lip, drawing blood, and his tongue claimed my mouth, it was hard to pretend. A shudder chased cold through my body, but my pussy was red hot, pounding a frantic beat as Wynvail growled into my mouth and kissed me thoroughly. Blood coated my tongue and his, but it tasted like need and satisfaction.

He dragged his mouth from mine and grazed my jaw with his sharp teeth, breathing fast. "Take as many knives as you like, honey. If I get to kiss you like that each time, you can strip me of a hundred weapons."

Shit. I tore away from him with a knife in my hand, the blade feeling less like a prize now. He knew what I was doing; he *let* me kiss him. Even when I made the first move, I felt like a pawn in his game.

"I want a blood vow," I told him, clearing my throat when it came out husky.

"I thought you would," he agreed easily, holding out his arm as if a blood vow was nothing. As if it didn't lock both people into a promise until death.

I licked my dry lips, hating that I tasted blood, tasted *him.* Shuddering—definitely with revulsion—I slashed my forearm, and then Wynvail's, and fought back a shudder when his fingers intertwined with mine after zero prompting.

"I, Lord Wynvail Locke, vow no harm upon the mates of my mate, and upon receipt of a tiara, Emlyn, Malakai, and Harveil will be released from their cells." He met my hard gaze. "To whatever end."

I swallowed. What did that mean? "I, Halwen Vakhara, vow to retrieve the tiara from Lucifer's palace in return for my mates' freedom."

Wynvail grinned as power roped around our forearms, lashing them together for a long, long moment. It was barely visible as a shimmer of opalescence in the air, but it was as strong as steel rope. My stomach knotted, foreboding crawling down my spine.

"Shall we seal it with another blistering kiss?" Wynvail

asked, his molten eyes gleaming. "I think another will send me over the edge, I'm so fucking hard from the taste of you."

The second the magic released us, I tore my arm away. "Fuck you."

"Your body wants to," he taunted.

"It wants to kill you," I corrected in a snarl, scanning my arm. The vow was barely visible with the curse mark already on my forearm; there was just a cluster of promise dots above the moon at the centre of my tattoo.

"That's your mind, honey," Wynvail replied with a laugh, squeezing his cock through his trousers. "Your body wants something *very* different."

"I assure you, my body also wants to stab you in the eye."

"I'd fuck you better with a single eye than all those brutes put together."

I turned and stalked up the tunnel without bothering to reply. My whole body was on edge. Violence, bloodlust, terror, and explosive desire made me shaky.

Wynvail followed me like a shadow.

I flinched away from the thought, remembering the shadows wrapped around me when Locke killed us. Wynvail was broken and cruel now, but those shadows had been protective and kind—loving. Was this cruelty the start of his deterioration? Would I become a stranger to him, like I was to the others?

I was alive now, but what if it was too late to stop Wynvail's descent? What if there was no way to reverse the others' either?[1]

Wynvail didn't talk the whole walk down the tunnel, but he followed closely enough that I felt the heat and intensity of him against my wings. He only spoke when we reached the stairs back up to the house where I'd woken up, chained to an attic wall.

"Wait, Halwen."

I paused only because he didn't snarl the order and it felt more like a request. I watched, my arms crossed over my chest, as he ducked into a kitchen and retrieved—my swords. My heart stumbled; I snatched them out of his hands and held them to my chest.

"They mean so much to you," he observed, his eyes narrowed. Jealous.

"Yes," I bit out, driving them into their sheaths where they belonged. I felt better with their weight on me, like I was carrying my mates with me. I'd find a way to bring them back to themselves. As long as they were out of the cells, I'd find a way to reverse what my death did.

"I'm keeping the pin, though," Wynvail told me, remorseless. "And this is for luck."

I was too emotional to realise he'd sidled closer. His lips pressed to my forehead; I felt his smile against my skin.

I slammed a fist into his stomach, and when he doubled over with a grunt, I fled.

36

*P*aranoia burrowed under my skin and made me itchy as I strode down the tall, bright hallways of Lucifer's palace. I had every right to be here, but I was so scared someone would take one look at me and know *why* I was here.

I held my breath every time I rounded a corner, expecting cruel gods to throw Callahan or Cerny into my path. I didn't know how I'd explain losing the bone pin. I could get thrown in the dungeons for all I knew, and I didn't have that kind of time to waste.

My mates were suffering, traumatised and abused, forced into a fighting pit regularly. I needed to get them out of there. I'd figure everything else out when they were free. And fuck Wynvail. Just ... fuck that guy.

Your body wants to.

I shut out his words, struggling for breath as I walked deeper into the palace. I didn't know where to find an all-powerful tiara, but the vaults seemed like a good place to start. Thank fuck for Tali's guided tour; I sent a silent apology to my friend for abusing the information she gave me.

But this was for Kai, Em, and Harvey.

I inhaled sharply when images shattered through my mind; Em's feral eyes, the new scars on his bearded face; Kai's complete and utter lack of humanity, his hunger for my death; and Harvey, a beast of nightmares made of fur, claws, and teeth. The pain he'd inflicted on me...

I had to get them out of those damn tunnels. Had to get them somewhere safe.

I didn't know where we'd go, but getting out of Alphaven was more important. I'd figure everything else out later. At least we'd be alive, and together again.

"Hey," a male voice called from behind me, and my stomach turned over even if his tone was friendly, not furious. "You're Halwen, right?"

I turned slowly, dread blooming from my gut to the rest of my body. My hands shook as I assessed at the brown-haired, thirty-something man opposite me; I pressed them flat to my thighs.

"That's me," I confirmed, frowning. He didn't strike me as a threat, but appearances could be deceiving.

He pushed his glasses up his tanned nose and said, "I'm Russ; my brother, Cerny asked me to talk to you about—"

"Look, I'm really sorry, Russ, but I'm in a huge rush. Can we talk about this later? I'll be free in a couple hours."

When I'd be safely out of the palace.

"Uh, yeah sure." He frowned at me, his brown eyes pinching. "Are you okay? You look sick."

I gave him a thumbs up, because my awkwardness was at an all-time high.[1] "I'm great, thanks. See you later."

Ugh, gods smite me.

I turned and hurried away before Russ could question me further.

I wasn't great; I was cold and clammy and close to passing

out. But I wasn't about to tell a stranger that and rouse suspicion.

The vaults were next to the armoury where Renna had brought me to return my knives, but neither Renna nor Tali's tour had told me how to get *in*. I paced down the hallway, staring at the spot of solid, white brick where the vaults lay, and didn't know how the hell to open it. Where even was the door? It was just pure brick, no handle, nothing.

If I still had the pin, I had no doubt I'd be able to force my way in with brute power alone. But without it, all I could do was skim my hands over the wall in search of a seam.

"What are you doing?" a husky female voice made me jump.

I spun, my hand going to the hilt of a knife as awareness of being caught sent shivers down my arms.

Shit. Queen Lili stood there with her lips in a flat line and her eyes darting between me and the wall, like she knew exactly what I was doing.

"I'm lost," I blurted, dread crushing the air from my chest.

When her dark wings snapped tight to her back in clear disapproval, my stomach dropped hard. "No. You're not."

I shook, turning halfway to look at the wall. I needed to think fast or I was dead, Wynvail would win, and my mates' suffering would never end. I couldn't bear it, everything that was happening to them. The emptiness and harrowing rage in their eyes. There was nothing I wouldn't do to get them out of there.

"Renna told me to meet her here," I breathed, nowhere near strong enough to be believable. "She needs to give me something for my next job."

Lili took a slow step forward, her dress barely rustling, the expression on her face frozen with wrath. "Are you stealing from us, Halwen?"

"No," I argued, putting enough force into it that it *might* be believable. I backed up a step when she advanced, power bleeding into the air. It was enough power to make my bones ache and my skin tingle with warning.

I caught my breath, the aches in my body flaring a thousand times worse than when I'd woken in the cell with Wynvail.

"After we took you in and gave you a job, and a *home*. After we made you our friend and ally—you'd betray us like this? *For what?* Money? Status? To brag that you could break into Lucifer's vaults?"

"No!"

I trembled harder, the sensation of being caught, trapped making metal head spin. The emotion that had been ravaging me since I realised it was Emlyn who attacked me blazed through my chest, pressing against my weak spots. Everything that had happened in the last twenty-four hours was too much. It pressed on me until I felt something in my soul collapse.

I *needed* this damn tiara; without it, Wynvail would do fuck knows what to the others.

Lili advanced on me, and I was so busy falling apart I didn't get away in time. She grabbed my arm and dug her fingers in.

"You better start explaining yourself, Halwen, or I'll show you why I'm known as the Justice of Hell."

"I can't," I gasped. What would Wynvail do if he found out I told the queen of Hell about him? "I can't tell you why, but I *need* to get inside the vaults. *Please.*"

Lili shook her head, a glint of ruthlessness in her brown eyes. "Not good enough, Halwen."

"I found my mates!" I blurted.

Her pretty face swam as the pain in my ribs and shoulder flared, my soul copying the sudden surge with a sharp slice, making me gasp. A surge of cool shadow crashed through me in response, and it felt like worry, like blinding fear.

"They're captive," I went on breathlessly, her grip painful, "and I can only free them with a tiara in these vaults. *Please.* The psycho who has them will *kill them.* He's been torturing them for a hundred years and—and something's wrong with my mates."

A sob broke up my throat, and I lost complete control of my voice, my breathing. Tears blurred my vision until all I could see were smears of light.

"They attacked me. They shouldn't even be able to hurt me, but they wanted to *kill me.* Something broke them, and I don't even know if they can be saved, but I need—I need to try—"

I hated breaking down in front of other people, but I couldn't stop now I'd started. My chest collapsed with cries, my heart breaking out in the open for anyone to see.

"Which tiara?" Lili asked, releasing my wrist, a deeper frown blurring her golden face.

"I don't know, it used to belong to a goddess," I rasped.

Lili nodded and stepped around me, pressing her palm flat to the seamless wall. I wiped my eyes to see a ring on her finger glow faintly, like it was a key. Or maybe a master key for every door in the palace.

She didn't say anything else, silently ducking inside the room. Tall ceilings made her soft footsteps echo.

I pushed my way through the door as dread swelled to fill my chest. But my breath caught with a gasp of awe at the huge, golden shelves that spanned from the floor to three storeys high, filled with so many different things that I couldn't begin to imagine what they were.

Lili strode right for a glass cabinet, her skirts trailing on the ground. She was terrifying. Soft spoken, elegant, and kind, but terrifying. I hesitantly followed her past three dozen waist-high bookcases that bowed with the weight of globes, astrolabes, and objects of unknown power. I eyed the strange and varied collection like it would grow teeth and bite me. For all I knew, it would.

My heart slamming against my ribs, I kept a hand on my knife as Queen Lili opened the cabinet. I waited for the axe to fall. Would it be handcuffs? A cursed bracelet? A crown of rusty nails to punish me?

She was right; they'd taken me in and given me a home, given me kindness and friendship, and here I was driving a knife into their backs.

I turned for the door. What had I been thinking, following her in here? She had every right to murder me.

"Halwen." She stopped me before I could leave.

I swallowed the lump in my throat and turned, instinct burning at having my back to the most powerful woman in Hell. I jumped, what breath I had left abandoning me when I saw what she held out to me:

A tiara with glimmering white and red gems and beautiful, scrolling silverwork.

I swallowed, wiping tears from my cheeks and looking from the tiara to her face. "You know giving me that could put its power in the wrong hands, right?"

Oh, my voice was so not sexy. The word *clogged* came to mind.

Queen Lili crossed the room to me, nothing but understanding in her brown eyes. "I would burn down the whole world for my men. It probably makes me a bad person for putting them above everyone else, but I would. So go get your mates."

The metal was cold when she pressed the tiara into my numb hands, the pain ravaging my shoulder and soul easing, like the tiara's magic already seeped into me.

"Was it really owned by a goddess?" I whispered, my heartbeat loud.

Lili nodded, sweeping soft brown hair over her shoulder. "Eos. Lucifer's mother."

I blinked. Wait..."His mum's *a goddess?*"

"I know," Lili laughed, a smile rounding her cheeks. "Crazy, right?"

"Definitely," I agreed, staring at the tiara in my hand. The tiara that had been worn by a goddess and had her power still within it.

The thought of Wynvail having all that power made me sick. He already had the bone pin, and control over demons. What would he do with this? Something far worse than fighting pits and tunnels full of prisoners forced to fight.

"Do you need anything else to free your mates?" Lili asked, nothing but understanding in her husky voice. She looked one move away from pulling me into a hug.

I turned the tiara over in my hands and swallowed. I had an idea—a very stupid, reckless, suicidal idea.

"Actually," I replied, "I need one more thing."

37

*T*his time, I approached Alphaven with so much steel and iron on my body that I rattled with every step. I didn't crouch in the trees to scope out the road into the city; I blew into the place like a storm and snarled at anyone who got in my way.

"Well, well," a sneering voice remarked as I strode up the road, fixed on the giant fire burning in the middle of the fighting pit until four people stepped into my path. "Look who's back."

The raiders who grabbed me the last time I was here crowded around me, obviously thinking they could cage or intimidate me. I didn't bother with conversation; my heart had slowed to a sluggish beat and a cold, brutal calm filled me. It had been a long, long time since I'd felt this lethal calm.

By the time the raiders reacted to me drawing my beloved blades, I'd slashed the throats of two of them and buried a dagger in the stomach of a third, leaving them to a painful death. The fourth—the biggest, smartest one—stumbled back, but I slammed a dagger back into its sheath and grabbed him.

"Take me to Wynvail."

"And you won't kill me?" he asked.

Yeah, something like that.

I kept my other dagger as an incentive for him not to piss me off, but the ice cold wrath in my expression must have been enough because he didn't even look at me. He scurried quickly across the city, leading me through the warren of streets, past houses too intact, too perfect to show the rotting underbelly of Alphaven.

A rotten core my own mate was responsible for.

I was starting to think whoever had cursed my memories had been doing me a favour.

"Thanks," I told the raider when he led me to the door I'd fled eight hours ago. I'd have been back faster if the cloud cover hadn't fucked with my visibility in the skies. I'd had to *walk,* and I wasn't happy about it.

I slashed my knife at his throat, fully meaning to kill this asshole too, but he dodged the move like he'd been expecting it. Without looking back, he sprinted away, kicking up a cloud of dust on the dirt road.

I shrugged. I'd let him live; with any luck, he'd live in terror for the rest of his life. Serves him right for working for a twisted psychopath like Wynvail.

I adjusted my grip on my dagger, reached for my blood magic—swearing when I failed to grasp it—and then kicked in the front door with my heavy boots.

"Hey, asshole, I'm back!"

WYNVAIL WAITED for me in the kitchen. He didn't get up from his seat at the table when I crashed through the door or stalked down the hallway. Cold spread deeper through me, icing my emotions until every part of me felt sharp like broken ice. With mechanical movements, I swapped my volcanic dagger for a regular blade.

The little smirk on his face made me want to slam my knuckles into his nose and draw blood, but I locked down that rage and just stared at him. He stared back with unflinching silver eyes, cocking his chin in invitation.

"Take a seat," he ordered, that smirk growing.

My expression went flat. There was only one chair and he was sitting in it. All the others had been removed; he'd planned this.

I wasn't about to drop onto his lap, so I gave him a psycho, little smile that should have made him piss himself in fear, and stalked to the countertop by the small window, hoisting myself up.

I swung my feet back and forth, satisfaction beating in my heart when a vein throbbed in Wynvail's bronze forehead.

"So you failed," he said after a long pause, his fingers knitted together on the tabletop, knuckles white. His irritation threatened to show. It seemed he was trying to get a rise out of me, and my icy calm was driving him mad. Good. "You didn't bring me the tiara."

I tilted my head, assessing him with a cold gaze. "I'll give it to you when you release my mates. That was our deal."

His smile was sudden and as sharp as a razor's edge. "Why would I free them without evidence?"

I didn't look away from his cruel, sharp-planed face as I reached into the leather satchel at my waist and pulled out the tiara. I settled it on my head, inhaling a sharp breath like I had when I first touched the bone pin. My hands visibly shook; I curled them into fists.

"Its power corrupts," Wynvail said, rising from his seat like a predator marking its prey. "It takes over its host entirely, until they're nothing but mindless magic."

He drew closer, hands gliding up the outside of my thighs until I jumped, my heart slamming fast. "How does it feel, honey? To hold unlimited power?"

That was as good a time as any to drive my dagger all the way through his shoulder. It took more force than I expected to bury it deep, like I punched through a shield as well as skin.

Wynvail cried out in pain, staggering back in surprise. Nostrils flaring, his face frozen with rage, he lifted his hand where blood poured freely from his shoulder. It darkened his white shirt, ruining the fabric. *Aww, so sad.*

"Like I said. Release my mates."

Wynvail stared at me with an intensity that shared me, his chest rising and falling fast. Like he wanted to own me, *devour* me. "I could slit your throat and rip that tiara off your head right now."

I bared my teeth in a smile. "So do it."

His eyes flicked up to the tiara, burning bright silver, and returned to my face. His stare lingered dangerously on my mouth. "I'll return your mates to you."

My heart pounded faster. I couldn't let my relief show.

He grabbed my chin in a vicious grip and tilted my head up while I shook, overcome with power. "They're waiting in the pit. But I warn you, Halwen, they're wild beasts. If I release them, they might kill you."

They're my mates; they can't kill me. Unless they were too far gone to even feel our bond...

"Maybe they'll kill you instead," I replied, matching his viciousness. I wrapped my fingers around the knife's hilt and tore it free; he drew back with a hiss but there was no concealing the obsession in his eyes.

His smirk hooked deeper. "I can't wait to watch them tear you apart."

"Likewise," I spat, and shoved him away so I could jump down from the counter. "I'll meet you at the pit. No fucking way am I walking those tunnels with you again."

He laughed, standing in the kitchen like a god, unaffected by the blood pouring from him.

"Brave of you to turn your back on me," he taunted when I stormed from the room, ripping the tiara from my head, "when I want to break you so badly."

"As if you could," I threw over my shoulder, crushing the terror that tried to form in my gut. He wanted me alive for whatever reason. He'd have killed me already if he didn't.

I shoved the front door open—and sucked in a sharp breath, stumbling into the wall when a long, carnal touch stroked down my soul.

Fuck, was that—?

Wynvail's low laugh behind me confirmed it.

Oh, gods.

I knew he was my mate all along; everything about his story made too much sense, and felt *right,* but I didn't want to believe it.

I'd hoped I was wrong.

"Safe flight, honey," he called from behind me.

I scrubbed a hand down my face and pulled myself back together, but it was impossible to grasp the emotionless ice from before. My temper was too hot, emotions too fiery. I grabbed a throwing knife and spun, judging his location by the sound of his voice.

I grinned when it sank into his existing wound. I might have been dead for a hundred years, but I was still a damn good shot.

Wynvail grunted, his eyes flashing. But he pulled the

knife from his shoulder and ran his tongue along the blade suggestively.

"I can almost taste your fingerprints," he purred.

"I hope you die in the tunnels," I spat, and kicked off the ground, pumping my wings to carry me across the city.

Something was going to go wrong. I could sense it, warning prickling my skin even though I had the tiara safely stashed in my bag. The feeling grew, throbbing behind my skull, instincts *screaming* at me to turn back, to run, to—to find something. *Find what?*

The feeling grew, making my heart race and sweat prick my palms. I was missing something, and I didn't know what. And the longer I ignored that gnawing sense, the bigger it grew.

I needed the icy calm back, but I struggled to grasp even *regular* calm as I raced across rooftops, weaving in a manic path to the open-roofed arena at the heart of the city. The bonfire blazed high enough to leave scorch marks on the highest edges of the roof; I avoided them as I flew closer.

I was so focused on the flames, I didn't see the arrows firing right at me until one lanced through my wing. I screamed, a mingled sound of pain and fury that made my throat hoarse. Another arrow tore my shoulder apart when I tried to twist out of its path, and a third slashed a burning line across my chest.

I filled my lungs with air and did the most reasonable thing a person could do when they'd been impaled by three arrows. I threw my head back and bellowed, *"Cock-sucking motherfuckers!"*

My wing was pierced. The dishonourable bastards had *shot my wing.* My breath shattered in panic when my next wingbeat faltered, too much pain slicing through the delicate membrane beneath my feathers.

"No," I whispered, trying to catch enough air to slow my descent, but the sky tore at me as I plummeted.

I flung my arms out, as if they could stop my fall, but they were useless. I plummeted straight through the fire, screams bruising my throat. It took me a long, terrifying moment to realise they didn't burn my skin, didn't make my flesh bubble and melt. Oh.

I caught my breath, snapping out my good wing to gain some control of the descent, but I was *far* closer to the ground than I realised. I only had two seconds to twist my body so I landed on my shoulder and not my face.

When I slammed into the fighting pit, a piercing scream ripped up my throat, sounding utterly foreign. The arrow in my wing had torn on a jagged angle, and the one in my shoulder pushed deeper.

"Ouch," a smooth voice remarked high above me. "That looks painful, honey."

I snarled, trying to push to my feet.[1] "I'm going to kill you."

"I look forward to it," Wynvail replied. "Bring me her bag."

Hands reached for my bag and snapped the strap; I kicked out, but my leg was too weak to land a blow.

I took a tight, stabbing breath and shoved my body off the floor, baring my teeth at the pale-skinned demon who crossed the arena to give my bag to Wynvail who ... *fuck,* who sat on a throne like a dark king.

I wanted to cry. Instead, I panted for breath and summoned a sneering laugh from beneath my pain.

"Who do you think you are, Wynvail? You're *nothing.* Nobody. The son of a dirty politician that no one knows anymore. You look—ridiculous on that throne."

I panted by the time I finished talking, but it was worth it for the dark, livid expression on his bronze face—and for the way someone snorted in the crowd.[2]

"Hold her down," the psychopath snapped at the pale guy

who'd stolen my bag. Oh, no, wait, there were three more of them. Quadruplets? They all had the same damn face. "I want her forced still for this punishment."

He rifled through my bag as his eerie goons came for me. I was forced to drag my stare away from the cruel bastard to defend myself. No way would I let them grab me and hold me down for—what? What would Wynvail *do*? Were there any lengths he wouldn't go to? Any lines he wouldn't cross?

A hush went through the audience, and for a moment I thought it was because the bastards had reached me, but from the corner of my eye I watched Wynvail raise the tiara to his head.

"I'm not sure it's your style," I remarked breathlessly, and slid a knife from my leather trousers, jamming it into my pale assailant's throat before his hands could touch me.

Shit! He landed *on* me, blood pumping hot from his throat until I was drenched. I was too weak, pain scorching through all the places I'd been shot, to push him off.

"Did I say you could touch her?" Wynvail asked in a calm, still voice. It was the sort of quiet rage that carried across an entire arena.

A sudden rush of movement to my right preceded the dead man being hauled off my bleeding body. I groaned, arrows shifting in my flesh.

My abhorrent mate paused above me, seeing the dagger in his goon's throat, realising I'd been buried under dead weight. He stared at the pale man with such hatred, his chest rising and falling, like he wanted to reanimate him so he could kill him himself. "She's *mine*."

Wynvail tossed the man aside and reached for me.

I reacted on instinct, throwing my palms out, sweat dripping down the side of my neck and temple. A deep crimson light exploded from the tattoo on my arm, glowing through my jacket and lighting up my hateful mate in shades of blood and violence.

The formerly hushed crowd erupted into sudden noise, and I flinched, stroking my head against the floor.

Cursed One...

She's cursed...

Cursed marks...

She'll kill us all...

Great, these bastards knew me as well as Bevan and his little band.

Even Wynvail staggered back, staring at me like he'd never seen me before. "You..."

"Me," I agreed with a grin that was—easier to fake. Huh? What happened to my agony?

I wasn't sticking around to find out answers. I vaulted off the floor and drew a dagger, driving it into Wynvail's unmarked shoulder. *Might as well make them matchy matchy.* I gouged a nice, deep line before tearing the blade out and plunging it under the ribs of another pale bastard when he lunged at me. The tip pierced his heart; I watched the light leave his eyes.

"I suppose I should be grateful you didn't stab *me* in the heart," Wynvail mused, his arms locking around me from behind. Shit, how did he sneak up on me?

I kicked off the floor, throwing all my weight into him to dislodge his grip. It didn't work. *Fuck.*

"I should warn you," he said, lips brushing my ear in a warm caress that made my toes curl. "Physical combat turns me on."

I turned my shudder into one of revulsion. "Gross."

He laughed, breath tickling my ear. "You *ache* for me, don't you, honey? You need this cock stretching you out, filling you up with every inch of me. I can feel your need, throbbing in your soul. Does your cunt throb, too?"

I gritted my teeth and stretched my arm down, panting fast as I reached for a concealed knife. The second my fingers connected, I drove it into his thigh and—felt his cock throb against my ass. Shit, fighting really did turn him on. Injuring him earlier had been little more than foreplay.

"Let me go," I hissed when he dragged his teeth up the line of my throat, his tongue hot and wet on my skin. Everything tightened inside me, my clit pulsing even though I was so close to being murdered by him.

"Give me one good reason I shouldn't thrown you down on the floor and fuck you in front of all these people. I could make you scream my name, Halwen. I could make you come harder than you ever have, until the only cock your body craves is mine, until you exist only for the pleasure *I* can give you."

Cool fingers stroked my wing, grasping the arrow piercing it and tearing it free.

I screamed so loudly it echoed around the arena. His cock jerked madly against my ass.

But both my cursed marks flashed red, burying my pain until I had enough strength to elbow Wynvail in the gut and hurl myself out of his arms. I could barely breathe.

I brought my knife up to kill the remaining pale demons but—they were already dead. Their eyes were nothing more than burned red sockets, mouths hanging open in pain. Had he done that ... or had my curse?

"I'd rather die than touch you," I hissed at Wynvail, turning to face him, my heart pounding at the predatory, intense way he watched me. I clenched my jaw, panting, and tore out another arrow before he could do it himself.

"Gods, I love the way you fight me," Wynvail groaned, a bright fanaticism on his face as he pulled out the knife in his thigh and tucked it into his pocket, blood spurting to the ground. "Will you fight me when I'm buried in that sweet, aching cunt? Fuck, I hope so."

"Where are my mates?" I snarled, the back of my neck burning as the crowd stared at me. I reached for the last arrow and yanked it free. The magic in my curse marks soothed the pain as soon as they were out.

"I'm the only mate you'll ever need," he replied, but there was a bite in his voice and his face tightened. He was angry that I had other mates?

"Where are they?" I demanded, my nostrils flaring. "That was our deal. You release them if I bring you the tiara."

He tilted his head, observing me in a way that made my skin crawl. "Kneel, and I will."

My breath stuttered. I glanced at our audience, and quickly looked away from the hunger in their faces. They didn't chant for Wynvail to kill me, but I could see the desire for blood in their eyes.

"What?" I breathed.

"You heard me," Wynvail replied, a smirk on his cruel mouth. "Kneel."

I licked my dry lips. My heart thumped so hard I felt each beat through my body and—no, that wasn't my heart. That was *magic*. It pulsed in time with the glow in my curse marks.

"Kneel before your master," Wynvail purred.

I gave him the middle finger, and focused on that ebb and flow of power, my breath syncing with the magic. Five answering thumps went through my blood, shocking my soul with power and—life.

I jolted back a step, magic unlocking inside me that had no right to be there. I didn't have the pin, and my blood power was locked down, cursed away, so—where the *fuck* was this magic coming from?

Wynvail laughed, strolling towards me, covered in blood. "Well, isn't that interesting?"

"Fuck you," I hissed, keeping my eyes on his face as I grasped that power. What the hell was happening?

Rage filled my soul, blisteringly hot; I flinched away from the sudden intensity. I felt clawed hands curl around cold iron bars, and a muscular shoulder slam into a cell wall, and invisible snakes coil protectively around frail shoulders, and a body curl into a tight wall, fresh cuts throbbing on an arm already littered with scars, and cold, cutting rage swell to fill a chest as—as Wynvail stalked closer to me.

Shit! I twisted aside, throwing up my glowing arm to ward him off, but he only grinned.

"That won't hurt me, Halwen. You can't harm your mate."

"You can't harm me either, then," I panted, the ache that had bruised my soul ever since I climbed out of a grave growing viciously, making my legs buckle.

Wynvail made a contemplative noise, his boots stopping in front of me as I bent over myself. "I suppose I can harm you, but not kill you. The same goes for you killing me."

I made a throaty sound, my curse marks pulsing faster, the light casting further. I could feel the cold bite of cells, feel the strength of stone walls, the suffocation of being trapped, always trapped.

"I don't need to kill you," I breathed to Wynvail, wrapping fingers around those bars like they were my own. Magic throbbed faster, power sinking through my fingers into iron. It made no sense, but I wasn't about to question how the curse mark's power travelled down my soul to my mates.

"*They* can kill you," I rasped, and felt the bars collapse—not just in my mates' cells but *every* cell under Alphaven.

"What did you do?" Wynvail demanded, grabbing my arms and dragging me to him.

I grinned, snapping my teeth at his face as alphas and beasts burst through the tunnels into the arena. "Your move, *honey,*"

38

*M*y victory was undermined by the pain that ravaged my chest and weakened my legs, but it was satisfying to watch the blood drain from Wynvail's face.

"They'll kill you, too," he hissed, already storming away, leaving me to the mercy of alpha beasts.

I gave his retreating form my middle finger. "Coward!"

He spun with a hiss, teeth bared, ruining his smug, aristocratic mask. He opened his mouth to retort, but his attention caught on something behind me and panic widened his eyes.

I spun, throwing my hands out in front of myself, not sure how to wield the power of my curse marks. But I had no doubt this glow was magical. The curse had blocked my blood power, but there was no way I'd be able to unlock all the cells without magic.

Who the fuck cursed me?

"Shit," I gasped when I spotted the giant running straight at me, his meaty fists outstretched like he was going to grab me up.[1]

He wasn't deterred by my curse marks, but the next crea-

ture—a snarl of shadows, black fur, and vicious teeth—
flinched away when the light spilled over him.

"Harvey," I breathed.

He didn't even look at me.

"We're getting out of here, Buttercup," I told him,
shrieking as I threw myself out of the path of the giant's hairy
hand before it could crush my bones. Harvey paused at the
sound, his head tilted.

"This way," I yelled over the sudden snarls, growls, and
roars filling the arena. A muscular body jostled me; a huge
woman with tusks shoved me aside. I kept my eyes on Harvey
the whole time, not letting my heart sink at his lack of recog-
nition. "Where are the others? *Harvey!*" I shouted when he
stalked away from me.

He didn't know his own name. A lump rose in my
throat.

"Stop!" Wynvail yelled from above. He must have made it
into the stands without being murdered. Fucking pity. "All of
you, *enough!*"

A bull-demon beside me chuffed viciously through his
nose. I didn't think he thought it was enough; quite the
opposite.

Someone else shoved past me, knocking my shoulder so
hard I went flying to the ground, pain cracking up my wrists
as I landed awkwardly. Shit, I was gonna get trampled down
here.

"Get up, Halwen!" Wynvail roared, a sudden yank on my
soul making me gasp. "I want to kill you myself, not watch
you get murdered in a stampede."

My heart skittered. The crimson glow of my curses illumi-
nated boots, bare feet, and hooves, all running frantically,
coming too damn close to my face.

When a shapely leg landed beside me, I used it as a
crutch to heave myself back to my feet—and came face to

face with Kai's livid face, his nostrils flaring and crimson eyes bright with murder.

"There you are," I sighed, grabbing his shoulder to keep him from running off.

He stared at my arm, and inhaled a sharp breath when he saw my curse marks. "Yeah, this is a whole thing."

For a moment I thought he recognised me and he was worried because his mate was cursed, but the next moment he tried to wrench himself out of my grip, his invisible snakes brushing over my skin with a mix of sparkling pain and soft familiarity. Kai didn't recognise me, but he was *afraid* of me.

"Stop fighting," I barked, hauling him away from a sudden brawl, blood spraying the air. "I'm trying to rescue you, you difficult fucking damsel."

He bared sharp fangs.

"Yeah, yeah, whatever," I muttered, scanning the melee for Harvey and finding him on all fours not too far away, snarling in the face of any alpha that came too near to him. "Harvey! *Hey!* Fucker!"

I swallowed down the lump of emotion in my throat when he didn't even look my way. He really didn't remember me at all.

None of them did.

"Well, I remember *you,* you bastards," I snarled, and dropped my arm to Kai's hand, linking our fingers to haul him across the arena to Harvey, craning my neck for Em's broad-shouldered frame and salt-and-pepper hair. "And I'm not leaving you here to Wynvail's mercy."

Kai's snakes tried to harm me and failed. He hissed, deep and throaty at my touch.

"Yeah," I agreed. "Wynvail needs to suffer. But not now; we need to get out of here."

He threw me a wary look, trying to extricate himself from my grip and failing. *Nice try, buddy, I'm as clingy as an octopus.*

"Em!" I screamed, finally spotting him rolling on the floor, knocking ten lumps out of a demon that looked like a gorilla.

It was bizarre to see my quiet, introverted gentle giant fighting like a wild animal. His anxiety must have been going crazy right now. I reached for him in the bond and—found nothing but shreds of our tether. Pain cracked through my middle.

"Stop!" Wynvail boomed again, some of the alphas responding with snarls but others pausing with their fists and paws frozen.

I shoved past them, hauling Kai with me, and grabbing Em's shoulder. When he growled in my face, I bared my teeth and growled right back, my wings ruffling and giving away my nerves.

"You need to come with me. We'll be safe."

Em pulled away, using his superior strength, but Kai let out a foreboding hiss and Em's blue gaze snapped to me, finding the curse mark on my arm. Were they ... communicating?

My bottom lip wobbled, but I shoved the vulnerability behind an iron wall. I didn't have time for it, even if I was *so damn relieved* they could talk to each other, that they might have been together all this time, as our family—not alone in their cells.

"We need Harvey," I shouted over the noise, surprised Emlyn wasn't running anymore. I grabbed him again, just in case he got any other ideas. "Harvey!"

Wynvail's laugh had me turning, my breath catching in my throat. He ruled over the chaos and violence like this had been his grand plan all along, a smirk on his gloriously arrogant face.

I tried to connect with the ruddy power in my curse marks, to push it out towards Harvey. It had worked once; it had to work again.

I staggered as a heavy boot slammed into my stomach, rearing back to crunch something in my chest, then drive into my face until my nose broke and blood flowed. Every hit made my head spin, my body throbbing and howling.

I stumbled where I stood, my knees buckling, but a hand tightened around mine, ripping me out of the vision.

"Harvey's in trouble," I breathed, which was such a familiar statement that I nearly sobbed.

I wrinkled my nose and found it unbroken, not bloody. Not mine, then. Harvey's.

I wish the wounds were dealt to me. My chest cinched tight at the realisation he was being beaten at this very moment.

Emlyn rumbled something in my direction, his brow low over his eyes and gaze darting to my forearm, then to where I touched him, and back to my face.

"This way," I barked, tucking my wings in tight and towing both my mates across the arena.

The handy thing about them being mindlessly violent was they punched everyone out of our path. The less handy thing was they kept trying to escape from me, and they looked at me like I was a bigger monster than the man with lobster claws for arms and crab legs. He scuttled sideways to escape a wolfy woman; actually, it was kind of cute.

Em grabbed a winged demon that looked shockingly like me and—and tore her wings off before casting her side like she was rubbish. Phantom pain sliced down my back, stealing a gasp.

"He's this way; I can feel it," I breathed, which was useless to them, so I tugged Kai and Emlyn left. They moved like obedient horses under my reins, but I knew it was because they were afraid of my glowing arm and not because they remembered and trusted me.

Fuck, how was I going to get their memories back? I didn't

care if they stayed like this, driven by base instinct instead of rational thought, but I needed them to *remember* me. If I had to live as a stranger to them for the rest of my life, it would kill me.

I gasped when an elbow jammed into my throat, my steps stumbling as I fought for breath. Mother*fucker,* that hurt.

"Careful, Halwen," Wynvail barked—closer but still in the seats ringing the arena. Fucking coward.

"Fuck you," I shouted back. Oh no, my voice was hoarse and low. My voice better not be forever changed.

Emlyn rumbled his agreement. He might not have known his name or who I was to him, but he certainly seemed to understand the sentiment of *fuck you.*

A cruel smile lifted my lips when Kai's snakes tore into the man who elbowed me, dropping him so fast he didn't even scream.

Hope isn't dead, I promised myself, forging on through the violence around us. *I'll get them back. I just have to get out of this place first.*

Wynvail had his damn tiara. He was vow-bound to let us go. It wasn't my fault if he didn't realise I'd faked the whole *overcome by uncontrollable power* thing. He'd bound me to fetch him *a* tiara. So, I had.

A sudden stench of sulphur and brimstone made me recoil on my next step. Lucifer, someone *stank.* Please don't let it be Harvey...

The first thing I'd do when we were safe would be find a bath if that gross smell was coming from—oh, thank fuck, it was coming from the gorilla he fought.

Well, the gorilla currently turning him into mincemeat.

The growl that burst up my throat was deep and furious and not entirely under my control. Instincts buried for a hundred years erupted.

"Stay here," I ordered Kai and Em, not expecting them to listen.[2]

"Hey, asshole!" I roared at the huge black gorilla, charging right at him and drawing my long daggers in each hand.

He—I presumed the beast was a *he* because of the giant balls dangling between his legs—didn't blink at the blades, but his attention caught on the red light coming from my arm.

"What the hell are you?" he demanded, shocking the hell out of me.

"Holy fuck, you can talk."

He bared his teeth in a blunt grin. "I'm new here."

So the longer you stayed, the more of yourself you lost. And my mates had been here for a hundred years. *Gods.*

"Good for you, buddy." I jumped between him and Harvey, ignoring my mate's low complaint, probably at my proximity. "You're beating the shit out of my mate."

"He started it. He grabbed me and punched my nose.

To be fair, that did sound like Harvey.

"Find another punching bag," I replied, a hard edge to my voice.

"I like the one I've got, thanks," the gorilla replied, matching my tone.

I sighed. Here I was thinking it would be easy.

"Dakarh," Wynvail yelled from the crowd.

"Oh, fuck off," I shouted back without looking at him, hoping it pissed him off. I wasn't connected to him beyond that first flash of emotion so I couldn't know for sure.

"Kill the monster and I'll reward you," he told Dakar. Whoever Dakar was.

"He's not a fucking monster," I snarled, turning despite myself to bare threatening teeth at my evil mate. "You're the only monster here, Wynvail."

He shrugged, standing at the edge of the seats in a dusty

suit, his eyes fixed on me and gleaming molten silver. Harvey's eyes.

You have two Locke brothers as your mates.

I wished he wasn't my mate and felt sick for the wish. I *wanted* to love him, wanted him to love me back, but whatever memories I had of our epic love were gone. All I knew was the cruel, heartless man I wanted to stab in both eyes.[3]

Harvey sucked in a short, pained breath, and I knew his ribs were at least bruised, probably broken. I twirled my knives to warn the gorilla off, refusing to let anyone close. When Emlyn and Kai slunk closer, their eyes full of violence, my stomach flipped. But they only protected Harvey's vulnerable back.

They knew him, and still acted like a family unit. I swallowed the lump in my throat, and slashed at the gorilla when he dove at me with a low, warning sound. Wait, should gorillas have had seven-inch claws? And fangs that were half the size of my arm? Those hadn't been there before; now he spoke with a lisp.

"Nothing personal, sweetheart."

I stabbed him for that remark, more because it was cliché and clichés pissed me off than any offence caused. Also, he left his left side right open, swinging his arms around like that; it was his fault I stabbed him, really.

The roar he let out when I tore my dagger out of his body made my ears ache. I winced through the discomfort and followed up the first cut with a second and third, my training kicking in. It was as if I hadn't been rotting underground for a century.

Harvey let out a pitiful sound on the ground, wheezing with each breath.

"Stay down," I barked at him, distracted long enough for the gorilla to get a solid, blunt blow against my jaw. "Bastard!"

"Like I said," he grunted, intelligent eyes following my

movements, "it's nothing personal, but I need to kill that thing behind you."

Thing?

All my anger stilled. Froze over. It drowned out everything except the whoosh of blood in my ears. The red glow splashed higher on my arm as I dove at the gorilla—apparently Dakarh—driving the full force of my strength into the blow. My body might have been aching, but rage gifted me strength.

I kicked off the concrete floor and slammed my wings up and down, jumping above the gorilla and driving a long dagger straight down.

I missed. Shit, how did I miss?

"Another! Don't let her leave me," Wynvail yelled, his voice reaching right into my chest and gouging my heart.

Heat and fire flashed through my wings, and I caught my breath, losing height. What the fuck? I twisted, scanning my dark feathers until—a wooden shaft stuck out of my tender membrane. I'd been shot again.

Son of a bitch!

I gritted my teeth, a sound of deep, unyielding rage building in my throat as I snapped my wings open, clawing my way higher.

"Up here, asshole," I panted at Dakarh.

He laughed, dismissive of the half-angel demon flying around his head, refocusing his attention on Harvey. *Big mistake.* I didn't miss this time; I gripped the pink hilt of my dagger and drove the wavy blade through his hairy skull until it met his chin and forced its gruesome way out.

No one screamed or raced towards him. No one mourned him at all, and instead of satisfaction, sadness filled my chest when I landed unsteadily.

"Watch my back," I breathed to Em and Kai, hating that

the familiarity and camaraderie between us was ruined. But as long as we were alive, we could rebuild it.

I sawed at the wooden arrow in my wing and ripped it out, beyond glad I hadn't been shot *twice* despite Wynvail's barked command. That fucking bastard. What was I supposed to do with a mate I hated, who wanted me dead every bit as much as I wanted to kill him? I threw the arrow aside, blood spilling down my feathers.

"Come on," I gasped, ignoring the rough pants of my own breathing and focusing on Harvey's rough, wheezing breaths as I sheathed my knives. I bent and grabbed him under his shoulders, trying to heave him up. I couldn't do anything for his injuries here, but if I got him somewhere safe he could heal them himself.

I'd have struggled to lift him in his other form, but his beast was even more muscular and damned heavy. I couldn't pick him up. I couldn't get him out. All of this was for *nothing* because there was no way I could leave him behind, even to get Em and Kai to safety. A sob escaped my clenched teeth.

A sudden growl made me flinch; my hands were knocked away.

My vision wavered in shades of blood red, and suddenly I was staring at myself with narrowed eyes, confusion and unease beating against my chest.

I staggered back when the vision released me, knocked aside when Emlyn scooped Harvey into his arms.

Either my mates realised I was their ticket to freedom, or they were just too afraid to go against me. Whichever way, I was so fucking relieved when Em picked up Harvey, both of us glancing up at the open sky at the same time.

"Stay with me," I pleaded, hoping he understood, hoping he'd listen, but holding absolutely no hope. His eyes darted to the curse mark on my forearm and he swallowed.

"There's nowhere you can go that I won't find you,"

Wynvail shouted from the stands, leaning against the barrier with the tiara clenched in his fist. Judging by the rage on his face, he'd figured out it was a fake. "Do you hear me, Halwen? You are *mine*. You don't get to leave. Launa, get them! Don't let her escape!"

"Shit," I hissed, and reached for Kai, gritting my teeth against the sharp lance of pain through my bloody wing when I moved.

I didn't know what attack would come next—more arrows? another ferocious beast?—but I braced for pain as I wrapped my arms around Kai, my contrary mate already struggling to free himself. He hissed, eyes flashing and magic twisting in tattooed text around his throat.

"Stay still, or I'll drop you to your death," I snapped at him, tightening my arms and exchanging a glance with Em— who was already in the air, flying away with Harvey.

Fuck, *fuck*. So much for us being a family unit; they'd straight up abandoned Malakai.

"Stop fighting," I growled at Kai, unable to take off with him wriggling and hissing.

Fuck it.

I slammed my mouth into his and kissed him hard, willing him to *remember* with every press of my lips. He parted his mouth to hiss at me, and I jumped at the vicious zap of his snakes as he wrapped them around me, constricting my chest, shocking sparks into my tongue. I kissed him deeper, forcing Kai into submission, and leant into his magic's touch as if it was pleasure and not sharp, biting pain.

I missed you so much.

When I drew back, his ruby eyes were wide, stunned. Good. That was all the distraction I needed to kick off the ground and pump my wings in a rapid beat, catching enough air to shoot a few feet into the air, then more, and more.

My nostrils flared as wicked-edged shards of pain travelled down my nerves, cutting through muscle and membrane until I was gasping with every wingbeat. Kai hung limply in my hold, not fighting but not helping me carry him either. Couldn't he use his snakes to make a damn sail? *Anything* to catch the air and help us fly faster.

"Good luck finding safety," Wynvail shouted as we passed him, his voice carrying easily. Wicked cleverness filled his tone, along with something cruelly amused. "You're cursed to kill each other, Halwen, and if my calculations aren't wrong, you only have thirty days of mated bliss before you all murder each other."

He paused, enjoying my gasp, watching my wings falter for a moment before I flew faster, dragging my body and Kai's through the air. A low growl of pain shook my throat, the sound constant.

"Of course, mated bliss will be difficult when they don't even know your name," he added, wholly unnecessarily. "But you don't need them when you have me. I'm all you need."

I didn't have any breath to spare on calling him delusional, so I just panted and slammed my aching, bleeding wings through the air, hauling us higher. I avoided the fire as much as I could, but its heat licked my skin like a threat.

Kai dragged in a sudden breath, his arms latching around my middle when we reached the top of the arena.

"Oh yeah, vicious fear of heights," I gasped out, wasting air I didn't have to spare.

I groaned, forcing my wings to keep flapping, Kai's body so heavy in my lead-weight arms that I came dangerously close to dropping him. But now he held me back, and it was enough for me to carry us out the open roof and down to the other side of the arena.

I stumbled when my feet touched down, my knees buckling. Wynvail's voice filled my head like a nasty echo.

The curse marks—one to nullify my power and memory, but the one on my arm? The one they all kept staring at? It cursed me to kill my mates?

We were free, but a far worse and painful threat loomed like Cassander Locke's shadow.

"Where are the others?" I rasped, holding onto Kai and refusing to let go even when he released my waist, looking decidedly less green-faced on the solid ground outside the arena.

He hissed at me, his forked tongue lashing out, which was not helpful but did throw me back into a dozen different memories. I clutched his shoulders, wavering on my feet.

"Harvey. Emlyn," I reiterated. "Where are they?"

The names meant nothing to Kai. I wasn't sure the words did; he gave no indication if they did. I let my head fall on his shoulder with a groan. How was I going to do this? With three mates who didn't know me, didn't remember how to speak, and who I was cursed to kill?

"One foot in front of the other, Haley," I breathed to myself, patting Kai in thanks for not shoving me off him. I'd needed that moment of physical contact. Of course, when I drew back he was staring at my curse mark with narrow, wary eyes.

I turned and picked a direction at random, hoping my instincts were guiding me. I opened my mouth to tell Kai to follow, but he was already jogging up to me and—catching my arm to slow my stumbling steps. The physical contact made my bottom lip cave in.

His brow knitted, lips pressed thin as he let go of me and reached for the hem of his shirt.

"Now's not the best time for a—striptease," I finished with a gasp, instantly spotting what he was trying to show me: the exact same curse mark sprawled over his too-defined ribs. I knew that body, and knew his ribs had been covered in a massive, inked raven surrounded by roses. But now it was the same brutal mark I had on my arm.

My eyes stung as I looked at it, awareness of its power burning through my bloodstream.

"You're cursed too," I choked out, Wynvail's words repeating in my head like a taunting echo.

You're cursed to kill each other, Halwen.

Each other—not me cursed to kill them. We were cursed to kill *each other.*

"I can't do this," I sobbed, reaching out to trace that mark on his ribs, his hot, velvety skin so damn familiar.

He inhaled sharply, and I tore my fingers away, eyes burning.

"Does it hurt? When I touch you?"

Kai only watched me intensely, the same expression he wore when he was either thinking about skinning someone alive or stripping me naked. I didn't know which one it was.

"Let's find the others," I breathed, turning back to the road —and flinching when a shadow dropped from the sky with a growl of warning.

I skittered back, narrowly avoiding being crushed by—by Emlyn, carrying Harvey.

A weight fell off my shoulders; I drew a full breath. But relief was a double edged sword. I became more aware of the injuries burning across my body, pain driven like arrows through my skin.[4]

"You're both okay," I breathed, staring at Em and wondering why he had two heads. That was weird. Maybe because I'd lost a scary amount of blood? "I'm not, by the way. Someone should probably catch me."

No one caught me when dizziness dropped me, but I did successfully slump into Malakai so I called that a win.

"Got my daggers back," I told him, annoyed that my voice

was thick and clunky. "They weren't lost. Renna preserved them."

The words were meaningless to him.

We all jumped when a sudden chorus of roars and barks warned the rest of the alphas were breaking free of the arena.

"Time to go," I slurred, forcing myself to stay conscious. I couldn't pass out. Not yet. Not until we were safe. "The forest," I told them, pointing at the trees at the edge of the city.

Em followed my line of sight and nodded. He quickly rumbled something at Kai, but I was too busy passing out to see if they broke into a fight.

Warm arms caught me before I could hit the floor. Aww, did Em tell him to catch me?

That was so sweet.

I tried to tell him he was sweet, but blackness snapped shut around me like a trap. Safe in my mate's arms, I didn't fight the tug of a deep healing sleep.

Everything else could wait until I woke up. Sure, we were cursed to kill each other, they didn't know me at all, and I had no idea where we were going to go, but that could wait.

I did it. I found them.

39

Wane

The shadows were whispering her name again. The woman I refused to forget, the woman *he* tried to torture from me. It had been a hundred and two years, three months, and twelve days, and he hadn't given up. I broke years ago, probably when he had me held down while two of his cruellest warriors snapped my horns off. I didn't know the name of the titan who held my leash, who called me his wicked pet. People whispered *he* and *him* and *the titan.*

Titans were supposed to be dead. They weren't supposed to have warrens below the earth or cells so pitch black it was easy to forget your own name. I'd forgotten mine so many times, but not hers.

I felt for the shard of metal I was using currently. Before, it had been glass or broken pipe or even a claw ripped off my wings during torture. Both wings were gone now, the wounds still hot and bleeding decades later. *He* didn't let them heal.

The cuts pulsed in time to the name I repeated over and over, refusing to let *him* take it.

My shadows whispered again, holding onto her name with a ruthless possessiveness. Her name was mine. *She* was mine. A hundred years of torture hadn't stolen her from me —not like the curse written on my back, ringing both severed wings, had stolen me from the memories of everyone else.

Only the titan and his servant knew me now.

I dug the metal point into my skin, writing her name over another scarred slash of her name. I wrote it deep, so it wouldn't fade easily. My whole body was covered in that name, scarred flesh overlapping scarred flesh. The titan called me a freak, called me ugly, a monster.

As long as I never forgot her name, he could call me anything he wanted.

A memory of a lazy morning chased through the true darkness of my stone room, and my fingers tingled at the remembered feeling of silk-soft skin. My mate had let out a soft, sleepy sound and curled into me, like a flower seeking sun. But my brother was the sun; I was cold starlight and shadow.

My mate was fire and rage.

I fell into the memory as I wrote her name on my body. I wouldn't forget.

I wouldn't forget.

I jumped, a gasp torn from cracked lips when metal clanged against metal. I was broken beyond repair, but there was no denying I was still alive. I was afraid of more pain, and scared of the fear itself.

Would I give in one day?

No, the shadows whispered. *Halwen.*

Yes, I agreed as the door to my room swung open with a low creak.

"Come on, pet. He wants to see you."

See you. That meant hurt. It meant *tear apart,* meant *push to exhaustion* so he could laugh at my misery.

Halwen, I reminded myself as I was grabbed and hauled through the warren. *Halwen.*

THANK YOU so much for starting a new crazy adventure with me. This series has lived in my head for YEARS, so I am so damn happy to finally share it with you. **Midnight Descent, book two, will release next month so there's no huge wait until the next book!**

There is SO much in store for these guys, and I can't wait to delve deeper into this world of demons and mythology, and to throw more plot twists at you. (Trust me, you won't see the Wynvail one coming.)

WHILE YOU WAIT for book two, go read the Lili Kazana series - it's complete and set in the same world. You'll recognise Queen Lili and her harem of demon mates.

Thanks again for reading a new series from me. It means the whole damn world that you keep picking up my books. And if you're new, hi! I promise I'm not a psycho in real life. Come join me in my reader group.

Leigh x

INSANELY PRETTY SPECIAL EDITION HARDBACK!

If you're like me and LOVE a stunning collector's edition, check out this GORGEOUS Killer Crescent hardcover, with brand new covers, character art, and killer merch goodies!

Find the hardcover exclusively on Kickstarter!

THANK YOU FOR READING!

If this is your first Leigh Kelsey book, I have lots more books for you to sink your teeth into, and three completed series. I've got vampires, wolves, shifters, angels, and demons - and of course plenty of growly alpha males with tragic backstories.

Reviews make the world go 'round - or at least they do in my world. If you loved this book and you can spare a minute, please leave a review on Amazon or wherever else you like to review. Even the smallest, one-line review has an impact, and helps me reach new readers like you awesome people.

Thank you to everyone who's already reviewed. Your words mean I can keep writing the books you love!

Where the men are psycho but the women are wicked

FREE VAMPIRE ROMANCE STORY!

Hybrid's Curse is a stand-alone paranormal romance.

As a vampire-witch hybrid who can never be killed, Emilio is used to pain and suffering. But when Aislin, an innocent faerie healer, is kidnapped because of him, Emilio will do anything to stop her suffering too. Especially because she's been dreaming of him for seven years, and claims to be his mate.

If you love romantic stories with a healthy dose of suspense, and pairings of dark, gloomy men and sunny, optimistic women, you'll enjoy this happily-ever-after story.

JOIN MY MAILING LIST FOR YOUR FREE STORY

COMPLETE TWISTED PARANORMAL RH SERIES

Here's a tip: don't mess with the demon girl who kills people for a living.

The four self-proclaimed kings of Orchid Vale apparently never got that memo, and now my self care retreat is about to become a bloodbath.

READ FREE IN KINDLE UNLIMITED

SIGNED LEIGH KELSEY BOOKS!

LEIGH KELSEY

Want my books on your shelves?

You can find all my available print copies in my online book store, plus books from my cowrites and pen-names, **and all orders come with swag and a dedication from yours truly.**

VISIT THE STORE: https://payhip.com/snarkystabbybooks

ABOUT LEIGH KELSEY

Leigh Kelsey writes about psychos with questionable morals and addictions to shiny, stabby objects, but she's perfectly harmless, she swears. She can be found in Yorkshire, England listening to K-Pop, watching serial killer documentaries, and writing as much spicy paranormal romance as she possibly can in a day. (Where's that Time Turner when we need it...?)

LEIGH KELSEY

Where the men are psycho but the women are wicked

FIND THESE OTHER PSYCHOS BY LEIGH KELSEY!

All solo books free on Kindle Unlimited

Feared by Monsters: A stand-alone twisted paranormal romance

Killers and Kings series

(Complete Twisted Paranormal Demon RH)

Crazed Candy

Sweet Violence

Sugar Rush

Kissed By Brimstone series

(Twisted Paranormal Demon RH)

Hellborn Angel

Midnight Descent

Eternal Night

Cursed Dawn

Shadow Fall

Rebels and Psychos Duet

(Complete Twisted Paranormal RH)

Complete Series Box Set

Killer Crescent

Blood Wolf

Lawless Angels series

(Dark Biker Apocalyptic RH)

Vicious Legion

Sick and Twisted series

(Twisted Death Gods RH)

All Hallows Night

Broken Alphas series

(Complete Rejected Mates Dark Paranormal RH)

The Omega's Wolves

The Omega's Mates

NOTES

Chapter 1

1. Ugh, that sounded pitiful even to me.
2. Maybe, and I was just spitballing here, but maybe all the red flags and signs not to take this job were actually trying to tell me something? I was a dumbass for not heeding them.
3. It was disgusting, like drinking fermented paint water
4. It hadn't worked, as you could probably tell.
5. I had visions of my nose being ripped off and almost whimpered. I didn't want to be known as No-Nose Halwen for the rest of my life!

Chapter 2

1. It would've been nice to hide in shadows sometimes, like when I was having a traumatic flashback or someone was trying to teach me maths; I envied him that.
2. I couldn't help myself. I wanted to know what he'd do when he snapped. I was hoping he'd do *me*. I'd always had a thing for maniacs.
3. Ughhh, this was a soul mate thing, wasn't it?
4. Not sexually. Definitely *not* sexually.
5. Weird. Very fucking *weird*.
6. Please—*please*—tell me why my chest threatened to collapse at the thought of that.

Chapter 3

1. It's multi-purpose. Man attacking you? Knife to the dick. Aggressively hitting on you and won't take no for an answer? Knife to the dick. Stuck his cock in another woman? *Knife to the dick!*
2. And let's be real, if I was going to settle down with a big, strong protector, I couldn't do much better than the woman currently strangling me.
3. Good name for a gang, that. Blanket of Menacing Death. Their minions could be called the Blankies.
4. Ooh. Did he have a pet parrot?

Chapter 4

1. Uh-oh. Someone call the Sensible Police because the horny parade going off in my body right now was worrying. I needed someone to remind me of all the reasons why I didn't get involved with anyone. Stat.
2. Despite it being, y'know, a room. Irony was a bitch.

Chapter 5

1. That got us this month's rent, thank you very much.
2. But if they watched me being a psycho and thought to themselves *that's the kind of crazy I want,* who was I to question their strange tastes in women?
3. Butterflies. Legitimate butterflies. I fought a swoon.
4. And why wasn't I stabbing Malakai? *Come on, Haley, get it together!*

Chapter 6

1. Even the inches I felt throbbing under me. Especially them.

Chapter 7

1. She had a point. Books were boring when everyone just stood around chatting. Much better to insert a fight to the death.
2. Like brain matter—heart matter was a thing, right?

Chapter 10

1. And by play, I meant murder.

Chapter 11

1. Mostly I sensed Wane's; he'd vanished into shadows to protect himself, only his bound hands visible. I wished he'd taken me with him.

Chapter 12

1. On the negative side, it was furnished with an *army of the dead* décor theme, complete with cutlasses, axes, and skulls spiked on the wall above the bed in the large, attic room. I was suspicious about the dark staining on the deck outside, too; either it was a cherry red wood staining or blood, and I was betting the latter.
2. If *I'm fine* meant, *I'm a huge mess of emotions and hatred and fear, and I don't know if I'll ever feel safe again.*

Chapter 16

1. My face could personally attest to its structural integrity. The builders did a 10/10 job with construction.

Chapter 17

1. I just came back from the dead; sue me.
2. Because I had more space to attack Renna in the middle of the road...

Chapter 18

1. Do you think I could get away with a rebirth party, like people had birthday parties? I could use an excuse to gorge on cake and drown myself in ale.
2. She was *a queen;* I wasn't about to tell her she had my name wrong. She seemed sweet, but rulers were all the same. One moment it was pleasant chats over tea and cakes, the next it was beheading for treason.

Chapter 19

1. Heated, recycled air had to be a demon's invention; it was as bad as brimstone's stench.

Chapter 20

1. I didn't even get them halfway. My girl was all grown up now.
2. If I hadn't lost my mates, I'd say it was almost worth dying to get coffee this good because *holy shit.*
3. I had to hand it to the metal box—it certainly knew how to brew a cup of coffee.

Chapter 21

1. He was onto something. I'd be trying that as soon as I found my mates.

Chapter 22

1. Haha, just kidding.
2. Cock and Claws—whatever. Mine was a better name. Maybe when I found my mates and we were safe again, we could buy a pub.
3. It would be a *tad* alarming if two teenagers had gone out hunting criminals.
4. And by track I mean kill, but you're clever so you knew that.
5. Let's just say my backside would be so red and stinging, I wouldn't be able to sit for *days.*
6. Honestly, this was doing wonders for my confidence. Two days ago I'd been a corpse, but now I was hooking big, burly alphas. *Still got it!*
7. I loved a psycho man, but this was taking things a little too far.

Chapter 23

1. Probably not my smartest move, but sometimes you just had to call someone a dick.
2. Other times I thought I was insane, which was *much* more likely.
3. Flying would be awkward as fuck if I was.
4. Seriously. No face. Just a smooth surface where eyes, nose, and a mouth should be. It made my stomach squirmy.
5. Well, minus a hundred or so years.
6. Well, minus a hundred or so years.
7. Great, there went two more knives.
8. I wasn't one to judge but *yuck.*
9. She ate the limbs one by one and left the torso. I really could have lived without knowing that about my friend. Some things were better left as a mystery.

Chapter 24

1. If you're thinking I rode Tali, you'd be correct. I couldn't fault her speed but the comfort could stand to be upgraded. Would she let me put a little seat on her back like she was a camel?
2. Definitely not murdered. Nope. No, sir.

Chapter 25

1. See, the good thing about being dead a hundred years is no hair growth! I ought to have had an out of control bush, but it was still neatly trimmed. I should die more often.

Chapter 26

1. With admittedly better, more wicked senses of humour.
2. What a fuchsia dress was doing in the bowels of Hell, I didn't know, but I wasn't about to complain.
3. Or get Tali to do the honours for me. I still couldn't forget her crunching through that skull.
4. I *did* learn about a gentleman called Scraggy Nave who'd been cursed to have a squid instead of a dick, and his wife Zillah who'd fucking loved it. You do you, Zillah.

Chapter 27

1. You guessed it; I wasn't invited to the tea party.
2. Don't ask. Really, don't ask.
3. As long as I had this rage in me, it would never pass. The guy was a grade A moron. Pretty, though.
4. Life hack, my friends, life hack.

Chapter 29

1. I shouldn't sneer though; that probably took someone all two of their brain cells to come up with that name.
2. Okay, so some mistakes had been made. This was not my finest hour.
3. Please be unconscious and not brain damage. Please be unconscious.

Chapter 30

1. But I wasn't brain dead! Thank Lucifer.

Chapter 32

1. Not sexy dominance, but true, powerful dominance that even alphas would bow to. Although now I think about it, that's pretty damn sexy too.

Chapter 33

1. Just kidding, they were still urging him to kill me.

Chapter 35

1. I loved them no matter what, exactly as they were, but them trying to kill me over breakfast would be awkward as fuck.

Chapter 36

1. I could thank Tali for teaching me that gesture, despite her lack of opposable thumbs.

Chapter 37

1. Hell, I'd take pushing onto my knees right now; being facedown was not a fun experience. Well, not like *this...*
2. Because yes, he'd invited people to watch me fall to my death.

Chapter 38

1. It was bad that I hoped he wanted me for my power and not a light snack.
2. They never did before; why change the habit of a lifetime?
3. No seriously, it was on my list of things to do before I died. First, restore my mates' memories. Second, have insane, mind-blowing mated sex. Third, stab Wynvail in his smug little eyes.

4. Maybe because arrows *had* been driven through me. Fucking Wynvail.